MUSE

Susie M. Hanley

Pocket Kitten Productions
P.O. Box 2436
Corvallis, OR 97339

First Edition: September 2012

Cover design by Susie M. Hanley
Cover photographs © Susie M. Hanley
Cover © Susie M. Hanley

Pocket  Kitten

For my husband, Kacey, who's made all my dreams come true.

Acknowledgements

This book was four years in the making and would not have been possible without the help and support of countless people.

First, I have to thank my husband for his never-ending support, for letting me spend hours bouncing endless ideas off him, for picking up the slack when I was in "Shelbyville", for reassuring me at every turn, and for letting me cry on his shoulder when it all seemed too impossible. There would be no book without you.

I'd also like to thank my kids. For being so patient and accepting, for doing their best to keep quiet while I worked, for reminding me what I was supposed to be doing when I got caught up .... and for being a fountain of inspiration for this story. Thank you, a big part of this book is just for you.

Special thanks to Bruce McAllister, my amazing writing coach, who was always patient and kind, yet honest in his attempts to help me write the best book possible. Thanks to Donna, my editor, who took the time to help make this book as error free as possible, and who worked so hard on the epigraphs: those horribly painful epigraphs. Neither of us will ever forget them. Thank you both, I learned enough from you two: I could write another book just about writing.

Thanks to my parents for raising me to believe that I could do anything I set my mind to. Thanks to my little brother Spencer for handing me the book that inspired me to finally go after my dream and become a writer. You've always been a good friend and I miss having you around. Thanks to my friend Jeremy, who listened to me ramble for hours and hours, who read chapter after chapter, revision after revision, and only complained a little. To my sister Julia and our friend Anna who were the first to love this story and tell me it was something worth writing. Thanks to my friends Lacey, Jamie, Jennifer, Leighana, and Danielle your excitement and enthusiasm still makes me smile.

Lastly I'd like to thank all the women who've inspired me throughout my life and shown me what it really means to be a woman, a mother, and a friend. You've been family, friends, teachers, and mentors, but most importantly, you've been shining examples of strength and beauty. I wouldn't be who I am, and there certainly wouldn't be a book, without you.

It has been such a long road, I am sure there are some people I forgot. To you I apologize and thank you for any part you may have had in helping me make this book a reality.

MUSE

Muses and Guardians are subspecies of Homo sapiens that have existed alongside ordinary human beings since prehistory. Although distinct, these two groups are irrevocably linked, neither surviving without the other.

Apart from their supernatural abilities, Muses and Guardians closely resemble mortal humans. They coexisted on the planet Earth without detection until the late twentieth century when technological advances made concealment difficult.

While the majority of Muses and Guardians demonstrate a dedication to humankind, some have been accused of using their powers against mortals.

—"Muses and Guardians," *World Look Encyclopedia*

1

Muses are born of mortal, Muse or Guardian parents and present with talent in an art form or craft at a young age. At age twenty-five, a final transition occurs that is characterized by distinct physiological changes and a marked increase in talent. After this final transition, they receive the title of *Muse*, bond with a Guardian and use their talents and energy to inspire humans.

—"Muses," *World Look Encyclopedia*

When I was a little girl, my dad would pull quarters from behind my ear. When I asked, "How?" he said:

"Magic."

Then he died. The magic went with him.

When I was fifteen, a boy in my class pulled a coin from behind my ear. I thought I loved that boy.

Some years later, I learned his magic wasn't real either. Love, it seems, is just as rare a find.

I found my own magic. Then again, perhaps it found me. I can draw and sculpt, but with a paintbrush something incredible happens. Something basic to my very being. Something that is my very own magic.

Love, I also had to find myself--though it could be argued that it, too, found me. My children are that love. Like any mother, I'd die for them, give up my own magic to see them safe and well. They are what matters most.

I could be content forever with my magic and my love, but it seems the universe has bigger and more dangerous plans for both. Those plans, too, are about to find me.

I am, after all, twenty-five.

Even when we think our mundane lives are of no importance, someone is always watching.

I was really really late.

"Shit!" I bit my tongue. Been trying to clean up my language since Julian started mimicking me at school.

Rinsed out my brush, dried it, put it in the case, then peeked around my easel into Irene's office. She was watching me.

"Crap." I muttered it this time and decided to make a break for it. I threw on my sweatshirt. Messenger bag over my head, I grabbed all my stuff and headed for my locker. Stuff in, I clicked the lock shut and turned around to find myself toe to toe with Irene, my program advisor who also happens to be head of the art department.

Irene is average height, average build, over fifty and going soft around the middle. Dark curly hair and hazel eyes make her intimidating in that elementary-school-principal way. Underneath she's a sharp old bird and made a point to keep more than one eye on me.

"Leaving so soon?" She raised an eyebrow.

I left at this time every day and she knew it.

"My kids have basketball today. I pushed past her, my Converse getting me a few steps ahead towards the door. She had to hurry to keep up in her heels.

"The auction's only two weeks away. I thought you were getting some help?"

"I'll be back tomorrow." I was almost at the door.

"Shelby," she said sharply.

I turned to face her, blowing out a breath and reminding myself this wasn't worth an argument.

She closed the distance between us. "Your piece is looking good, but you need more time here. You have talent; I don't want to see it go to waste."

"I'll see what I can do."

"See that you do." She gave me another stern look and walked away.

I moved towards the door again. I reached for the handle....

"Oh, and Shelby?"

I tensed, hand on the door. I'd almost made it.

"Happy birthday."

I wheeled to face her. She was smiling, and all I could do was intensify my confused look.

She clomped back to her office.

I gave myself a little shake and pushed through the door out into the freezing January air. I made my way to the student parking lot feeling both flattered and blindsided. I never told anyone about my birthdays. Why bother? I'm turning twenty-five. It wasn't like I was a Muse. Not that I'd want to be one anyway. They're just something you hear about, no one you know is ever one.

So, no big deal. Just one year closer to thirty. My sister hadn't called, nor had my brother. My parents had been dead a long time. Irene, had made a point to look up my birthday and wish me a happy one. I smiled despite myself.

In the last few hours, black clouds had moved in. The temperature had dropped and frozen Oregon's perpetual rain into thick sheets of ice. It would melt off before morning. But getting home was going to be a nightmare made hellish because my usual rig, an SUV with four-wheel drive, was in the shop getting a new starter. I was stuck driving a plastic compact rental now covered in ice.

I pulled a card from my wallet and started scraping at the ice. I was already running late so I did a half-assed job and climbed in, cranking over the engine and setting the heater on high. No time to wait for the windshield to clear. I rolled down the window and joined the barrage of vehicles headed off campus.

Later, I'd look back with no one to blame but myself. I was speeding on an icy road surrounded by pedestrians, but that wasn't what I was thinking about; any second my kids would get home from school to find a locked door. And if that wasn't enough reason to give the gas a little more oomph; it was also their first day of basketball practice-- and we were going to be late.

I was distracted, trying to make a plan to get them out the door in record time, the windshield was fogged, and I didn't see the brake lights ahead of me.

Time slowed like a bad commercial as the red Jeep in front of me bloomed like a rose caught on speed film. I kicked at the floor, looking for the clutch. I couldn't find it. A half-second later I was two-footing the brake, but I'd hit a patch of ice and the car was sliding out of control. I turned the wheel, but the ice had me. I slammed into the Jeep.

The first thing I processed was the sound: metal tearing, glass shattering. I heard some of it rain down as the airbag threw me back in my seat.

The air bag deflated, leaving me hunched and stunned. There was a moment of silence where I tried to focus, tried to see if I was all right. A moment was all I got. A car horn blared. A glance in the rear view mirror showed me another car barreling towards me. I couldn't even brace. The impact smashed my head into the steering wheel.

Things went away for a while. When I woke up again, warmth was running down my face. I put a hand up, looked at it. Blood. The stench of gasoline. Hands shaking, I unbuckled my seatbelt and reached for the door handle. I pulled it and pushed. Nothing. I hit it feebly with my shoulder. Still nothing. My left leg hurt like hell, and I couldn't get leverage.

I could see, through the shattered windshield, flames licking from my hood to the Jeep. I needed out-- right now. If I could crawl out through one of the windshields....

I pulled on my leg, but it wouldn't budge. I screamed and pulled harder as more flames licked up the Jeep.

All I could see was my parents burning to death in their own car accident, unable to get out in time, like me. But *I* couldn't do that. *I* couldn't leave my kids to be raised ... to be raised by relatives worse than strangers.

I screamed again as I pulled on my leg, but it was caught in the wreckage. If I pulled harder would I damage it forever? Did it matter? As long as I could crawl away and live to care for my children: nothing else did.

I braced myself, ready to pull until it came loose no matter what.

There was movement outside my window.

I didn't believe it at first.

A man swathed in black was looking in at me with the bluest eyes.

Then he was ripping my door off its hinges, throwing it impossibly far and bending down to look in at me again.

Through the fog in my head, I heard "Are you hurt?".

"My leg," I heard myself answer. Was that me sobbing, too?

He gripped the steering wheel and did the impossible.

He snapped it off the column like a twig off a branch, freeing my leg. Then he lifted me from the car, and the next thing I knew we were hundreds of feet away. I was sure I'd only blinked. Was he that fast? We looked back just as there was a pop and my rental went up in flames.

I should have been thinking *Guardian!* But they're no more real—no more in anyone's life—than Muses are. So, I simply looked at him and blinked. I was in shock, wasn't I? I was hallucinating the whole thing. I'd somehow gotten out of the car—no door ripped off its hinges, no steering wheel snapped off by a normal-looking hand— and he was merely a bystander, wanting to help, but not knowing how. I'd wanted to be saved, and I'd imagined him helping.

"No," he said. "You didn't ... imagine it."

I kept blinking, but nothing was clear, not who he was, not what it all meant. It was all too impossible.

Emergency vehicles arrived, and he carried me towards them. In retrospect, I should've thanked him, asked him a question—anything—but my leg was hurting so bad all I could do was clutch at it and sob.

The man set me on a stretcher and disappeared. Not that I saw him vanish. I looked up from an EMT adjusting my leg and he was just gone. I looked around for him, but what I found instead was the last person I expected.

Standing across the scene, some three hundred feet away, was Cal. Also known as my ex-husband. The one who knocked me up in high school, married me, knocked me up again, divorced me and then disappeared into the military, never to be seen again.

I blinked and looked again. He was still there, standing in the distance dressed in jeans and a dark brown trench coat. The EMTs started moving me into an ambulance, but despite my pain, I twisted around to get another look. He was gone. One man appears and does the impossible. Then another man—one I know—appears and disappears. It didn't mean anything because I was still hallucinating, right?

"How's your head feel? Does your vision seem blurred?" The EMT shined a light into each of my eyes as the ambulance doors closed and we started to move.

"It hurts."

My mind reeled back to Cal. Could it have been him? No, last I heard he was on the East Coast doing his Special Ops thing for the government. He sends me a child support check every month and I imagine his foster parents send him pictures of the kids, but he's never contacted us and that's how I like it. He's never even wanted to see his kids.

The kids!

"Oh, my gosh! I need a phone. No one's home to watch my kids." I looked imploringly at the EMT, who seemed startled by my outburst. "Please, just let me call my friend. She can track them down. I just need one minute."

He shot a glance at the driver and unclipped the phone from his belt. "One minute. I *should* make you wait till we get to the hospital."

I grabbed the phone and dialed my friend, Diane. She was horrified I'd been in an accident, but I turned her attention to the fact no one was with the kids. I'd taught them to go to the neighbors if I wasn't home, but I wasn't sure they'd remember in a true emergency. She agreed to see check up on them and to send her husband to the hospital to give me a ride home.

I gave the EMT back his phone and tried to relax on the stretcher. I tried not to think about how dismal my health insurance was and how much all this was going to cost me. I tried even harder not to think about my hallucinations: a Guardian who saved me and my ex-husband's impossible appearance.

"Who saved you?" the EMT asked said as he hooked me up to an IV and a sci-fi array of monitors. "He sure didn't stick around. Everyone's saying he's a Guardian, the way he pulled you from that car."

"What?" I had to hear someone say it even to *begin* believing it.

"You know, a Guardian."

"A what?"

"You've been through a lot, ma'am." He was smiling a wonderful smile, perhaps looking a little guilty.

"Is my leg broken?" I said, needing something real to grasp onto.

"We're taking you to the hospital. The doctors will be able to tell you."

I didn't know whether it was shock or pain medication. It didn't matter. I was a mess and babbling. "Do Guardians suck the life out of people? Is that how they get their power? I heard that once. I hate Guardians."

He smiled again but didn't answer.

I started in again. "Did he really do those things? Did he save me? Somebody did. I don't know who, but somebody...."

Still smiling, he adjusted my IVs and I finally shut up.

2

Guardians are unique human beings whose abilities include strength, speed, healing, intuition, telepathy and invisibility. These preternatural abilities, evident early in childhood, will eventually assist Muses in carrying out their tasks. Each Guardian is linked to a particular Muse, whom he or she must guide and protect. They undergo rigorous training in order to fulfill this mandate.

—"Guardians," *World Look Encyclopedia*

At the hospital, they wheeled me into a little curtain-lined room, and a doctor came in to do the flashlight-in-the-eyes again and to order an X-ray.

When I got back, a man was sitting in the chair in my little room. He looked up as they wheeled me back in, and I was horrified to find it was Cal. When I envisioned myself seeing my ex again, it wasn't with me in a hospital bed, soaked and filthy. I was barely dressed, let alone presentable.

"What are you doing here?" I asked.

Standing, he flashed a badge at the nurse. Her eyes went wide, and she did a double-take to his face and back to the badge.

"I'll get the doctor." She hurried from the room.

He tucked the badge away, looking me up and down. "You look like hell, shelly-belly."

"Don't call me that." My head was throbbing. Once upon a time, that had been his favorite pet name for me. "What are you doing here, Cal? Visiting you parents and thought you'd drop in on me after seven years?"

He adjusted my blankets and scrutinized my forehead where the EMT had applied a bandage. "You're my new assignment."

What could the government want with me? Before I could get the question to my lips, the doctor walked in. He looked serious and stiffer than he'd seemed before. The nurse followed, looking nervous.

Cal pulled out his badge and an official-looking letter, handed them both to the doctor and waited while he looked them over. The nurse read over the doctor's shoulder.

"Will someone please tell me what's going on?" I tried to sound annoyed. I was the patient here. As far as I was concerned, Cal was an intruder.

"It seems, your husband here—"

"Ex-husband." I interrupted.

"All right." The doctor took a deep breath through his nose, handed the badge back to Cal and looked at me. "It seems this man is a Guardian of some note."

A Guardian? Was I still hallucinating? I'd been with Cal for four years; I'd known him in high school. All that time he'd just been ... he'd just been like anyone else. Ordinary people aren't Guardians.

I looked at Cal, my ex-husband—the one who'd left me alone to raise two kids when I was only eighteen—and all the betrayal I'd ever felt from him multiplied a thousand-fold.

Lies. More and more lies. People are people, whether they be super or mundane.... They're all the same.

Even more unbelievable was two Guardians. Two in one day? Even if it were true, it was improbable, laughable and made no sense.

"And, according this letter," the doctor went on, interrupting my thoughts, "he's authorized to administer any and all of your healthcare the way he sees fit,"

My mouth dropped open. Now I knew I was hallucinating.

"And he's authorized to remove you from my care and act as your steward with full power of attorney." He said the last bit as if he couldn't quite believe it himself.

"What!" I couldn't help but shriek. "I didn't authorize any of this, and I don't want him near me."

The doctor was still looking at Cal. "Mind if I observe? I've never witnessed one of these. It was after my time."

Cal inclined his head and stepped towards me.

"No, no, no!" I tried to sit up. "He needs to leave." I may have been willing to tolerate his presence when he was just my unwelcome ex, but being a Guardian moved him into the "dangerous" category.

"Please concentrate, Ms. Hammond. I know you've been through a lot today, but we need you to think clearly. Everyone here wants the best for you. This man has the power and the willingness to heal you. For everyone's sake, please let him."

This was impossible. Cal couldn't be this person. He was a jarhead for the government. I'd seen pictures of him in uniform. A Guardian? Guardians are self-centered, heartless monsters. If he was a Guardian, no wonder he'd left us the way he did.

"No. I don't want him here." I folded my arms across my chest and stared in the opposite direction. If I could've gotten up and left, I would've.

"Ms. Hammond, your leg is broken in three places. If you don't let him heal you, you're going to have surgery and an extended stay in the hospital. You won't be walking for at least three months."

That got me. I started thinking about my kids and the three sets of stairs in my house, then about my pathetic health insurance and how much debt this would rack up. I'd have to drop out of school until I healed. I didn't want to think about the auction. I wouldn't even be able to go grocery shopping. My closest relatives lived two states away, and they wouldn't help me. My friends could help me, but I couldn't ask them to give up their lives that way.

Could I live with being healed by an already treacherous Guardian?

I looked to the doctor and he nodded in such a reassuring way that I cracked. I looked back at Cal. "Why'd you lie to me?"

"You never asked if I was a Guardian."

I opened my mouth to retort, but nothing came out. I mustered as much irritation as I could. "Can we just get this over with?"

Cal stepped forward. "Try to relax; focus on your breathing. I'm going to touch you, and you may feel some tingling as I examine your wounds."

All he got in response was an indignant huff.

He placed his hand on my forehead, palm down.

All at once my body relaxed. Any pain I'd had evaporated in a rush of relaxation. It was so abrupt I started to panic, but Cal was right there in my ear.

"It's all right; I'm relieving your pain and analyzing your wounds. You're safe. You're calm." He repeated the last bit in a quiet voice a few times, and I closed my eyes trying to believe it. "You're safe. You're calm."

Less than a minute went by and Cal spoke again. "She has a hairline fracture to her skull, several bruised ribs, a broken femur and both the fibula and tibia are broken just below the knee." He looked down at me, his chocolate eyes exactly like I remembered. "You might also be interested to know your triglycerides are on the high side of normal and you're going to ovulate tomorrow." He said that last with a little smile.

"Would've been nice if you'd known that little trick before."

"After our uh ... debacles, I made a point to learn." He blushed.

"How nice for all the women you've screwed since our divorce."

The doctor interrupted our little trip down memory lane. "Fascinating. You can tell all that from just a touch?"

A crowd had formed behind the doctor. Several more doctors and at least five nurses had squeezed in near the door.

"Yes, and a lot more if I took the time to look." He looked down at me. "I'm going to manipulate your leg to set the bones before I heal them."

I gulped. That sounded painful.

"You won't feel any pain. I can block that, but I need you to relax and let me work."

I just nodded.

Cal pulled back the sheet revealing my jeans had been cut away. My T-shirt and, to my further humiliation, my thong, were all that covered me.

"I'm sorry, but I need to be touching your skin." He moved his hands down to my bare knee.

I didn't look closely at my leg; one glance told me it had swollen huge and purple. I looked away while Cal worked.

He manipulated my leg. "You'll feel some tingling as the bones heal. These are severe injuries. It may feel intense but don't move or the bones won't heal in proper alignment."

I took a deep breath, tried to focus on not moving and nodded.

"Here we go," he said.

It started with tingling in my leg, concentrating in the areas Cal mentioned. It was definitely "intense." Instead of a slow ache like my foot might feel waking up, it was a faster paced throbbing, but not in a painful way. The tingling spread up through my torso, lingering in my ribs before making its way up to my forehead, where it gave one last jolt and ebbed away. All told, it took maybe three minutes.

Cal released me, looking ashen and struggling to breathe, as he stumbled to a chair. We all watched in silence as his color slowly returned. He got up and went to the sink for water. It wasn't until he looked back at us, seemingly himself again that the doctor came to examine me.

He removed the bandage from my forehead, shined the light in my eyes and bent my leg around, asking me if it hurt. All the while, the light of discovery was in his eyes. I recognized that light and cringed inside. The same fascination with Guardians had killed my parents. I wanted to warn him, but I held my tongue. He was an old man, who wouldn't take my caution seriously anyway.

He finished my examination and a strange smile lit his face. "You're perfectly healed. If it was up to me, I'd say you could go home." He directed the question at Cal.

Looking better, Cal nodded and stood.

He and I were going to have a serious talk about this supposed paperwork that gave him control over my health. I might need a lawyer, but I had no way to pay for one.... One problem at a time; I needed to get away from Cal.

"I'll take care of the paperwork," the doctor said, shaking Cal's hand, "Thank you very much for allowing the audience."

"Of course. Shelby, we should be going."

I gave him my most incredulous look. "I don't know what this *we* stuff is, but I'm going home. My ride should be waiting."

I looked around for some pants, and a nurse appeared holding a pair of loaners. Knowing I had little modesty left—Cal had seen it all before anyway—I hopped off the gurney.

I felt great, so nimble, light, and, of course, healed. The swelling was gone, and he'd even cured my troublesome hamstring. Cool. I pulled the loaners on and moved towards the door.

Cal stepped into my path, all six feet four, two hundred sixty pounds of him blocking my way. His deep chocolate eyes—the same ones as my son--gave me an instant disadvantage.

"I saved this for you." He handed me my purse, which doubled as my school bag.

As much as it killed me, I had to say thank you. If it weren't for him, I'd be in traction for the next few months and without any of my necessities. "I appreciate you helping me, but, please, just leave us alone. I don't want you in my life." I tried to step past him.

He countered my move, "There are things I need to tell you...." "I tried to step around him again. "You need protection." He countered my move.

I made the mistake of meeting his gaze again and had to tear my eyes away. Damn, he looked good.

"The only thing I need protection from is the weather and overwork, things I can handle on my own." I finally pushed past him into the hallway. I needed space and time to digest what had just happened. I never expected to see him again. That he was a Guardian, I couldn't even fathom.

Diane's husband, Johnas, spotted me in the waiting room and looked worried. Then he spotted Cal on my heels and the look turned to confusion. Johnas and Cal were once best friends.

The confusion quickly turned to anger.

"What'd you do to her?" He stepped between us, getting in Cal's face. Johnas towers over Cal by about four inches. They're well matched in appearance, since both are half Native American.

"He didn't do anything, Johnas. Let's just go." I pulled at his arm.

He backed away, not taking his glare off Cal.

We made it into the car without Cal following us. Johnas sat behind the wheel, the anger rolling off him in waves.

"What was he doing there? And what the hell happened to you? You look like a truck ran over you."

"I don't know why he's here ... and it was a compact, not a truck."

Johnas did a double-take as he turned the engine over. "A compact? You were hit by a car?"

"My stupid rental hit some ice and then it hit a Jeep and then a compact hit us." I waved a hand as if this were an everyday occurrence.

Johnas's mouth fell open.

"I'm fine. Cal healed me." And then, because I couldn't deny it any longer, I said it: "He's a Guardian, Johnas."

He took his hand off the shifter, but said nothing. I knew he, too, was trying to figure it out: what had really happened, whether I was hallucinating from shock and meds.

"Talk to the doctors," I said. "My leg was broken. Badly. Now it's not. I don't believe it either, Johnas, but I have to.... Guardians don't get involved in the lives of ordinary people. You know that. I know that...."

Still no answer. His eyes were focused on something outside or maybe nothing.

"Take me home, Johnas. I'll tell you and Diane everything when we get there. We don't have to talk about it now. I need some time to think it through myself."

I leaned back in the seat, exhausted. "I need to get as far away from Cal as possible."

"You and me both."

He was holding something back. I could tell. But what?

We didn't say much on the way to my house. I could see Johnas's jaw working as he clenched and unclenched his teeth. I wasn't the only one Cal had betrayed when he went into the military, filed for a divorce and cut ties with all of us. Johnas and I hadn't been the same since.

"Did Diane find the kids?"

"They were at the neighbors like you thought. She took them home and ordered some dinner."

"Thank God." They were safe; I was going home well and whole. This day could have gone so much worse.

We pulled up to my house and I jumped out before Johnas could turn off the engine. I needed to see the kids and make sure they were all right, make sure Cal hadn't got to them. I'd never told them about Cal. When they asked about their dad, I told them he was in the Army and couldn't visit. I knew that answer wouldn't work forever, but how do you tell five- and eight-year-olds their dad doesn't come to see them because he doesn't want to?

I burst through the door and found Diane and another friend, Kali, standing in the kitchen, digging into plates of Thai food. The kids were at the table, chomping on bean sprouts and Pad Thai.

When they saw me, Kali and Diane went wide-eyed, and then I dropped the bomb. "Has Cal been here?"

It'd been years since any of us had mentioned Cal, so it took a moment for them to realize what I meant. Johnas came in the door behind me, looking grim, and they finally reacted.

Diane put down her plate and went to Johnas.

Kali met my eyes and the words passed unspoken between us. *We're in for a world of shit.*

"You saw him?" Diane asked.

"Wait," I said and went to the dining room to hug my kids. I knelt down and pulled them both towards me, one filling each arm. After a long squeeze, I tucked a strand of dark hair behind Chloe's ear.

"Where were you Mommy? We missed basketball." She stuffed another forkful of bean sprouts into her mouth.

"I had a little car accident, but I'm okay."

She made an affirmative noise and turned back to her food. Chloe's the most easygoing person I know. It takes a lot to faze her.

Julian tapped my shoulder, and I turned to him. Cal's molten eyes—complete with long black lashes—stared back at me.

"Mommy, what's wrong?"

I gave his forehead a long kiss, taking in the smell of his aloe shampoo. Could my sweet little kids really be the offspring of something so evil?

"It's just been a long day, buddy." I looked into his eyes, trying to see the differences, rather than the similarities between him and Cal.

"I love you."

I hugged them both again, encompassing a million unsaid things in the gesture. *I'll protect you from those evil people and make sure you don't become like them. ... I'm sorry I was so careless with who I chose to be your father....*

Julian gave me a strange look.

"Everything's fine," I said, more to myself than him. "Finish your dinner, please."

"Okay, Mommy. He turned back to his food.

The adults were waiting for me in the entryway. Johnas had explained about seeing Cal with me at the ER, but that was all he knew. They looked impatient for the rest of the story, so, as best I could, I explained about the accident, the guy who had to be a Guardian saving me, seeing Cal in the distance and then him showing up in my room. I told them about the badge, the paperwork, him healing me ... everything. When I finished, Diane and Johnas just stared at me and Kali looked at the floor.

Diane found her voice first.

"Shelby, ... you're a *Muse*."

Johnas piped up. "I knew it."

My head snapped in his direction.

"What? Nobody wields a brush like you, and today is your twenty-fifth birthday."

Muses supposedly came into their full power around age twenty-five, but I wasn't a Muse so it didn't matter.

"That's right." Kali put in. "You're a Muse."

"I'm *not* a Muse! But Cal is a Guardian. He heals people. Is that where he's been all this time? And why didn't he tell me? Isn't that something you mention when you're dating someone, when she's having your child or maybe before you marry her?"

"I don't think you have a choice about being a Muse. Isn't it just something you're born with?" Diane looked to Johnas for the answer.

"That's what I thought," he said.

So much for my attempt at deflection.

I was saved by a knock at the door. I took a few steps toward it before I realized who it must be. I looked out the peephole and saw Cal on my doorstep. Damn.

I whispered to my friends. "It's Cal. What should I do?"

"Let him in," Diane whispered back. She did love a good intrigue.

"I'll do it." Kali walked toward the door.

I retreated to stand next to Johnas. He puffed up his chest. At least he was getting an ego boost out of this.

Kali opened the door. "What do you want?"

"Hello, Kali, good to see you're well." Cal said from the darkness beyond the door. "I'm here to see Shelby."

"I think you've seen her enough for one day." She started to close the door.

Cal's hand flew up to stop it, and he whispered something only Kali could hear.

Whatever he said worked. Kali let the door swing open and retreated to stand next to me. Cal stepped through the door and closed it behind him.

"Johnas ... Diane." He nodded to both of them and turned to me. "Shelby, can we talk in private?"

I crossed my arms over my chest. "I'll tell them everything you say, anyway."

He tugged the hair at his temple, his tell for when he's thinking or stressed. Some things never change.

Chloe and Julian wandered in from the dining room. "Mommy, who's that?"

Panic shot through me. *What should I tell them?* I searched the faces around me, frantically looking for an answer. Several people seemed about to say something.

"Nobody answer that!" I narrowed my eyes at Cal. His mouth had opened, but no way in hell would I let him say *anything.*

I turned back to Chloe and Julian, startled after my outburst. "It's all right guys; he's just an old friend. Would you get ready for bed, please?"

Chloe shrugged and skipped off, but Julian and Cal stared at each other. Cal had left when Chloe was eighteen months old. He'd never met Julian.

"Hi Julian," Cal said more heavily than I expected.

"You have hair like mine." Julian said, tugging at his black curls.

"It's good hair," Cal said.

"Julian?"

He pulled his gaze from Cal to look at me.

"Ready for bed, please."

He nodded and left. I let out a breath I hadn't realized I'd been holding. Cal had finally met Julian.

"We're gonna have to do this later." I said, throwing my head in the direction the kids went.

"What time do they go to bed?" Cal asked.

"Not tonight. It's my birthday, and you're not invited."

"Tomorrow then. What time do they leave for school?"

"I have a meeting in the morning. I can give you an hour around eleven." I crossed to the door and held it open for him.

Something flashed in Cal's eyes, but he maintained his professional tone and stepped toward me. "This isn't a game. There are things you need to know, things you need to do,"

My eyes narrowed. "Why should I trust you?"

He looked at Kali, and my knees got weak. I'd never seen a look like that pass between them. Did Kali have something to do with this?

"Tomorrow then," Cal said, and was gone.

3

A Muse-Guardian relationship begins after a Muse completes his or her transition. A natural attraction begins between the Muse and one or more Guardians until a bonding occurs. In ancient times, Guardians fought and even killed one another over a Muse. Once bonded a Muse and Guardian cannot live more than a few days without the other, and in certain situations only hours.
—"Muses and Guardians," *World Look Encyclopedia*

After Cal left that night, Johnas disappeared and returned with vodka. He and I went a little overboard with it. I wouldn't let anyone talk about Cal or the fact that I was, supposedly, a Muse now.

I just didn't believe it and nothing they could say would convince me. To be regarded as a Muse is a HUGE deal. It means I have something to offer the world and need to be protected because of it. Me? Yeah, right.

Twenty years ago, the Guardians tossed their trench coats, so to speak. With technology advancing so quickly, they couldn't protect Muses without being caught on surveillance. At that point, some of the most prominent people in the world were exposed as Muses. Finding out the vice president had metaphysical abilities was a big deal, but it was the power Guardians have that worked everyone into a tizzy. Powers like super strength and healing abilities. Being able to write a perfect symphony or negotiate peace treaties was old hat. Even I preferred to hear about the Guardian seen flying like Superman through New York City. They even have their own international agency called MAGRA or the Muse Affairs and Guardian Regulative Authority, but most people just refer to it as the Authority.

Guardians, however, conceal the most important thing about themselves. Guardians will do *anything* to protect their Muses. They will kill, run from battle, even allow innocents to die. *Anything* to protect those they deem "more important" than the general public.

Is a Muse dancer more important than a mother of three young children? If you ask Guardians, they will tell you, "yes," and choose the dancer over anyone else, even a small child about to be hit by a car.

Befriending a Guardian killed my parents. Had that Guardian considered everyone equal and been a protector of the innocent—like all superheroes should be—my parents would still be alive. Instead, when I was five, my sister, brother and I went to live with my dad's stepsister. Our aunt wasn't a bad person, but she had three kids of her own and her husband wasn't a kind and generous man. It was hard for her. The day each of us turned eighteen, we left, understanding we would never return.

The father of my children is a Guardian. Not good news. I hate him for abandoning me, but this? Unforgivable. Finding out I could be a Muse? Being pulled into one of these unethical and amoral relationships is not something I can live with, even if it's supposed to keep me alive. There are people more deserving of protection and healing. Cal should be curing cancer in little children, not following me around making a nuisance of himself.

What about the Guardian that saved me? That was out of character. Guardians don't run around saving people. They look the other way, staying on the alert to keep their Muse safe. The blue-eyed Guardian is a mystery, an enigma.

That I could be thrown into this with only Cal to catch me was too preposterous to believe and frightening to boot. It seems more likely a plot made up by Cal to weasel back into our lives, and there's no way I'm letting that happen. The divorce states I get full custody. He waved visitation rights. If he thinks this will get him back in our lives, he's gonna be disappointed.

It took two aspirin and fifty ounces of water to clear my head the next morning. I got the kids out the door and staggered down the driveway, painting in tow. Diane was taking me to get my rig from the shop.

"You look about like Johnas this morning," Diane said, as I slid into her green Prius.

"Sharp, witty and ready to face the day?"

"Like turds warmed over."

"Turds aside, do I look ready to sell my first painting?" I indicated my black dress slacks and elegantly done up-do. Not too much make-up, either.

We stopped for a light and she scrutinized my appearance in that best-friend way, honestly without sounding harsh. Handing me her purse she said, "Tweezers—inner pocket, left side."

Rolling my eyes, I started the ritual of auxiliary hair removal, using the well-named vanity mirror. Being a single mom doesn't leave much time for frivolous grooming. Diane would faint if she knew the last time I shaved my legs.

We were half way to the repair shop when Diane checked her rear view mirror for the umpteenth time.

"Your pool boy following us or something?" I asked.

Diane is a petite gorgeous red head. Despite a huge diamond and a huge husband, men hit on her everywhere we go. She doesn't have a pool boy, but if she did, he'd probably stalk her too.

She smiled, unapologetically, at my joke, but then looked worried again. "This Fed-mobile has been following us since we left your neighborhood. He's not even bothering to stay a couple cars back."

I looked back. It was Cal, looking smooth in sunglasses behind the wheel of a black SUV. He saw me looking, smiled and waved.

"Cal." I said, making it sound like a groan. I slammed the vanity mirror shut. He'd watched me pluck my eyebrows for twenty blocks. So much for my confident cool persona. Car accidents and eyebrow hair were ruining my image. "Why's he even following us? I told him I'd see him at eleven."

Diane cleared her throat.

"What?"

"He's guarding you, Shel. You know, following you around and making sure you're safe."

I glared at the side of her face until she shot a glance at me.

"Come on, Shel. You're a Muse now; you need protection. Sucks that it's Cal, but aren't you excited?"

"I am not a Muse. This is Cal's plot to get back into our lives. It's not going to work. We're over. I moved on. The kids moved on. We don't have space for him, and he's just gonna have to get over it. Not to mention I would never take part in such an amoral endeavor anyway."

Diane chewed her lip and glanced back again. "Is it so hard to believe you could be a Muse? You're talented enough and twenty-five is the age you find out. It all fits, Shel. As for the amoral part, is this about your parents?"

"It's not about my parents; it's about the stupid Guardians using their stupid abilities to help everyone. Not just people they think are 'worthy'." I used air quotes to emphasize my point and folded my arms across my chest. Diane didn't push the subject and soon we were at the repair shop.

Before I could remove my painting from the back seat, Diane surprised me by throwing her arms around me.

"It's gonna be okay. Whatever it is, whatever he does, we'll be here for you, just like last time."

"It's not gonna come to that. I'm not letting him get that close. He'll be gone in a week, never to darken our doorsteps again."

"I just want you to know that we're here for you. You're not alone."

She knew how much that meant to me. "Thanks, Di."

She rubbed my shoulder. "Don't worry about him anymore. Go deliver that painting!"

She was right. "I got this. No worries."

"Oh, I know. I've never had any doubts about you. Go get 'em!" She let out a whoop and threw her hands in the air.

I blushed, but appreciated her enthusiasm. She drove away, and I found myself scanning the street looking for Cal's Fed-mobile. It wasn't in sight, but that didn't mean he wasn't watching. He was always a sneaky one. Another reason not to trust him.

The Beast, as my kids affectionately refer to my SUV, is one of those mid-size SUVs that rolled off the line somewhere in Asia, sometime in the mid '90s. It has gleaming deep red paint, huge tires and an even bigger engine. I've driven it since before Julian was born and, a few routine maintenance things aside, it had yet to fail me. When the mechanic drove it around, I felt a weight lift off me.

Five blocks later, Cal slid into traffic behind me. Did he have low-jack on me or something?

I snagged a parking space in front of the coffee shop. Cal passed me. He'd have to circle back to find a parking space on the crowded street. If I hurried, he wouldn't see which shop I went into.

4

The Muse Affairs and Guardian Regulative Authority (MAGRA), popularly called *the Authority,* originated in 400 B.C. when small factions of Guardians and Muses unified to protect and govern themselves.

The agency formed rules of conduct and chose leaders from among their most powerful to enforce them. Each geographical area has its own faction; faction leaders gather biannually to discuss issues, share information and exchange Guardians or Muses best suited to serve the mortals in their areas.

MAGRA initiated the public emergence of Muses and Guardians in 1982. The agency continues to monitor their public behavior and to manage issues among Muses, Guardians and mortals. The organization also trains Guardians and matches them with Muses deemed best suited for their abilities.
　　—"Muses and Guardians" *World Look Encyclopedia*

Isabella's is a cafe named after the owner, a little Italian lady in her fifties. It's over-priced, the atmosphere stimulating and the sweet rolls to die for. When I can, I do my homework here. One day, bored of studying, I pulled out my sketchpad. Isabella herself walked by and noticed my work. She pulled me to a bare wall near the register, gesturing and speaking in her heavy accent. I could barely keep up, but I understood enough. She'd been looking for art for the space for a long time and would pay me to paint a landscape for her. Isabella wanted fifteen square feet of Tuscan valley.

At first, I declined. Sure I want to make a living as an artist, but this was a big project. Maybe too big, but Isabella wouldn't take no for an answer. She grabbed my sketchbook and flipped through it, praising each sketch, telling me my proportions were perfect and my use of light dramatic yet smooth. Honestly, it wasn't her praise, it was the thought of extra money in my budget that convinced me. We agreed on a thousand dollars for the painting, and she cut me a check for the first half. I'd packed up and gone home feeling more apprehensive than excited.

Today was the delivery date. A wave of anxiety washed over me as I walked into her little shop. This could be big for me. If Isabella liked the painting, she might give me a referral. I had some business cards printed, just in case. If all went well, I'd leave a couple with her.

A little bell announced my entrance. Isabella was behind the counter talking to an employee. She looked up at the sound of the bell, gave me a smile and signaled she'd be right with me.

I took a moment to look around the shop and better take in the clientele. I was scanning the little tables when my eyes flashed across a familiar face. It was the Guardian who'd saved me the day before. He was smiling at me. I smiled back and headed towards his table. I at least needed to thank him, I told myself, but he was a curiosity to me. Why'd he save me? Where was his Muse?

"I'm glad you're all right," he said in the deep voice I remembered. This was definitely the same guy.

"I am, and I wanted to thank you. I wouldn't have made it out of there without you."

"It was my pleasure. Would you like to sit down? Have a cup of coffee with me?" He had a cup of espresso and a newspaper in front of him. His shoulders were unnaturally broad and his suit looked expensive. I put him in his late twenties or early thirties. His strong jaw line was clean-shaven, accentuating full lips. His eyes were a luminous blue, and his hair light blond against tan skin. In short, he looked good enough to eat.

"I can't,"

His smile didn't falter. "Perhaps another time then?"

Isabella's arrival saved me from having to make up an excuse. "Shelby darling, you brought my painting," She pulled me into a tight hug, kissing the air next to each of my cheeks.

"All finished, just like I promised."

"Fabulous. Shelby, do you know Malcolm? He's an old friend." Isabella looked delighted to introduce us.

"We met yesterday" I stuck out my free hand and he gripped it. His touch was warm and on the firm side. Not too firm, though.

"Malcolm. Nice to meet you."

"Oh, wonderful! Shelby is an amazing artist. I had to beg her to help me with the shop."

Malcolm's eyebrows went up as he released my hand. "An artist?"

I blushed and nodded.

"Open it, Shelby. I want to see. Malcolm, you look, too."

The table next to Malcolm was empty, so I set the three-by-five foot painting on it. With shaking fingers, I peeled back the heavy brown paper and propped it against the wall. Malcolm stood and stepped back next to Isabella. I was so busy watching for his reaction, I almost missed Isabella's.

Her face went from elegant serene to utter shock faster than a stoplight changes. I'd done what she asked me, perhaps improving on it a bit, but her reaction had me worried. I looked over the painting thinking something happened to it in transit, but it was perfect, a scene of a Tuscan valley in spring. There were blades of grass in shades of green and yellow with a few oranges and pinks thrown in to set it off. Shaped spots looked like wildflowers riding the grass, the flowers an inspiration taken from the perfume Isabella always wore. The sky was blue with puffy white clouds riding the same breeze that made the grass lean daintily to the left. Set atop the hill was a stone cottage surrounded by an old wooden fence, a clothesline set out front. On the clothesline was nothing but a bright red dress billowing in the breeze. The red of the dress and the sparse hints of red given off by the wildflowers drew on elements of the elegant surroundings. I thought it would make a perfect balance for the ambiance of the shop. Perhaps I was wrong.

"Isabella, is everything all right?"

She sat abruptly in a nearby chair.

I looked at Malcolm. He was still looking at the painting, his eyes wide. He looked at me and his eyes seemed to glow. What had I done?

My first commissioned delivery was not going well. I knelt on the floor next to Isabella.

"Isabella, are you all right? Is there something wrong with the painting? Whatever it is, I can fix it. Just tell me."

I put a hand on her arm and felt a pull of energy so abrupt and violent that the next thing I knew, I was hearing Malcolm's voice in my ear and a warm hand was on my neck.

"You're all right; breathe," he said.

I gasped, not having realized I wasn't breathing. My eyes flew open and I convulsed. It wasn't painful, but terrifying.

"What's wrong with her?" I heard an accented voice say. It was Isabella. This was not going well.

"She's a Muse." Malcolm said in a very quiet voice.

Isabella had a sharp intake of breathe. "I had no idea. I wouldn't have—"

"It's not your fault. It's not even hers. She had no idea what she was doing. Check her wallet for some ID. I think I know what happened." I heard all this but couldn't speak. I was convulsing again, and my jaw felt glued shut. Between spasms, my body went limp. As much as I tried to move, I couldn't. I watched Isabella hand Malcolm my driver's license. I wanted to stop him: The picture was terrible.

It's amazing what asinine things go through your head when you could be dying.

"Her twenty-fifth was yesterday," he said, handing it back to Isabella. "She must have given him the slip. Can I take her upstairs?"

"Of course."

Not taking his hand off my neck, Malcolm lifted me. I could still feel a steady, warm trickle of energy flowing into me. Someone asked if I needed an ambulance, and Malcolm said my blood sugar was low. I was unable to speak or move, so Malcolm carried me behind the counter, through the kitchen and up a narrow flight of stairs. Like the day before, he moved as if I weighed nothing.

Isabella led the way to what must be her apartment over the cafe. "Can I do anything to help?" She looked nervous once we were inside with the door closed.

"She just needs a few minutes."

"I'm going to get the painting. I want to talk to her about it when she's better. You be okay?"

He nodded, and she left. He looked down at me. "How are you doing?"

The convulsions had almost stopped. I took a deep breath and tried to speak; my lips moved, but nothing came out.

He snuggled me in closer to his chest. He smelled musky, like fresh turned earth and sweet like crisp new paper.

I wiggled my fingers and toes and panicked, realizing I was incapacitated, alone in a room with a strange man ... a Guardian!

He must have sensed my anxiety, because he whispered in my ear that I'd be all right, that he wouldn't hurt me. I knew he was telling the truth. I could feel his sincerity in the trickling energy moving into me.

After what seemed like an eternity, I was able to speak. The words were slow and a bit slurred, but he understood me. "What happened?"

"You turned twenty-five yesterday. Where's your Guardian?"

My thoughts went to Cal. "Why?"

"He didn't tell you?" Malcolm sounded incredulous.

I moved my head so I could better see his face, my slow uncoordinated movements giving me time to think. "It's complicated," I said, not wanting to explain. "You didn't answer my question though. What happened? And what are you doing to me?" I could still feel a steady transfer of energy between us. Now that the convulsions had stopped, the feeling was almost pleasant.

"I don't know what he told you but the short of it is, you're a Muse."

I cringed.

"When Muses turn twenty-five, they gain abilities," he continued. "And one of those is the transfer of information, understanding, feelings— whatever the situation may call for—into others ... often with a touch." He paused for a moment and let me absorb that. "With the transfer goes energy. Your energy, your life force, if you will."

Okay. I guess I could see that. It was pretty much what I'd felt. "It was like all the life just left me?" He nodded, and some of the color left his face. "Now you're transferring it back into me?" He nodded again. "What would've happened if you hadn't been there?"

"You would've gone into a coma and eventually died if a Guardian didn't come along to help you." His fingers moved against my neck.

I wiggled in his lap and he took the hint, setting me on the couch next to him. He moved his hand to the inside of my forearm to maintain our connection, his hand's warm weight somehow more intimate on the sensitive skin there.

I wiggled a bit more. A man hadn't touched me in a long time. I wasn't sure how to handle it. "So when Isabella got upset, I touched her to try and make her like the painting?"

"Unconsciously. Your Guardian will teach you how to do it consciously and how not to dump all your energy when you do it. He'll also stay close enough that you'll be able to pull energy through him when you're ready."

My head spun with images of doing all that with Cal. I couldn't even imagine Cal touching me to transfer energy like this.

"What if I don't want a Guardian? Can I send him back to MAGRA or donate him to the public good or something?"

He gave me a puzzled look. "A Muse can't live without a Guardian. I don't know what your situation is, but surely you want to do what you can for humanity?"

"Me? What about you? What about all Guardians? You people have amazing abilities and you squander them following around uppity, semi-talented jerks. You should all be working for the good of everyone, not just a few select."

He continued to look confused. "Shelby, that's why Guardians protect Muses, for the good of all humanity, not just for the sake of the Muses." His voice was calm and smooth as if he were explaining breathing. It was just that simple to him. He brushed the inside of my arm with his fingertips.

I shivered as the sensation sent tingles up my spine. I looked up into his eyes, trying to be angry and accusing, but I couldn't hold onto the feeling. Like a drug, calm was coming in with the energy. Questions buzzed through my mind. He'd saved my life, again, and all I'd done was go off about my issues.

"Who do you guard? Isabella? She seemed to know a lot about this."

It was his turn to look uncomfortable. He stopped stroking my arm and looked away. "Isabella's daughter is a Guardian. That's how I know her and I uh ... I ... I don't ..." He cleared his throat. "I don't work for MAGRA, I mean."

"Really? Why not?"

"It's a personal choice." His hand curled around my arm as if to remember to keep it there.

I was excited. A Guardian with no Muse, a Guardian who helps everyone? Like a real super hero or something? I decided not to press the subject. He seemed sensitive about it.

"So, Muses like me ..." I tried it out and didn't cringe. "We can touch people and influence them?"

He nodded, still not meeting my eyes.

"Why haven't I heard this before?"

He turned to me, eyes searching. "Can you imagine what would happen if the public, if the government, knew you could do that? They'd round you up and send you to an island somewhere like they used to do with lepers. You want that to happen?"

I gulped and shook my head.

"I don't know what's going on with you and your Guardian, but you need to have a sit-down with him."

"Him? How do you know it's a man?"

"It always is." He stroked my arm again. "Women guard men, and men guard women. It just works better. The relationship is... intimate."

He added, "That is, unless you prefer women." His mouth tilted into a smile.

"Men are great, thanks." I stifled a laugh.

Isabella walked in with my painting.

Malcolm's hand went still against my arm. For a moment, she just looked at us curled up on the couch. I'd been feeling normal for a while; Malcolm could've stopped touching me, but hadn't. I didn't want to move away from him either. I'd analyze that later.

"You look better, Shelby. Malcolm has helped you?"

"Yes, thank you for letting us up here; it would've been awkward to stay downstairs."

She smiled. "It's no trouble, darling." She crossed to her little dining table and propped the painting against it. "Your talents have created quite the stir in my cafe. Everyone was buzzing around the painting when I went downstairs. I could hardly whisk it away for all the questions. It's going to be the perfect centerpiece for my little shop."

With her back to us, Malcolm's fingers started a slow line across my arm again. I watched his fingers in fascination. They were long, but broad, dark against the pale skin of my arm. Like his eyes, there was something familiar about them.

Isabella turned back to us, and his fingers stilled. "Can I show you something?"

I nodded, still nervous about what she thought of the painting.

She picked something off her desk and sat down in a chair near us. "When I was girl, I lived in the Tuscan Valley with my mother and father," she started in her thick Italian accent. "My mother was the most beautiful woman. She loved to pick wildflowers. There was always a vase of them in our home and some of my fondest memories of her are in the kitchen of our little house, kneading dough with the smell of wildflowers washing in with the breeze from the window, her hands covered in flour, her showing me how to work the dough. I will never forget the smell of sweet dough mixed with wildflowers." Isabella was quiet for a moment, and I tried to imagine that smell. It made my mouth water. "I've tried so hard to recreate that smell in my adult life, but I must accept that things can never be that way again." She was quiet.

"When I was nine, my mother died giving birth," she continued, struggling to find the words. "My father was so ... melancholy. He took me and we left the valley. By the time I was fourteen we were crossing the ocean, and I've been here ever since."

She handed me the framed photo. "This is all I was able to keep of my mother. I had to keep it out of sight of my father. He would've destroyed it if I'd insisted on keeping it in the open."

The photo showed a gorgeous woman and a little girl standing in front of a stone cottage in bright red dresses, holding bunches of wildflowers. I could just make out a clothesline around the side of the house. The cottage and the clothesline had been my own addition to the painting. She'd only asked for a scene of a Tuscan valley. How could I have known? I'd never seen the photo before. I'd never even heard the story.

"Isabella, I'm sorry. I can fix it. Just give me a couple days. I can have it how you asked. I didn't realize ..."

She made shushing noises at me. "You don't understand, darling. It is wonderful. More wonderful than I could've asked for. I wanted a piece of Tuscany, and you brought me a piece of *my* Tuscany. I hadn't known it was possible, but here it is." She turned back to the painting.

I just watched her, not daring to believe the truth of it.

After a long moment, she got up from the chair and crossed back to her desk. A few minutes passed before she crossed back in front of the painting. She looked at it again. "The wildflowers are perfect, the cottage, the red dress. I feel like I'm back there again." She smiled at me, a tear rolling down her cheek. She held a check out to me and I took it. Giving it a cursory glance, I nearly dropped it.

"Isabella, you made a mistake. It was supposed to be five hundred, not five thousand—"

"You deserve it. This is ... There are no words for this. Just take it." She looked back to the painting.

I looked at Malcolm, not sure what to do. His intense eyes met mine and through our connection, I felt something like admiration, only it felt like more.

He got up and slowly helped me to my feet. He spent a moment tucking my hand into his. I was still wobbly and appreciated his help.

We got to the door before Isabella noticed us leaving.

"Shelby?"

I turned, not letting go of Malcolm.

"Thank you."

The emotion in her voice caught me. "You're welcome."

Malcolm gave my hand a tug and pulled me from the room.

5

Musehood officially begins at transition, if it occurs. Due to deficits of character and intelligence not fully understood, only 50 percent of potential Muses accomplish the complete transition. Those who do transition choose their own paths, using either positive energies (like light, beauty and peace) or negative ones (like darkness, destruction and discord).

—"Muses," *World Look Encyclopedia*

Malcolm led me through the cafe onto the street.

"Where's your car?"

"Red SUV." I pointed a few cars down.

"Perfect." He pulled me towards it, leaned me against the passenger door and put a hand on my cheek. "The transfer of energy happens through nerves. The more nerves touching, the more energy we can transfer at once." To demonstrate, he put a hand on my other cheek. The power increased and with it came Malcolm's essence.

"I can feel you." I met his eyes. "Pages turning in a book, the hum of an engine, the burn of runners high ... and strength, so much strength." His eyes closed, and the strength washed through me in a wave and left ... sadness. It was such a small trickle and was gone so quickly that I put my hands on his face, trying to catch the last of it. Big mistake. The added connection doubled the energy. We both gasped. The energy ebbed within me and pushed back into Malcolm, seeking equilibrium.

"I can feel you now," he said. "Colors, all of them, so bright and ..." He didn't finish. He opened his eyes and looked at me. He had that same expression from when he saw my painting. Was it disbelief?

Someone moved in my peripheral vision, and I dropped my hands.

Cal, still in sunglasses, hovered over us.

Great.

Malcolm removed one hand and then the other. I didn't collapse or convulse. We were both relieved. Then I caught myself. How did I know Malcolm was thinking that?

"Cal." Malcolm gave him a nod.

"Malcolm." Cal returned the nod. Men and their weird non-verbals.

No one said anything until Malcolm broke the silence. "It was nice seeing you again Shelby. Perhaps next time we could meet under more pleasant circumstances?"

"Yeah, it would be nice if I didn't end up in your arms again." Then, realizing what I said, I blurted, "Not that I don't like being in your arms or anything." I felt my face burn with humiliation. This is why I don't date. It would be better for the whole world if I just didn't speak. I made a mental note to stick to painting.

"I know what you meant." Malcolm chuckled. "Until next time ..."

As soon as he was gone, Cal grabbed my arm and pulled me around my rig. "Do you have any idea how dangerous he is? You're not to speak to him again."

I wrenched my arm from his grip." I don't care how many pieces of signed, stamped, and approved paper you have that say you can butt into my health. Don't you ever grab me like that again." I straightened my coat. "And furthermore, you don't get to tell me what to do. I'm an adult and no possession of yours. I do, say and talk to whomever I want."

"You're not gonna make this easy on me, are you?" He sounded tired.

"You?" I started laughing. I couldn't help it. I laughed so hard it hurt. "You want *me* to make things easier on *you*? This out of the man who left me pregnant and crying with a baby in my lap when I was eighteen?" I started laughing again. "Then you show up here, storm my hospital room, show up at my house, interrupt my birthday and push your way in front of *my* kids." I took another moment to laugh. "You want *me* to make things easier on *you*?" I opened the beast's door. "No Cal, I'm not going to make anything easy on you. In fact, you can kiss my fat ass." I slammed the door in his face.

He stood there a long moment. "See you at eleven."

I sat back in my seat and took a deep breath. One minute, just give him one minute to get gone. When the minute was up, I let out a scream and beat the steering wheel with everything I had. This was not happening to me. He could not come into my life and turn everything upside down. There had to be a way to get rid of him. But I just couldn't think of it. I pulled away from the curb stewing, determined to think of something.

I made it home without spotting Cal in my rear view. He was out there, though. I could feel it.

I hung my coat in the closet and a black business card fell out. I picked it up and recognized the name: Malcolm Dixon. Just a phone number. No position or title, no business logo or fax number. He'd given me his phone number.

I tucked the card in my wallet. I wasn't gonna call him. Yes, he was handsome. Yes, he was probably rich and a super hero type, but I had enough guy problems. Cal's warning was there, too. Why didn't Malcolm have a Muse to guard? Why did Cal think he was dangerous? How do they even know each other? Do all Guardians know each other? Is that part of their thing?

I decided Cal was just jealous. He saw another man touching me and went all cave man. Telling me Malcolm is dangerous an easy way to keep me away from him, but why would Cal even care? He'd made it obvious he didn't love me anymore. It was just a territory thing. Stupid males. I wasn't going to call Malcolm anyway, so it didn't matter.

I found myself pacing back and forth between my entryway and kitchen, thinking about how to get rid of Cal again.

Maybe I could convince him he didn't need to babysit me full time. Then he could spend most of his time helping other people. I might be able to live with that, and it would at least keep him away from me until I could devise a more permanent solution.

Ten minutes later, I was out the door. I ran, pushing myself harder than usual. I needed the burn, the rush of endorphins and the control ... even if it was just for an hour and over something minor, like how fast I was running. When my life spirals out of control, an extra run—or ten—finds its way into my routine.

Home again, I went to the kitchen for some water. There was someone on my couch. I stopped, backed up and, sure enough, Cal. I made a mental note to lock the doors and take my keys from now on.

"Get out." I pointed a stiff arm at the door. "You're not allowed in my house unless I invite you in. I will call the cops. Get out."

Cal just stared at me. At least his sunglasses were gone, so I could read his expression. I'd call the look slightly confused.

"I was early and overestimated your hospitality. Of course I will go back outside and knock."

"Don't bother. Our appointment's not for another hour. You're not coming in 'til then." I know I sounded like a bitch, but I have boundaries and he was going to respect them. I wasn't his little wifey anymore.

For a second he looked like I'd slapped him. Then his face smoothed back to unreadable.

"As you wish." He got smoothly to his feet.

Damn he looked good, better than I remember. His boyishly round face had thinned to reveal a masculine profile. He was no longer floppy and clumsy in his long limbs, having filled out to match the length of his tall frame.

Not fair that he looks better than before, and I'm zigzagged with stretch marks and crow's feet. Those twenty pounds I still haven't lost since having Julian were there, too. "My fat ass" hadn't been an expression.

Cal met my eyes. "Despite what I said after your accident, you look good, Shel. You've turned into a real lady."

I harrumphed. I was in baggy, stained sweats, hair plastered to my sweaty face. There was probably mascara running down my cheeks, and I could only imagine what I smelled like.

He smiled at me again.

I looked to the door and then back to him, trying not to grind my teeth. If he didn't get out, I'd *show* him a lady.

He backed towards to the door. "We're gonna find a truce eventually. We both have a job to do."

I shook my head. "Not the way you think, Cal."

He opened the door. "We'll see." He gave me one last infuriating smile and was gone.

I locked the door. All three locks. He couldn't even pick his way in. I stomped up the stairs to the shower, where I shaved my legs. Not because there were men in my life again, but because if I went much longer, I was going to need a fresh blade for the second leg. The thought of Cal's hand on these beastly looking limbs at the hospital sent a wave of humiliation through me. I would never be caught like that again.

After my shower, I took stock of myself in the mirror. I'm around five foot three, weigh in at one forty and am proud to say that most of that is muscle, minus my ass, of course. My hair is dark brown and hangs past my shoulder blades. Despite my petite frame, I've always been on the bulkier side. My daughter, Chloe, just got the petite frame. Lucky her.

I like my face, though. Crow's feet aside, my eyes are big, dark brown and long lashed. I can get away with not wearing mascara and often do.

Staring at myself, it finally hit me.

I am a Muse.

I sat down on the edge of the bathtub and just watched my reflection in the mirror.

I couldn't be a Muse. I'm not special enough. I'm just a stupid girl with a couple kids who likes to paint. I don't even have family or fans or even fashion sense. ...

Muses are glamorous and busy, jet-setting the world, helping people, dodging crowds, holding tight to their Guardian.

What happened at *Isabella's* would be just the beginning. What else could I do now? I didn't even know. Muses are shrouded in mystery, their secrets kept well. You hear them speak, see their creations, watch them dance or act or play professional sports. You sometimes even see the after-effects of what they do. A huge charity donation on their behalf, countries that were at war suddenly declaring peace.

That was my job now. How to do it? I had absolutely no idea.

I needed a Guardian. After today, I couldn't deny it, but not Cal. Whomever it ended up being will have to understand that other people are important, too, and must be helped, saved. I couldn't stand by and watch people like my parents die, watch families be torn apart all for the sake of *my* life.

I looked in the mirror and tried it aloud. "I am a Muse."

I didn't feel any different. Maybe more tired.

I looked in the mirror again. My messy bathroom with its mismatched towels and retro paint job framed me in a way that was laughable.

I was suddenly overwhelmed with anxiety and fear, not sure I could do it, not sure I could handle one more thing. I have friends, but, really, there wasn't anyone to help me. Could I undertake such a huge responsibility by myself?

"I am a Muse," I said again. There must be a reason I was chosen, why it had to be me. I had to believe I could, somehow, do it all.

I have kids to raise, college to finish and a bathroom to remodel, but somehow I would do it.

I decided right then that no matter my responsibilities as a Muse, my kids come first. They're the reason I have to handle Cal the right way. I can't have him popping in and out of their lives. They need stability and predictability. Something Cal will respect or move on.

I left the bathroom feeling more tired than I had in a long time.

I dressed in jeans and a long-sleeved thermal, put my hair in a ponytail and forewent any make-up. No need to dress up for Cal; I didn't want him thinking I cared what he thought. I headed downstairs with twenty minutes to spare. Just enough time to make some coffee—which I wouldn't offer Cal—and eat some cereal before he knocked again.

I was ready. This time, Muse or not, Guardian or not, magical mystical abilities or not, I was calling the shots. This was still *my* life.

6

In a **Muse experiment** conducted by MAGRA in the early thirteenth century, suspected Muses were told of their abilities at an early age in order to begin preparation for their calling. The experiment failed. Every Muse informed of his or her talent before age twenty-five failed to complete the final transition. The repercussions nearly eliminated the Muse and Guardian population of Western Europe.

In addition, those misdiagnosed as Muses commonly developed mental illness before age thirty. Some committed suicide and others failed to thrive as human mortals, dying of natural causes by the age of thirty-five.

—"Muses," *World Look Encyclopedia*

Cal knocked right at eleven. Punctual is good.

I undid all the locks and let him in. He took the couch again. My coffee and I took my desk chair across the room

"First, I want to tell you that I've taken care of the police report and settled with the insurance company for you."

I blinked. "You didn't have to do that."

He shrugged. "It's done."

We were quiet for a minute. "What is it you want, Cal?"

"To see my kids."

"No." Okay, I may have been bluffing, but I wanted him to earn it.

He leaned forward. "Come on, Shel. I'm their father."

"Sperm does not a father make. You signed away your rights. That makes me sole guardian, and I say, no." I took a sip of coffee.

"I could have full custody by tomorrow morning. I'm coming to you out of courtesy."

After his little flash and dash with the paperwork at the hospital, I expected something like this. "You'd do that to them? You're a worse father than I thought."

"Of course I wouldn't, but I want you to realize you can't keep them away from me. One or both of them could be a Guardian. They need me."

I sat in shocked silence for a whole minute.

"How could you do this, Cal? To me? To them? You know how I feel about Guardians and what they're consigned to. This is ... worse than I could've imagined." I tried not to cry. My poor babies.

He sat back in the couch again and tugged at the hair around his temple. "I didn't mean for this to happen. Please believe I didn't know."

"How could you not know? You knew what you were."

"I didn't know what you were."

"Me?"

"Guardians can only have kids with Muses."

Cal and I met during my freshman year of high school and hit if off right away. Less than a year later, we were pregnant with Chloe. Cal had convinced me not to use birth control, and I'd been too naive to insist.

My aunt had kicked me out, her final act in proving how much she didn't care about me. Cal, also being an orphan, went to work for his foster parents and was able to afford us a little one-bedroom apartment. We continued to go to school and when Chloe was born, she went to the daycare our high school operated just for the students. Things were tight, but I'd thought we were happy. Cal finished school a year ahead of me, got a scholarship to the local university and continued to work when he could.

After I graduated, friends and family threw us a little wedding. Chloe was eighteen months old by then; Cal was doing well in college, working on an IT degree; and I'd started working part-time to help out, thinking I'd go to college when Cal finished in another couple years. We didn't have much, but things seemed to be coming together. Again, I was naive.

Despite our best efforts to the contrary, I got pregnant with Julian. That's when Cal changed. He got distant, started staying out late; sometimes he came home drunk, if he came home at all. He wouldn't touch me and ignored Chloe. I tried talking to him, but he just said he was stressed.

Finally one morning, I got up to find Cal sitting at our little table with its mismatched chairs. Chloe's high-chair was behind him, still covered in food from last night's dinner. There was a packed bag at his feet.

I remember standing there, stunned, my brain unwilling to make the connections.

"I'm going into the Army," he said. "I just need to get away. I don't want this life or you. I never planned to have kids either. I just can't do it anymore."

I remember thinking how that didn't make sense. He loved me; he loved Chloe. He'd been an amazing husband and father for almost two years. He'd told me countless times that he loved me, that I was his universe, that he'd never leave me, that he'd always be my family....

I took a step forward, put my hand on his shoulder. He shrugged it off.

"It's just a rough patch; we can work it out. I'll get a full-time job, and you can just focus on school for awhile, see how it goes."

Then he did something I'll never forget.

In one motion, faster than I could follow, he stood up and hit Chloe's high-chair so hard it flew across the room and smashed into the wall. It shattered, leaving a dent in the wall and scattering food particles across the room. "You're a slob, Shelby. The house is always a mess; you're always dumping all your problems on me, bitching about everything!" He'd never yelled at me before, never so much as looked like he might hit something, let alone threatened to. That he'd actually hit it had me stunned, unable to move.

Never in over two years had he mentioned any of those things, either. The house was often a mess, but it was small, we were both always busy and we had a baby toddling around. Neither of us had got more than six hours sleep in years. He'd often encouraged me to take time for myself, to paint.

As for complaining about my problems, he'd encouraged me to share things with him. After all the years at my aunt's where no one gave a shit what I thought, it had been hard for me to open up to him, but he'd been patient and always encouraged me to let out what was bothering me. I'd never had much growing up and not having much now didn't mean anything to me. I just wanted Cal and Chloe, a family of my own, a place where I belonged.

Chloe started crying from her crib in the bedroom, but I couldn't move. I was in shock, not having seen this coming, not even a little bit.

"Go get your whiny baby. The one you wanted so bad."

That felt like a slap. Of all the people who encouraged me to have an abortion or give Chloe up for adoption, Cal hadn't been one of them. He'd wanted to keep her, too. Promising he'd take care of us.

He picked up his bag and I flinched, my adrenaline still pumping from the high-chair shattering.

"You'll get divorce papers in a couple weeks." He started moving towards the door.

I didn't know what else to do, so I went to get Chloe. There were little frightened tears running down her cheeks, and that's when I realized I was crying, too. She stopped crying when I picked her up. I carried her out to where Cal was standing by the front door, his hand on the knob.

It was happening to me again. Everyone who ever cared about me, who ever loved me, left. I was five years old again, and a social worker was standing in front of me, telling me my parents would never come home again. That I needed to pick my two favorite toys and leave everything else behind to go to a new home with strangers who'd never love me, where things weren't mine and I'd have a million lonely nights where I cried myself to sleep and begged the universe to bring my parents back.

"You promised," I said. "You promised you'd never leave me, that we'd be a family."

"I lied."

Something inside me gave way and I fell to my knees, Chloe still in my arms. "Please," I begged. "Please don't leave me. I love you. I'll fix it, I promise, whatever you need. Don't leave me. I have no one. ..."

For a second, I thought he was reconsidering, just a tiny flicker in his eyes, but it was fleeting and his eyes narrowed again. "I don't love you, Shelby. I felt obligated to take care of you, so I tried, but it's not going to work." He opened the door and looked back. "I'm sorry."

He left. Just like all the others.

I was eighteen years old. Chloe was not even two, and I was four months pregnant with Julian. I had nothing and no one.

In the months that followed, I realized I'd always be alone, that I couldn't trust anyone but myself and that I'd never let anyone in again. Especially Cal.

Some of it finally made sense, why he'd said we didn't need birth control, why he'd tried to take care of me. He's Guardian; they take care of Muses, but why didn't he tell me?

"You must've known I was Muse after I got pregnant?"

He stared out the window. "I couldn't tell you and I thought I could keep it a secret from the Authority, but they figured it out. After that, I knew I had to leave. I went back into training. Artistic Muses are a ... high maintenance." He tried not to smile and failed.

"I don't understand. Why come back at all? When you left, you made it pretty clear how you felt about me. Chloe was an accident, so was Julian. They weren't a reason to stay together, and they're not a reason to get back together. Why are you here?"

His chocolate eyes drilled into me. "They're my kids, Shel. I can't have another man raising them. Not if I can help it. This makes things easier. I can be their dad and take care of their mom."

I harrumphed. "I don't need taking care of." Even to my own ears, I sounded twelve.

His next statement surprised me. "No, you don't, but you do need someone to show you the ropes and help you if you get into trouble. Let me do that much, Shel, please?"

It was my turn to look out the window. "You know how I feel about Guardians. I can't trust you after what happened, and I can't monopolize your talents. You should be on a children's ward curing sick little kids. Not following me around, crowding up my life."

"I can't cure illnesses, Shel. Only heal injuries."

"Then an emergency room. Think how many people you could save?"

"I wish it worked that way," he said to the floor.

"It doesn't?"

He shook his head. "Remember how tired I was after I healed you?" Working in an ER would kill me within months. I can help so many more people by helping you."

"I don't know about that," I mumbled.

"What were you doing with Malcolm this morning?"

"Huh? Oh ... I had a little episode and he uh... helped me with it."

Cal raised an eyebrow. "What happened?"

My blood pressure spiked. I should've refused to answer. That would have been the smart thing, but instead I opened by big mouth. "I delivered a painting this morning. The recipient had an unexpected reaction, and I touched her arm...."

Cal shot off the couch and came at me.

I cringed and spilled coffee in my lap, but all he did was touch my arm.

When he spoke, it was so quiet, so calm and so intense, I was afraid. "Do you have any idea what you've done? What this means? You've jeopardized everything."

He knew, somehow, he knew.

I pulled my arm away. "By doing what? Staying alive? You're acting like I had a choice."

He wheeled away and started pacing.

I watched in stunned silence. I'd never seen him like this.

"It's all right. As long as you stay away from him, it should undo itself. I should've been more careful. I should've insisted. I thought if I gave you time, if I gave you space, you'd learn to trust me again. "He continued talking to himself or, I guess, the floor, but it stopped making sense. He said something about rules and then more and more blame, mostly on himself. There were some statistics in there too, but it was all lost on me. He stopped. "Do you hear that?"

I recognized the muffled ringtone coming from my purse. Not again. ... I pulled out my cell phone. Meredith Brooks' *Bitch* filled the air. I picked up the call.

My kids' vice-principal's voice cut through the line like cold ice. I felt the twitch in my eye take off at record speed. "May I speak with Mz. Hammond please?" She loved putting the emphasis on my lack of Mrs.

"This is she," I said, trying to soften her up with my correct grammar.

"Mz. Hammond, Julian is in my office, again. He was running up the slide, again. When the playground supervisor tried to correct him, he ran away, again."

I put a hand up to still my eye. Not today, Julian. Didn't I have enough to deal with?

"She had to drag him into my office, and now he is hiding under the table, refusing to come out or speak. Again."

"I'm sorry, Mrs. Brooks," See the ringtone really is fitting, "I'll be right there."

Cal moved into my bubble, still scary. "What happened?"

I took a step back. "Julian's in trouble at school again. I gotta go bail him out."

"Let me guess, trouble with secondary authority figures?"

I stopped in my tracks and my train of thought about where I'd left my keys. I realized that was exactly what Julian had: trouble with secondary authority figures. He was a sweet, loving kid. Didn't have any trouble with me or even his teacher, but get him under the watchful eye of the cafeteria monitor or the playground supervisor and he went into a defiant fit.

"How's it possible you know that?"

"I'm coming with you. I can help, and I'm going to."

"No." I opened the door. I was not taking the whole dictatorial thing.

His hand caught the door. "This is one of the first signs of being a Guardian. Guardians see authority figures differently. He needs help learning to cope, someone who can relate."

I shut the door with a snap and wheeled into Cal's face. "This is my life. I call the shots. Not you. Not any agency. And I don't take orders. You want to work with me? I need to trust you. For that to happen, I need information. Not orders. You want to come? You want to be part of this? You take my orders. At least until I can trust you and we get some things figured out. Do we understand each other?"

Cal's nostrils flared and he took a deep breath. I felt my heart rate pick up again. Was he this menacing before?

"How do you wanna do this?" he said in a very controlled tone.

I felt my shoulders relax. "We can't just spring on the kids you're their long lost father. This isn't Star Wars. And I don't wanna tell them until I'm sure you're gonna stick around."

He looked angry again. "Do you have any idea how hard I worked for this? I'm not going anywhere, even if it kills me."

There was something in his eyes, in his tone that, God help me, made me believe him.

"Uncle Cal."

He started to open his mouth.

"Until I'm sure."

He took another breath and nodded.

When Cal divorced me and left for the "Army," Johnas's parents made me an offer. They run a property management company and had a house in need of "cosmetic repair." They let me live in it at a reduced rent if I provided the labor to fix it up. The house was in an older but still well-off neighborhood, perfect for raising kids and across the street from one of the best elementary schools in the state. What I didn't realize was the amount of ridicule I was going to endure in such a ritzy part of town. Being a young single mom doesn't earn you many points among the educated upper middle class of Corvallis, Oregon.

So, as I walked through the door of their school with a good-looking, obviously important man at my side I couldn't decide if it was a dream come true or my worst nightmare come to life.

Cal followed me into the front office.

"Ms. Hammond, Mrs. Brooks is waiting for you in her office. Sir?" The office assistant turned to Cal. "Can I help you?"

"I'm with her."

She looked startled but pulled herself together. She looked him up and down, taking in his brown trench coat, jeans and running shoes.

"Of course, if you'll both just sign in here." She indicated the parent sign-in. We were both given little badges identifying us as visitors before I led us back to the vice principal's office. I knew the way well.

The door was ajar, awaiting our arrival. I stepped through, not waiting for an invitation. Cal followed me. Julian was in his usual place, under the table in the corner. I stifled a sigh. Mrs. Brooks was busy at her desk. A common scene.

"Julian, come out of there," I said.

He obeyed, coming to stand at my side. We waited for Mrs. Brooks to give us her attention.

"This can't keep happening, Ms. Hammond," she said, without looking up.

I wasn't worth her undivided attention and, by association, neither was Julian. My temper didn't like that.

"I have the safety of all the students at this school to think of and one child running amok, one who won't follow rules or instruction, is a danger to us all." She still hadn't looked up.

"He just needs proper coaching. Something I'm taking upon myself," Cal said, causing all three of us look at him.

Mrs. Brooks did the same double take the office manager had. "And who might you be?"

He stepped forward and handed her the badge he'd flashed at the hospital. "Cal Hammond. I'm Julian's *uncle*."

He said the word "uncle" to make the point he was something more.

I could've stomped on his foot. This was not part of our agreement.

Mrs. Brooks looked bored, as she took the badge. Then her eyes went wide and she did a double take to Cal, back the badge, then another to me and then to Julian, her mind making all the connections.

"You're a ... ?" she asked, leaving out the obvious word, *guardian*.

Cal nodded slowly.

"And he's a ...?" she indicated Julian.

"Perhaps."

She held the badge for another moment. Cal reached out for its return. She seemed dazed, staring off into space, but handed it back.

"This is normal behavior for a child like Julian." Cal spoke with authority. "If you're agreeable, I'll come in a few hours each day and spend time coaching him. It should only take a week or so. He seems like a bright enough kid."

We all looked at Julian.

"Would that be all right with you, Julian? If he comes and helps you learn to control yourself?" I said, not believing the words were leaving my mouth.

Julian nodded, and my heart rate picked up. This could end so badly.

"Is it all right if I talk to him in the hallway?" Cal started to take off his coat. "Then he should stay and finish out the rest of his day. Getting to go home would be a reward. We want to avoid that at this point."

"All right," Mrs. Brooks said, sounding as overcome as I felt.

Cal took Julian's hand and led him into the hallway. Julian didn't seem to mind.

Just outside the door, Cal knelt on the floor face to face with Julian. They talked in light whispers. Julian seemed receptive.

Mrs. Brooks leaned in close and whispered, "Is that Julian's father?" She mouthed the last word.

I took a step back. Mrs. Brooks, who up until this moment had been the bane of my existence, was leaning into me and whispering like an excited schoolgirl. What planet was this?

I looked at Cal. He was wearing a dark brown T-shirt. His muscular chest and shoulders clearly visible. As he knelt, I could see all the muscles of his back, too. He was speaking to Julian the way I'd always imagined he would, like Julian was an equal and not a dumb child. Despite my reservations, I was suddenly proud.

"Yes, and Chloe's too."

7

A Muse's ability to influence mortal humans can begin months before his or her final transition, often without the Muse's awareness. Subtle changes in his or her physical appearance, scent and aura attract mortals in need of assistance.

—"Muses," *World Look Encyclopedia*

Back in my driveway, I realized it was time to face facts. Cal is Chloe and Julian's father. Julian seemed to need him, and Cal seemed to genuinely want to be their father. This didn't mean I trusted him or wanted him near my personal life, but there were benefits to being civil with him.

I looked Cal square in the eye. "You're really going to stay? Be father to Chloe and Julian?"

He didn't blink. "Yes."

"If you leave, become a bad influence or hurt them in any way, I'm not giving you this chance again."

He just looked at me.

"You've been gone almost seven years. I'm willing to accept it was so you could be in training, but that doesn't make it okay."

He shrugged. "Fair enough."

"There's one more thing. If you're going to insist on guarding me, stay out of my personal life, don't stalk me and, if it comes down to me or the kids or anyone else for that matter, I want you to choose them."

He seemed to think it over. "I'll play it by ear," He got out of the car.

I went after him as he headed towards his SUV. "That's not what I said," I shouted after him. "I need to know you'll make the right call. That if someone needs you, you'll help them."

He opened the door to his SUV.

"Cal, would you risk one of the kids, even for a second?"

He turned to me. "You just don't get it. I don't choose. You do." He shut the door and drove away.

A few minutes later, I was still standing in the street, in the rain. I stomped into the house and resumed pacing. *This is what I get. I give him a chance, and he starts talking in riddles. What does he mean, I choose? I choose what? Who he helps? Who he saves? That doesn't even make sense!* I paced some more until I heard Kali's ring tone.

"Hey, Kal."

"Hey, Shel. I was wondering if I could come by tonight? I wanna talk to you about something."

The anxiety in her voice pulled me from my rant. "Something wrong?"

"No, no, I just need to tell you something. Can I come by around eight, after the kids go to bed?" She sounded upset.

"You can come by sooner if you need to, or I can come to you. Would that be easier?"

"That's all right Shel; I'll just see you at eight."

"You sure everything's all right?"

"We'll talk tonight. I gotta go." She hung up.

Kali and I have been friends since high school. Diane and Johnas have been around longer—first grade—just after my parents died. Diane is my best friend, but Kali brings something else. She has an innate intuitiveness that has always kept me out of trouble. I'm not sure where I'd be without her. She's the stable one in our group, the one with the best ideas, and she's the unofficial leader. If she's having problems, it's something serious.

The next hour ticked by. I couldn't settle. I wanted to call Cal and rant at him, but I didn't have his number. I didn't even know where he was staying. Whenever I managed to push thoughts of him aside, Kali popped up. Between the two, I couldn't get anything done. It was a relief when the kids walked in the door.

I hugged them both and told them I loved them. I looked into their faces, hoping for an answer. Could I trust Cal, be a Muse, still be me?

"Was that man at school really my uncle?" Julian asked.

"Does that mean he's our dad's brother?" Chloe added.

"Yes, he's related to your Dad," I conceded. I couldn't keep this a secret forever, and I'd rather they heard it from me. I needed to make a decision soon.

"Do you have any papers for me?" I asked, changing the subject.

"My teacher says we're out of snacks." She handed me a note.

We needed a trip to the store anyway, not to mention the bank. I had Isabella's check to deposit, and Cal's child support had come in the mail yesterday, too.

I looked up the state-mandated child support once and found Cal paid me four times the required amount.

Between the child support, grants and loans from college, I'd never had to work a job. I didn't take it for granted, though, and I didn't brag or tell anyone. I thought if Cal knew he was overpaying me, he'd lower the amount. After today, I realized he probably did it on purpose.

I loaded the kids in the car, stopped at the bank where I deposited enough money for us to live on for at least four months and headed to the grocery store.

Chloe picked string cheese for her class. We wandered up and down a few more aisles. I was reaching into the cooler for some milk when I noticed him.

He was watching me and not being covert about it either. We were stopped in front of the breakfast cereal when he approached me.

"You're that girl who was in the accident yesterday."

Girl? He wasn't getting my number now, not that I ever give it out anyway, but still. "Yeah, I was, but I don't wanna talk about it in front of my kids." I threw my head in their direction.

"That was really something. The way that guy ripped the door off and pulled you out. It was like something out of movie. I wish I'd had a camera."

He'd ignored my warning. We were done. "I have to go." I gave him my best polite smile and started to turn back to my cart.

"Hey wait," he grabbed my wrist, stopping me. "Can't we just talk for a minute?"

I tried to pull my wrist out of his grip, but he held on. My adrenaline spiked, my pulse thudding in my ears.

"Please, let me go." I said more quietly than I normally would've. I didn't want to alarm the kids.

"I just wanna talk." He pulled me closer.

I took a moment to get a good look at the guy, just in case I had to identify him in a police lineup later. He was eighteen or nineteen, a college student no doubt. He was a tiny, maybe three inches taller than me, but rail thin. I weighed more and had more muscle. His face was rat like, his nose pointy and his eyes beady. He was attempting a mustache, but his lip just looked dirty, not helping the rat look. Even his hair was a dirty brown.

I leaned in close to him, and his grip loosened. "I don't want to make a scene in front of my kids, but if you don't let me go, I will lay you out on this floor and make damn sure the cops haul your ass away."

His eyes narrowed, and his grip tightened.

Wrong answer.

I was debating between a kick to the groin or a stomp to his instep, when a figure came up behind him.

"There a problem here?" a male voice said.

Rat boy shot a glance at the new arrival, only to do a double take and then release me. He took a step back. "No. We're just talking," he said to the man. "I'll see you later," he said to me, and left.

I watched him go until he was out of sight. When I turned back, I was startled to find a tall, nicely built man with dark chocolate skin staring down at me.

"You all right?" he said.

"Fine." I rubbed my wrist where rat boy had squeezed it.

"He was at the scene of your accident yesterday."

"'Scuse me?" I asked, feeling like I was in a celebrity nightmare. It was beginning already?

"You don't remember me. Detective Ross." He held out his hand. I took it, feeling relieved. "You can call me Daniel, though," he flashed a dazzling smile revealing straight white teeth. "Shelby, right?"

"Yeah," I said, smiling back. "Thanks for your help. It would've scared the guy for life if I'd laid him out."

He laughed, a jolly sound. "I should've waited. I'd like to see that." We both laughed.

"But seriously, be careful of that guy. I've seen his type before. Sometimes these boys get fixated and things can get ugly. Let me know if he becomes a problem."

"Mommy? I have to go potty," Chloe said, pulling my attention from Daniel.

"All right sweetie, give me a sec." I turned back to Daniel. "I will. Thanks again. You saved me a headache."

"My pleasure."

We said goodbye, and I took the kids to the bathroom. Then it was time to go home. In the parking lot, I felt uneasy. Like someone was watching me. I hoped it was just Cal, but the anxious feeling in my stomach told me it wasn't. Just in case, I took a long roundabout way home.

I fed the kids dinner, helped them with their homework, made sure they had a bath and read them a story before tucking them in. I flopped down on the couch, exhausted, just as there was knock at the door.

Kali walked in looking grim, and I steered her towards the couch.

She looked nervous, clutching her hands in her lap.

"What is it Kal?" I reached towards her hand, and she pulled away.

Odd.

"I should've told you this a long time ago. You told me about your parents and I wanted to explain, but I couldn't. Now Cal is back, and I'm moving to a new assignment soon. I couldn't leave without you knowing the truth."

I started to ask her what, when I heard her voice in my head. *I am a Guardian, Shel, I always have been. I was sent to keep an eye on you and help you if you needed it.*

"No ..."

A tear ran down her cheek. So many things made sense now. Her arrival right around the time Cal was probably planning his departure, all her "safe" advice over the years. She came with me on every road trip, to every major event. I thought she was just my friend, that she and I were both single so liked doing things together. I should've been outraged by her betrayal. I should've stood up and started yelling. Instead, I moved to the far end of the couch, pulled my knees up to my chin, laid my head on them and tried not to cry.

This was my fault. I should've known. I should've seen. I trusted too easy and now one of the most important people in my life was a traitor and leaving. I should've known.

This isn't your fault; there was no way you could have known.

"Stay out of my head," I said softly, but in my most dangerous tone. "Just get out. I don't want you here. Not ever."

"Shel,"

"Just leave. Tell Cal I don't want him near my kids either." How could I trust people who'd done nothing but lie to me? If I was going to make this work, I needed backup not backstabbers.

"You'll get sick and die without a Guardian to help you."

"I'd rather die than have you lying, selfish, evil monsters anywhere near me or my family." I picked up my head and looked her in the eye. "Get out."

I love you. I always have. You're like a sister to me. I could've just not said anything and you'd never know the difference, but I wanted there to be truth between us. You were never just an assignment to me.

"Stay out of my head!" I yelled, covering my ears.

Guardians take everything, even the privacy of your own head. I stared at the wall and repeated *get out* over and over again in my head. I heard the door shut but stayed where I was for a long time.

I have a little brother and an older sister on the East Coast. We never talk. Other than them, I have no family. Diane and Johnas often fill that role, but they can only do so much. Kali filled that other spot. Learning she'd lied to me, that she was one of *them* was like she'd died.

Then something hit me. Hit me so hard I could barely breathe. I had to know, had to see it with my own eyes. It was only nine o'clock. I called the neighbor girl that sits for me sometimes and headed out the door. My destination was a few miles away, but it took forever to get there. I kept going over what I was gonna say, how I was gonna say it. When I pulled up outside, I had a moment's hesitation. I could be wrong. Did I want to go in there all psycho? I took a moment to compose myself, marched up the front door and, despite the time, hit the doorbell. I wanted both of them to answer me anyway.

Diane answered the door in her robe, Johnas not far behind in pajama pants. "Shelby? Everything all right?"

"No."

She waved me into the house. I followed them to the living room, but I couldn't sit. I paced around looking for the right words. "Are you guys in on this too? I just need you to be honest with me. Did you know I was Muse? Did you know about Kali and Cal?" I stopped pacing and watched their reactions. There was surprise on both their faces.

Diane looked at Johnas before answering. "What about Kali?"

"You didn't know she's a Guardian?" I tried to make it sound like an accusation.

Diane sat. "She told you this?" If it was possible, she went even paler.

"She not only told me, she projected it into my mind. She's a damn telepath. She knows everything we're thinking, all the time."

Johnas's face did something uncomfortable. "You sure, Shel?

I walked up to Johnas and reached out for his hand. He didn't flinch away, letting me take it. If he'd been a Guardian, he wouldn't have let me touch him. I'm not sure why, but it has something to do with me being a Muse. I stepped away from him and did the same to Diane. She didn't so much as bat an eyelash. I sank into the couch and wrapped my arms around her. Thank God, thank God she wasn't one of them, and Johnas wasn't either. They were all I had in the world. I don't know if I could keep going if they'd betrayed me too.

"Please tell me you guys didn't know about either of them."

Johnas looked in a daze and shook his head. I knew him well enough to know he was being truthful. Diane, too, was honest when she said she didn't.

"I'm such an idiot!" I got up to pace again.

"You're not the only one," Johnas said. "But is it possible Guardians aren't as bad as you make them out to be?"

"Two of them have been lying to us for years. Before that, Cal abandoned us, all of us." I looked around at them and saw reluctant nods. "Even if they weren't responsible for my parent's deaths, I have enough reason not to trust them."

I kept pacing. "I'm not gonna let Cal see the kids. He's not a good influence."

"Can you do that? I mean, he's their dad. Can't he petition for visitation or something?"

"He can try, but he signed away all his rights in the divorce. It would be quite the hat trick." I didn't mention his threat. I had a feeling he was bluffing anyway, trying to get me to agree. Either way, it'd take him awhile, and I had some money now. I could hire a lawyer. I'd get a job if I had to. Johnas's mom was always offering to watch the kids for free. I wouldn't like it, but I could do it.

"Shel, maybe you should give them a chance. They both lied to you. Does that make them so evil? Being a Guardian is a big deal, not something you can easily share."

I forced myself to take a breath. "Being a Guardian *is* a big deal, which is exactly why you should share it with the people you supposedly love at the beginning of a relationship, not years later."

We were all thoughtful for a minute.

"Just think it over before you do anything rash," Johnas said, "please?"

"Why?" I was surprised him of all people would be saying this.

He looked at Diane. "If they were my kids, I'd want a second chance, too."

8

The life span of Muses and Guardians differs
markedly from mortals'. A bonded Muse and
Guardian pair stops aging at thirty-five. However,
because of their high profile and hazardous lifestyles,
most die before their fiftieth year. The oldest pair in
recorded history survived more than 170 years
before drowning in a flash flood. If a Muse dies, so
does his or her Guardian, and vice versa.
— "Muses and Guardians," *World Look Encyclopedia*

It was hard getting out of bed the next morning. I
needed an unheard-of second cup of coffee. I got the kids
off to school and forced myself out to run. I came back
drenched in sweat and gasping, not normal for me. I
showered, printed my pathetic English paper and went to
class.

I got there early and pulled out my sketchpad. I put
my earbuds in and let the music take me. After awhile, I
felt someone watching me. The feeling was familiar and
pleasant. I looked up right into Malcolm's face. He looked
amused. I didn't know what else to do so I smiled back,
tucked away my headphones and flipped my sketchpad

shut. Everyone was watching me. My confusion increased.

"Nice of you to join us, Miss Hammond," Malcolm said as he moved behind the podium. "I was just telling the class Professor Albertson has been called away. I'm taking over his classes."

A Guardian teaching college?

"I just asked if there were any questions about the revised syllabus when we realized you weren't with us."

"Sorry."

"Is it safe to continue?"

I bobbed my head and tried to sink lower in my chair.

Malcolm lectured on the Puritans and the influences on their literature. He was funny, well versed and kept a good pace; he stopped at appropriate intervals and asked if there were questions. Overall, the class seemed to like him.

When the hour ended, I lingered while everyone left.

He looked up, happy to see me. Why did this make me happy, too? He's a Guardian. I should've been the first one out the door.

"Did you enjoy my class, Miss Hammond?"

"You've saved my life twice. I think it's okay if you call me Shelby."

He smiled even wider, revealing straight white teeth and laugh lines around his eyes. "Shelby, then, did you enjoy my class?"

"It was good, for an English class. I can't believe you teach. Shouldn't you be running a security company or something?"

He glanced around the empty room. "I don't tell people I'm a Guardian. I'd appreciate it if we kept that between us. I just want a regular life. That could be hard if too many people know about me."

"Of course." I understood about wanting a normal life.

"This is just a temporary gig to help out a friend."

I nodded.

"We'll have to catch up next time though; I have a meeting."

I followed him out, and we parted at the stairs. My class had been on the second floor and by the time my feet hit the ground level, something was very wrong.

I felt anxious and panicky. My vision kept skipping, and I felt like I was spinning. I stumbled through the lobby, my chest heavy. I staggered out a side door in search of air. My vision tipped and I fell down the cement steps, landing in the alley that runs between buildings.

I sat up gasping, my ankle twisted and hurting. Things continued to spin until my eyes fell on ... the creepy guy from the grocery store?

He stared down at me where I sat in a puddle, clutching my foot. He looked amused, happy and smug. My panic increased.

The guy was talking to me. I tried to focus. The vertigo didn't diminish, but I could hear him.

"That was quite the tumble. You okay?"

All I could do was look at him.

"Let me help you up." He reached out, but I waved him off and used the steps to help myself up.

I put my weight on my uninjured foot and tried to gather my wits.

"Better?"

I nodded and tried to look composed. Focusing on his face seemed to slow the vertigo. I held down the panic. I didn't know what was wrong with me, but I had the urge to run, to get help, but I could barely stand. Running was out of the question.

Through the fog in my head, I heard him say, "I didn't get to introduce myself yesterday. I was too forward. You know how girls can be. If you're not in their face, they just ignore you. You're a lady and need to be courted. I'm sorry. Can we start over?"

This guy was unbelievable, but I was in no state to argue. I should've just told him to go away. I sat down and called Diane and Johnas. They were all I had now. The panic welled up again, along with a lump in my throat. I swallowed it down.

I swayed. "I'm not feeling well."

"I'm Jerry," he said.

This guy was unreal.

"I was wondering if you'd be gracious enough to accompany me to a party tomorrow night? It's at my fraternity, and I'd be honored if you'd let me escort you." Was he talking about escorting me to a kegger? I must have been hallucinating.

"I'm sorry." I tried to take a step and fell forward. Jerry caught me and when our skin touched, I knew what was wrong. It was him. He was dangerous. I could feel it coming out of him. It was making me physically ill. *Jerry is not a nice boy.* The upload of this information caused the worst wave of panic and vertigo yet. I wrenched myself from his hold, threw myself backwards and yelled at him to stay away from me. The panic was blinding, but I had to get away from him. I tried to move out of the alley where there were more people.

Jerry grabbed me by the waist and started pulling me back toward the end of the alley where there was a turn and some trashcans.

"Girl, you need to calm down. I'm not gonna hurt you."

Liar! Every alarm bell in my head went off. I lashed out and yelled. Jerry kept us moving. A few more steps, and he'd have me out of sight.

"Hey! Let her go." It was Malcolm.

Jerry set me on my feet. "I'm sorry, sir; she just started lashing out. I thought she was having a fit or something. I didn't want her to hurt herself. I was going to get help."

Liar!

Jerry let me go, and I flew into Malcolm's arms. The second we touched, everything disappeared: the panic, the vertigo, the altered vision and hearing. I'd been dangerously incapacitated. I wrapped my arms around him as tight as I could. The symptoms may have been gone, but some very real amounts of adrenaline and God knows what else were coursing through me.

"It's all right, luv," Malcolm said gently into my hair as he held me, pulling my arms under his shirt to the bare skin there.

I was trying not to shake and cry at the let up.

"If I catch you near my girlfriend again, when I'm done with you, you won't recognize yourself." I could feel how serious he was. Even the girlfriend part.

"Look, I don't want any trouble. She didn't tell me she had a boyfriend."

"Well, she does, so take the hint and take a hike."

Jerry fled. Every step he took away from me cleared my head even more.

"Thank you." I hugged him tighter, tears rolling down my cheeks.

"You're all right," He put a familiar hand on my face. "It'll pass. Keep breathing."

"What happened?" I said into his chest. He seemed to know what was going on with me.

"You have an alarm system. It creates symptoms of panic to let you know when to be careful or run. Sometimes it goes off by mistake. Is that what happened?"

I shook my head against his chest. "He touched me. I could feel what he was thinking. It was awful."

He held me a little tighter. "Where's your Guardian? He should be here to help you."

"I hate him."

I felt surprise, alarm, confusion and something else I couldn't identify coming from Malcolm. "Cal? You hate Cal?"

"It's not my fault they sent me my ex-husband." Not that I'd have been accepting of any Guardian. If Malcolm approached me and said he was my Guardian, I wouldn't give him a second look. Things were different now, though. I could feel his sincerity; he cares about me. He saves everyone who needs it, and he wants a normal life. He's different from the others.

Malcolm stepped back, almost losing his grip on me. "Cal is your ex-husband? When, where?"

I blinked. "Here. About seven years ago. He's the dad of my kids."

His eyebrows disappeared into his hair. "You have kids?"

I nodded. I could feel his surprise, but that was it. No disgust. No fear. Things I'd expect from a man attracted to me. No one wants the extra baggage of kids. Not at my age.

"Shelby, you need a Guardian. I can't always be around to save you, not that I mind, but guarding someone is a full-time job. You need protection. Hasn't enough happened to you that you see that?"

I felt chastened. He was right. How many times had I ended up in his arms, gasping for life? Three in three days? But I just couldn't. "They're all a bunch of self-centered, egotistical—"

"You're talking about people who devote every second of their lives to just one other person. One other person they may not even like or get along with. Every minute of every day, until the day they die."

I'd never thought of it that way, but it still didn't negate one fact. "They're all liars. They can't be trusted."

He hugged me again. "The liar part I can agree with, but trust is something you earn. Give him a chance." He let me go and put a foot between us. My ankle was feeling better. I could stand.

"I see your point, but I just can't. Not Cal."

Malcolm rubbed the inside of his right wrist. Nervous habit? I watched as his mind came to a conclusion.

"What did that guy want with you?"

I blinked in surprise. "He wanted me to go to a party at his fraternity tomorrow night." I tried to remember if there was anything else. "He went off about me being a lady and wanting to court me."

Malcolm got a sly smile.

"What?" Whatever thought produced that smile couldn't be good.

"Let me take you that party tomorrow night."

"What?" He had to be kidding.

"I've dealt with guys like this before. He needs to see that you're off limits. See you out, having a good time with a ... "--he smiled at this— "a more dominate male."

I didn't roll my eyes. "I like you and all, but I don't date." Especially not Guardians. "And I doubt flaunting myself in front of this guy is going to help. Probably just piss him off more."

"Fine, don't trust my years of training." He had an adorable tip to his mouth. It made stuffy professor into bad little playboy. I was a goner.

"It's not a date."

"Sure." He headed back into the English building, "But make sure you wear something sexy." He wagged his eyebrows at me. "I'll pick you up at eight."

"You don't even know where I live or where the party is."

"That's half the fun, luv." He gave me one last smile and disappeared into the English building.

9

Public school enrollment of Muses and Guardians was banned briefly by mortals in 1983. Young Guardians were the main concern because they develop abilities, attract energy and defy authority, beginning at age five.

MAGRA successfully fought to keep such children in normal school, arguing that the dangers of separating them were twofold: Ordinary children would learn to fear Muses and Guardians, and Muses and Guardians would fail to understand the value of humanity.

—"Muses and Guardians," *World Look Encyclopedia*

Two more classes and then I squeezed in an hour at the studio. Irene wasn't happy with me: She ignored me the whole time. I needed more time in the studio, but things were just too crazy. I was doing the best I could, and she'd just have to get over it.

Back in my driveway, I peeled my fingers from the steering wheel. I think I'd finally slowed down enough to absorb my accident and how close I'd come to dying. The familiarity of leaving the art lab and heading home to get the kids ready for basketball must have triggered it. Whatever the reason, I couldn't shake the anxious feeling that crept in.

The kids' practice was terrible. At one end of gym, Chloe's team practice seemed to go just fine. Julian's team, at the other end of the gym, was the opposite. Julian refused to do anything his coach said. After fifteen minutes of his coach trying to get him to comply, I jumped into the fray. When I intervened he did better, but what was I teaching him? That he only has to obey if I make him? I spent most of their practice trying to think of a way to help Julian without involving Cal. I didn't come up with much.

By the time we were walking home, I was beat and hungry. The anxiety from earlier was still going strong, too. I was ready to order a pizza and sink into a hot bath with a bottle of wine. Imagine my irritation at finding Cal leaning against his SUV outside my house.

I walked past him. I meant what I told Kali: I was done. He followed me up the steps. I stopped at the door, letting the kids in.

The door shut behind them and Cal grabbed me, slamming me against the house, pinning one arm over my head and crushing the other between us, his body holding me against the wall.

I cried out, demanded he let me go and get the hell off my property.

"Let me tell you what's gonna happen now." Cal's face was an inch from mine. "You're going to agree to cooperate or I'm going to cuff us together and swallow the key. You want me watching you take a damn grumpy? Go ahead and scream."

I struggled against him, testing his resolve. He pressed me more firmly against the house and I went still. Pressed chest to chest, groin to groin, with Cal was too intimate. The threat of being cuffed to him was more than I could handle. I'd die first.

"Don't do this, Cal." My voice was barely a whisper. "I can't do it." I couldn't let him in.

"I love how you think this is about you." He slammed me into the wall again. "It's not about you or me or the kids. It's about the whole fucking world, Shel, about all the people you can help."

I met Cal's eyes. Really? He wanted this, too?

"I want to make a difference in the world. If I can do that and have my family, too, I'm not gonna let you fuck it up!"

I cringed. Why did it have to be Cal?

"I've spent my life working for this assignment and you've all but handed it to Malcolm. He's a traitor, a self-serving narcissist. He doesn't wanna be a Guardian. You need to stay the hell away from him and if I have to cuff you to make that happen, I will." He reached around his back pocket and pulled out a pair of shiny metal cuffs. "Just think, Shel, sleeping together every night, taking showers together, having coffee and running together. It'll be just like old times."

He moved the cuffs towards my pinned wrist.

"What do you mean, giving it to Malcolm? Giving him what?" I was trying to buy some time to find a way out of this.

He stopped and gave me a long look. "A Muse can only have one Guardian, Shel, and she picks him. The more time you spend with him, the farther we move apart. I can't have that. I've worked too hard." The cuffs moved towards my hand again.

"Wait. I pick my Guardian? So I can choose Kali?" Anyone was better than Cal.

His thick black brows pulled together. "That's not an option for you and Kali." The cuffs were at my hand now.

"Okay! Okay, you can guard me." What choice did he give me? With Cal attached to my wrist, there was no chance of a normal life, let alone any dignity. "But, I have boundaries."

"Speak," he barked in my face.

I flinched but pulled up all my nerve. I wasn't going to let him intimidate me. "You can't stay in the house."

His eyes narrowed.

"And I don't want you shadowing me. I want space, a life."

"It's my job to stay out of your way, but I will be shadowing you."

I was quiet, trying to imagine that.

"Anything else?" He was growling now.

"Evenings are mine. I want them with my kids, to do my homework and have my life. If I'm going somewhere, I'll call you; otherwise you go be wherever it is you go."

He let out a breath. "This isn't how it works, Shel. I should've moved in with you by now, established our relationship.

"Please, Cal, I just need more time. I'll come around, I swear. It doesn't help that you're my ex-husband or that ..." I stopped. I was going to say that my parents died because of a Guardian ruining my entire life, but he already knew that. I could see the comprehension in his face and that was when I knew I had him.

He lowered the cuffs. "If you go out before eight a.m. or after five p.m., you call me?"

"I call you."

"If you notice anything weird or off, you tell me?"

"I tell you."

He exhaled again as I waited for his decision. "Shelly-belly, why do you do this to me?" His eyes went to my lips. We both just breathed, our chests pressing against each other in the limited space between us. He was warm and smelled just like I remembered. Spicy and rich, like something you could sink your teeth into.

He pressed me harder into the wall and then stepped back, letting me slide down until my feet caught the ground. "When are we telling the kids?"

Shit. Not tonight, and tomorrow night I was going out with Malcolm.

"Saturday. Come over for dinner and we'll tell them together." What choice did I have? He was still holding the cuffs.

"You're in for the night?"

I nodded.

"Give me your phone."

"What?"

He waved the cuffs at me again

"You don't have to be such a jerk about it." I handed it to him.

He started pressing buttons. "I tried being nice. You just walked all over me." He shot me a look. "I underestimated you. I won't be doing that again." He handed me back my phone. "The five key will autodial me." He pulled my chin up so I had to look at him. "My only job is to protect you, take care of you. Call me."

I didn't know what to say to that.

"Good night, then." He walked away.

An hour after the kids were in bed, I had an empty bottle of wine and zero ideas about how to get out of this mess. There was knock at the door. I swayed across the room to look out the peephole. It was Kali. I opened the door.

She took a good look at me. "Shit. I told Cal not to do it."

"Come on in, Kali." Why not add to my little pity party.

She came in and shut the door behind her. "You're drunk?"

"I tried. Only had one bottle." I went back to the couch and sank into it, resting my heavy head against the back of it.

Kali just looked at me for a long time. "I hate when you drink. You're so hard to read."

I rolled my head back and forth against the couch. "Stay out of my head. It's mine."

She sat down next to me. "He's not so bad, Shel. He's worked hard for this, and you need him."

"Lying asshole. Dumped me. Left me all alone. That's what I always am, alone."

"You sure you only had one bottle? You usually hold it better than this."

I started to say I was fine but realized it had never been further from the truth. Tears started rolling down my face. "What am I going to do? I don't want this. Not for me, not for the kids."

"You can trust him. Please, Shel, just give him a chance."

The last thing I remember was shaking my head.
***

I woke up in my bed, Cal's heavy dark arms wrapped around me, my head resting against his bare chest. My first thought was that he had more chest hair than I remembered. My second thought was that he smelled good, just like I remembered, and I snuggled in closer to go back to sleep. About ten seconds after that, I realized I was lying in bed, half-naked, with my ex.

"Omigod." I pulled away from him. His arms released me as I slid out of bed and stood next to it in horror of how this could've happened. Cal didn't stir.

I was wearing nothing but my bra and underwear. I pulled a T-shirt over my head, followed by a pair of pajama pants. It was six-thirty in the morning. The kids wouldn't be up for at least a half hour. I had to get him out of here.

"Hey, wake up," I said from the safety of my side of the room. *Please, God, don't make me have to touch him.* He still didn't stir.

Some Guardian.

"Cal, wake up," I said as loud as I dared.

He stirred.

"Oh, you're up. Feeling better?"

"I'm fine. How did you get in here? Where's Kali?" The last thing I remembered was arguing with her over whether or not to trust Cal.

"You don't remember?" He stretched out, wearing nothing but boxers.

Oh God, please don't let me have *slept* with him.

"Kali came over to check on you, and you'd had too much to drink. You went into some kind of fit, so she called me. You don't remember?

I shook my head, trying to decide if I believed him.

"You were sobbing, telling us how you were alone in the world and couldn't trust anyone. You said you were going to die alone and your kids would have no one, just like you didn't."

I cringed. Those were very real fears of mine. That I'd drunkenly shared them with Cal was humiliating.

"After that, you stopped making sense. You got better when I touched you. Kali helped me get you up here, and we both crashed."

"That's it?" I looked up and down his perfect physique again. If I'd been that drunk, it wasn't impossible I'd do something pathetic and desperate. It had been seven years since there was a man in my bed. ...

"Well, once I got you in bed, you did cry for awhile. I couldn't understand what you were saying, so I just soothed you. After a few minutes, you fell asleep."

I sat on the edge of the bed in a daze and looked over at Cal. "What happened to me?"

He sat up and moved closer to me on the bed. "We told you. Without a Guardian around all the time, you'll get sick and die. This is how it starts. At the end of each day, you look for the balancing energy of a Guardian. If you don't find it, you're balance is off at the start of the next day. After a couple days, the balance tips too far and things like this can happen."

I looked up at him. There was real concern on his face. A part of me wanted to wrap my arms around him and tell him he'd won, that he could move in, that we should start over and try being a family. Then I reminded myself that's not what he wants. He wants to guard me so he can be with his kids. He had no romantic desires with me and even if he did, I wouldn't allow it. He wasn't that person to me anymore and never would be again.

"So every few days I'll need an adjustment of Guardian energy on top of having you save my ass on occasion?

He looked serious. "At least every day, if not twice.

"I don't think that's necessary. How about every third day?"

His eyes narrowed. "Every other day and for two hours."

I'd just spent the whole night doing a balancing with him and felt pretty good. Would two hours be enough? I almost said he should just stay the night again but held my tongue. I couldn't go there ... yet.

"How about around nine or ten o'clock after the kids go to bed. I can just sit with you while you do homework or watch television."

"Deal. Now get the hell out of my house before my kids wake up and find you here."

"Our kids." He didn't move.

I exhaled and managed not to hurt myself as I relented. "Our kids."

He got up and started pulling on his clothes. I wanted to ask why we'd been practically nude but remembered Malcolm telling me the more nerves the merrier. Great. I hope he didn't insist on so much skin touching every time we did this. This was becoming quite the nightmare. Then again, it could be some stranger I didn't know at all. I couldn't decide which would be worse.

Cal was dressed and gone without the kids being any the wiser. I went to get them up and get breakfast started, still trying to wrap my head around the idea that Cal was going to be stalking my every move all day. This was going to be a long one.

10

Energy and bonding within Muse/Guardian pairs is reciprocal. Guardians access energy from the atmosphere, which fuels their abilities. The excess is transferred to their Muses. Muses combine this energy with their innate knowledge of "the will of the universe," which they use to inspire mortals. When a Guardian passes energy into a Muse, some of his or her own life energy is caught in the path and lost. Muses must bond with their Guardians periodically to restore that lost energy. Without this bonding, Guardians fade and die.

—"Muses and Guardians," *World Look Encyclopedia*

I spent the morning trying to be mad at Cal or even Kali, but I just couldn't. They had done nothing contrary to what I knew about the Guardian/Muse relationship. After my experiences with Malcolm, I saw how basic the transfer of energy is between Muse and Guardian, which explains why you never see one without the other. Not to mention that I felt great today, compared to yesterday.

Muses need Guardians. With our abilities, our chi falls out of balance at an alarming rate. Guardians keep it in balance for us. Guardians need Muses, too. Since

Guardians can only reproduce with Muses, naturally they need to protect the Muses to keep their species alive. In Cal's case, his kids also need a mother. By taking care of me, he gets access to them and makes sure their mother is around to take care of them, too. While I wasn't excited about waking up with Cal in my bed again, I could finally see his perspective. That didn't mean I'd give him full run of my life or let him leave the scene of an accident just to protect me, but it was good to understand his intentions.

After Cal left, I didn't need my usual coffee. I got the kids out the door with a smile and went for my run. I went twice as far as usual and even did some lifting when I got home. I showered and, refreshed, headed out the door.

Fridays, I just have botany. We taste-tested various types of coffee and chocolate to understand variety within a plant species. By the time I headed to lunch, I was buzzing with caffeine.

I was alone at a table in the cafeteria, halfway through a chicken salad, when a young man approached me. He was a tall gangly guy with short messy hair and hazel eyes framed by stylish glasses. He was closer to my age, twenty-three or so, a science major if I ever saw one.

"I'm sorry to bother you, but you walked in here with a smile that hasn't left your beautiful face since you sat down. I'm Nathan." He stuck out his hand.

I was surprised by his forwardness but wanted to try something. I took his hand and shook it. I could feel his emotions and intentions towards me. I marveled, wondering if I could do this with everyone now. He had nothing but nice things coming out of his head so I invited him to sit. I could use the company anyway.

Nathan was indeed a science major, environmental technology to be exact. He was twenty-four and working on his PhD. We had about ten minutes of polite conversation before Cal came looming over our table.

Damn, he was good. I'd forgotten he was shadowing me. He was in his brown trench coat and jeans, wearing sunglasses despite being indoors.

"Sir, you need to be moving along now," Cal said, sounding a little too secret service for my taste.

Nathan had been mid-story about his lab partner's new haircut. He stopped and looked up at Cal. "Are you talking to me?"

"Yes sir, you should be on your way."

"I don't know who you are, but the lady and I are talking." He turned back to me and I gave him my attention, hoping Cal would take the hint and buzz off. I didn't intend to spend time with Nathan beyond the cafeteria, but I wasn't so overflowing in friends that I could afford to turn down every nice, smart, funny guy that just wanted to have a conversation with me.

"Sir, you need to leave now or I'll be forced to remove you." Cal said, still standing there all cloak-and-dagger.

Nathan wheeled around as if to say something, obviously about to tell Cal to take a hike, but I spoke before he could.

"Cal, seriously, back off."

Nathan and I turned back to finish our conversation, and the next thing I knew Nathan was yanked out of his seat and slammed into the table between us. My tray, with what was left of my salad, flew into my lap, covering my sweatshirt in vinaigrette.

I got to my feet and, by some weird intuition, put my hand on Cal's shoulder. He instantly released Nathan and put a protective stance between Nathan and me. I didn't let go of Cal's shoulder, but I did step around him to face Nathan. Cal let me, and I grabbed his hand when I couldn't reach his shoulder. Somehow I knew touching Cal was keeping him under control.

"I'm sorry, Nathan, but maybe you should go."

He looked from me to Cal and back again. He was livid, probably beyond humiliated. "What are you?"

I lowered my eyes in confusion. "I don't know." And it was the truth.

He seemed to take that as an answer and stormed off.

I let go of Cal and started to clean up the mess he'd made. I returned my tray and walked out of the cafeteria without a second glance at him. We'd been lucky no one called security. Once outside and around a deserted corner, I wheeled on Cal.

"Are you out of your ever livin' mind?" I yelled at him. "What in God's name makes you think it's okay to go all macho on my friends?"

He just stood there in his sunglasses.

"Take those fucking things off and talk to me," I screamed at him, stomping my foot like a two-year-old.

He pulled them off. "You were flirting with him."

"And?"

"I wasn't going to stand there and watch the mother of my children make herself into some kind of floozy. He's not the kind of guy you should be with."

I let my anger boil up and then down again. I rubbed my temples. I definitely wasn't telling him about my outing with Malcolm tonight. "Who I spend time with is none of your business. I can bring a hundred men waltzing in and out my front door and there's nothing you can do about it."

He started to open his mouth.

"I said I didn't want you in my personal life. That in there," I pointed towards the cafeteria, "was you up close and personal with my private life. He wasn't going to hurt me, and if you'd taken two seconds to stop and think before all that testosterone kicked in you'd have realized that, and I wouldn't have to be all pissed off and embarrassed right now." I shook my head back and forth trying to clear my anger, trying to make sense of it all. "I was starting to trust you, too. Good job, Cal." I turned on my heel and stormed off. This time Cal didn't follow me.

Once safe in the art building I called Diane.

"Sorry to ask you last minute, but could you keep the kids tonight?"

"Guess so. Why? "

"Somewhere to be."

"With Cal?"

"God, no."

"All right, when are you picking them up?"

"Tomorrow morning?" I cringed, waiting for her response.

"Mmmmhmm. Where are you going?"

"A party," I mumbled.

"Really?" She sounded excited. Was my social life that dismal?

"Where? With who?"

"I'll tell you later. Cal may be listening."

"Gottcha."

"Pick up the kids at six thirty or so?"

"Oh, I'll be there." She sounded far too excited.

I'd been afraid she'd react this way. "See you then."

We disconnected. I looked around to make sure Cal hadn't eavesdropped. Knowing him, he was invisible or hovering a few inches above my head. I looked up, feeling like an idiot, just to make sure he wasn't up there. I made a mental note to get the full workup on his abilities. As much as I didn't want to know and didn't want him around, it would be smart to know what I was dealing with.

I spent three hours in the art lab, by far the most constructive time I'd ever spent there. I was still on some kind of high from having spent the night getting a chi balancing from Cal. It spilled into my work and just in time. My painting hadn't been going well. It was a stylized version of a tree, nothing but forking branches. The bottom portion of the painting had been a mound of earth and grass with the tree coming out of it. The trunk expanded into branches that filled every corner of the canvas. The branches were dark brown. The background, a rainbow-colored sunset. It was already one of my best paintings, but no matter how much I worked on it, there was still something missing.

Today I found the missing piece. I extended the roots below the ground, making them white against the dark earth. It worked. The painting popped to life and more than a few people, including Irene, stopped to look at it as they made their way through the studio,.

She gazed at it, her face going through a strange set of expressions.

"Shelby, could I see you in my office?" She didn't wait for a response, just took off in that direction. I put my brush down and followed her, trying to keep up with her brisk pace.

Once in her office, she snapped the door shut and indicated a chair for me. She remained standing and paced. "Is there something you want to tell me?"

I glanced around her office looking for clue. "No?"

She shot me a glare. "You haven't found anything out in the last couple days?"

How had she known? Not sure where she was going, I didn't say anything.

"Not again," she muttered. "I can't do this again."

I just watched her.

"The work you did on your piece today was phenomenal. I expect you're almost done?"

I nodded.

"You don't see it do you?"

I shook my head.

"Where's your Guardian?"

Whatever reaction played across my face must have been the one she was looking for.

"I knew it. I knew it. I was waiting for this." She didn't sound happy. She sat down in the chair adjacent me and took my hands. I could feel sorrow and worry coming off her. "When I was in college, one of my girlfriends turned twenty-five and found out she was a Muse, too. It didn't end well."

I felt my breath catch. "What happened?"

"She was engaged at the time and one night on their way back from a movie, they were mugged. Her Guardian pulled her from the scene while her fiancé tried to talk down the attacker. There was a struggle, and the Guardian refused to help him. She managed to escape her Guardian's hold and went to help her fiancé. She was shot and killed."

The story was so much like what happened to my parents. I leaned back and tried to breathe normally. Stupid Guardians refusing to help anyone but their Muse ... this had to stop.

"I just want you to know what they're like. I started thinking about those little kids of yours, and I could never live with myself if I didn't put you on your guard.

I didn't want to tell her about my parents. It wasn't a story I often shared. "I'll remember and don't worry, I'll be careful."

She nodded and stood. I followed suit. Before we left her office, she gave me a long hug and told me if I ever needed anything to call her.

I left campus that day sure of two things. One: I couldn't trust Cal or Kali. Two: I was going out with Malcolm tonight and I was gonna have a good time.

11

Motivation is critical for Muses and Guardians. Following MAGRA regulations, potential Muses are raised as ordinary humans, unaware of their destiny until their transition. Growing up in mortal society, Muses receive the foundation to understand the importance of humankind and of inspiring it.

Guardians spend the majority of childhood in mortal society, knowing they are different. MAGRA regulates their education, guiding them toward their purpose: to help humankind. A minority of factions believe Guardians and Muses should rule society instead of serving it.

—"Muses," *World Look Encyclopedia*

Right at five o'clock, my doorbell rang. Thinking Diane was early, I opened it. It was Cal. I squashed my surprise. "What's up?"

"I want to apologize. I did exactly what you asked me not to. Can we start over?"

I chewed my lip, thinking. How was I supposed to sneak out with Cal being so nice? I teetered back and forth about telling him and then decided not to. He's not my keeper, damn it. Plus, I'd be safe with Malcolm. No harm done.

"Sure." As if I could say no.

"Good." He seemed to relax a bit. "It's Friday night. You sure you're in for it?"

"Yep, just dinner and movie with the kids. Then some homework. "I tried to sound bored with it all.

Cal tugged the black curls near his temple. "I'm staying at Kali's, and she works tonight. I could stay if you'd like."

I looked away into the distance. He was not allowed to do this to me. I refused to feel bad. Not for going out and not for excluding him from my fictitious family activities. "I gotta get dinner started. I'll see you tomorrow?"

"Yeah, give me a call if you have any errands. Otherwise I'll see you around four or five?"

I made an affirmative noise and closed the door with him still standing there looking hopeful. I said a silent thank you that Malcolm was picking me up. My beast would be in the driveway all night in case Cal decided to do a drive by, or seven.

At six on the dot, Diane waltzed through my front door. I realized she'd always done this. She even had a key. So did Kali. Crap. That meant Cal probably did by now, too. I made a mental note to call around and find out if it would be worth the price to have my locks changed.

Diane cornered me in the kitchen. "All right, girl, where are you going and, for the love of God, tell me who you're going with." She opened my fridge and poked around. "Spill it," she said from somewhere near my crisper.

I stirred the macaroni and tried to think of way to tell my best friend I was going on a date with a Guardian. "Remember my accident?"

Diane appeared with a carrot in one hand, a cheese stick in the other. "Yeah ..."

"Remember the Guardian that so uncharacteristically saved me, even though I wasn't his Muse?"

She looked at the ceiling, thinking. The light hitting her green eyes seemed to make them glow more than usual. "Oh yeah."

"Well, it turns out he's teaching my English class and happened to be there when I needed a little help, again. He's taking me to a party tonight."

Diane's mouth fell open, "You're going out with a Guardian who teaches college? You sure know how to find 'em."

"It's not a date. It's business. He's gonna help me with this guy that's been bothering me." I shuddered at the memory of Jerry. I couldn't get him off my tail soon enough. What if he figured out where I live and came to the door? What if he broke in? No, a few hours on Malcolm's arm were worth making sure that never happened.

Diane nibbled the end of her carrot. "This is the Guardian that doesn't have a Muse? The one that saved you?"

I nodded.

Her mouth tipped into a coy smile, her eyes alight with a mischief I knew only too well.

"Oh no, whatever you're thinking just forget it."

"Is he cute?"

I fidgeted.

"Ohmygod! He's gorgeous." Diane knew me too well.

I didn't say anything, confirmation in itself.

"This is it. You get this guy to fall for you, he'll be your Guardian and then you can get rid of Cal once and for all.

He already has the right code of ethics and everything. He'll help other people, not just you. It's perfect."

I opened my mouth to speak, caught myself on a couple thoughts and tried again. "Firstly, no one is falling for me, because I'm not falling for anyone. I don't need or want a man. Not to mention I don't have time for one."

Diane started to interrupt me, and I put up a hand to stop her.

"Secondly, Malcolm doesn't want a Muse. Not to mention Cal is ... you know." I tossed my head in the direction of the kids.

Diane gave me a skeptical look.

"Being a Guardian is genetic," I whispered. "They may need him."

"No. Way."

"It gets better," I said. "Guardians can only have kids with Muses. He knew what I was back in high school when he knocked me up with Chloe."

"He never told you?"

"Nope."

"Bastard."

"Yep."

We stood in silence for a minute.

"I don't envy you, Shel, although I would give a pretty penny for a chest like yours."

I made a scoffing noise. She knew my stance on this subject already. No boobs were better than sad ones. She disagreed.

"I need to help you get ready, and don't even try to tell me you don't need help. I have seen that bag of neutral colors you call make-up, and we both know you don't even own hair spray."

She followed me upstairs to "approve" my outfit and then spent a good half hour in the bathroom with me. She wouldn't leave until she was satisfied with my make-up and hair. Around seven, I got her out the door with the kids.

The next hour ticked by. I paced around, checked and rechecked my hair and make-up, made sure the house was decent and, at a quarter till, put on my outfit. If you could even call it an outfit. It consisted of my tightest, lowest cut pair of jeans and a low cut, deep red, button-up blouse. Something about button-up shirts just screams, "Open me up like a Christmas gift!" I put on a matching red thong and bra. The thong kept peeking up over my low jeans, but my shirt covered it well enough. The color of my lacy bra about matched the shirt so if someone did catch a glimpse of it, I wouldn't look too trashy. Diane had helped me straighten my long hair and then foof it up with way too much hair spray. Between that, some black eyeliner and mascara Diane spent ten minutes on, I felt like I was bursting out of myself. This was so not me, but Malcolm had said sexy and I didn't own a little black dress. I didn't even own a little black skirt. I tried not to imagine what he was going to think. This mommy doesn't do sexy. Poufy hair and too much eyeliner were going to have to do.

Malcolm knocked five minutes early.

I opened the door and let him take in my appearance. He's about six foot and so broad in the shoulders he filled my doorway. He was wearing white Adidas, pre-faded loose-fitting jeans, and a tight black T-shirt with a skull and cross bones on the front under a black windbreaker, his lack of Guardian-typical trench coat making a loud statement. His short white blond hair was spiked up, making him look years younger. The overall effect put him around my age. My eyes landed on his face, and the look I found made me wish we were touching so I could feel what he was thinking.

"You look ... perfect." His eyes roved up and down me again, and I had a feeling "perfect" wasn't the first word that came to mind.

I tried not to blush. "You look good, too, and ... younger. How'd you do that?" None of his students would look twice unless someone pointed him out.

He shrugged it off. "What can I say? I'm a master of disguise."

"Do you want to come in for a sec? I'm not quite ready."

"Sure," He stepped into the house and closed the door behind him. There was something terribly right about seeing him in my familiar surroundings.

I shook myself, trying to get a grip. This wasn't even a date! "Did you have trouble finding me?" I asked, trying to pull some normal between us. As if.

"I have access to the university database. That's how I found your friend's fraternity, too."

"So you know where we're going?"

He gave a tight nod.

"How are we getting in? It's not like we're invited."

"It's taken care of."

He stepped out of my entryway and glanced into my living room, a desk with computer on one side, a couch with end table on the other. He walked in and turned the corner into my dining room. Against one wall was a small table with three chairs, against the other, a counter with drawers and cupboards. I'd installed it to give all my art stuff a home. Leaning together at one end of the counter were some paintings. Some finished, some not. These pulled Malcolm's attention.

He looked at the first few then moved them aside to see the ones behind.

"How long have you been painting?" he asked, not taking his eyes off them.

I shrugged. "Forever."

He nodded. "You never guessed you were a Muse? Sometimes they figure out before we tell them."

"I never considered it. I ..." I stopped. Could I tell him about my parents? He was the enigma Guardian. Perhaps he would understand. Then again, that wasn't a first date conversation. Not that this was even a date. "I just never thought about it."

"You're very talented." He stepped away from the paintings and glancing into my hastily tidied kitchen.

"Thanks. I'll get my coat and we can go."

I stuck my ID, some cash, my debit card, my keys and my phone into my jeans. No need to drag around my mommy purse all night. I pulled on a short jean jacket Diane bought me last year in an attempt to spruce up my wardrobe. If I could get away with it, I'd wear sweats and sweatshirts all day, every day.

I left a couple lights on just in case Cal drove by, locked the door and said a silent prayer that this plan would work.

12

Happy is the man whom the Muses love: sweet speech flows from his mouth.

—Hesiod

Malcolm was parked at the curb, the streetlight shining into the visible engine compartment of his car.

I came to a sudden stop and willed my knees not to buckle.

"This is an Audi R8."

Malcolm looked surprised. "You know cars?"

"It's an old hobby." I said breathless. The car was worth a quarter million, easy.

Malcolm beeped the doors, unlocked and opened my door. "I'm impressed, Ms. Hammond."

I still couldn't move. Really? I got to ride in it? "This thing can go zero to sixty in 4.4 seconds. Does it have the magnetic ride?"

"For that, you can drive." He tossed me the keys.

I caught them in disbelief. I got to drive it? Was this Christmas or something?

Malcolm opened the driver's side door for me. "I've a weak spot for women who take the wheel." He wagged his eyebrows at me.

The keys in my hand were unlike any I'd seen before. I looked in through the open door, just taking it all in.

"Can you handle a stick?"

That earned him a look.

He chuckled.

I pulled myself together. "Better than I drive an automatic." I slid into the supple leather seat.

"Good. This is last year's concept model. It has a diesel V12. Be gentle with her or she'll take you off the road faster than you can say redlining."

He smirked as my mouth fell open again. The car just went from a quarter million to multi-million. Shit.

He closed my door, went around the passenger side and slid in.

"How do you even have this car?" I was still holding the keys, my faked coolness gone.

"A buddy of mine hooked me up. We should get going." He buckled his seatbelt. "We're gonna be late."

He had a buddy at Audi who got him a multi-million dollar concept supercar? I leaned back in my seat and let that sink in.

"Who are you?"

"I told you; I'm a businessman. I helped a friend and this was part of his thank you."

"A car?"

"No, the connection to get the car. The car I paid for."

Holy. Crap. "What kind of business are you into?" Please don't say anything that could sound illegal.

"I inherited some companies when my dad died last year, mostly insurance and a few factories."

I let that, too, sink in. "I'm sorry about your Dad."

He grimaced. He was holding my hand and I felt a strange combination of emotions. None of them sadness. Was it remorse?

Malcolm didn't say anything else so I took it the subject was closed. I slid the key into the ignition, put in the clutch and turned over the engine. I remembered at the last second to brace myself as the engine roared to life behind my head—deafening at first—but then it idled down to a subtle purr.

Trying to look like I knew what I was doing, I put it in first, let out the clutch and gave it just a little gas. The car rolled forward, the engine just rising above its idle hum. I turned the wheel and made a perfect, tight U-turn in my cul-de-sac. Everything the car did was effortless, as if it didn't need me to tell it what to do. We pulled onto the main road and, as the beastly growl of the diesel engine combined with the smooth ride and acceleration, I couldn't help the hot, heavy, blissful feeling that settled me deeper in my seat. This was going to be a great night.

Malcolm was so impressed with my driving skill he let me take his multi-million dollar concept car out on some back roads. I'd like to say I opened her up, but the engine was so powerful I had a feeling it would tear off the chassis if I revved it above 3000 thousand RPMs. Still, it was the experience of a lifetime. By the time I parked the car a few blocks from the party, I was excited. I turned off the engine and leaned back in my seat to look at Malcolm. We were both smiling and, for the first time in a long time, I felt like everything could work out. My sneaking out aside, I had an understanding with Cal, I was falling into step with being a Muse and I'd made a great new friend who had my back *and* let me play with his toys. I could handle this.

"You ready?"

My good mood sank. "I have a confession."

He raised an eyebrow.

"I've never been to a party."

His eyes went a little wide.

"Like any kind of party. Not a dance club or house party. I didn't even make it to prom."

"Really?"

I nodded, embarrassed. "I was a mom at sixteen, not a lot of time for that stuff." I blew out a breath. "I was in a bar once though and can hold my liquor." At least normally. Last night didn't count ...

"So you don't know how to dance?"

"I've watched MTV and plenty of movies. I just thought you should know I've never actually done this before." I let out a shuttering breath that gave away how nervous I was.

Malcolm put his hand on mine. The faint flux of energy was soothing, as were the emotions coming with it. Emotions are subtle, the nuances hard to differentiate. I imagined it was something I'd pick up with time. I could tell he wanted to say it would be all right.

"Do you trust me?" he asked instead.

That was the question, wasn't it? After all the times he'd saved my life or even just my butt. God help me, I did. "Yes." I tried not to gulp.

"Good, then we're gonna have a great time. When you wake up tomorrow, this guy will be nothing but a distant memory." He got out of the car and, before I could blink, he was opening my door. Super strong and super fast. I could get used to this. He took my hand, twining each of his fingers between mine.

We walked down the residential-looking street and stopped in front of a building that could be a small church built in the seventies when that brick look was so popular, only that wasn't organ music drifting through the thin glass.

Malcolm walked up to the door, pulling me along. He didn't knock, just stepped right in. Inside the door, a guy looked up at us.

"Hey Tom, did the party start without us?" Malcolm held his hand out to the guy. I saw a flash of green as the guy met him in a shake hello. Cash? That was our in? Nice.

"They're just getting started. Who's your lady friend?" Tom looked me up and down, licking his lower lip.

Okay, gross.

"This is my girl, Shelby," Malcolm said, sounding like the twenty-something frat guy he wasn't. "She's lookin' for a good time. Thought I'd show her how the Greek boys do it." He gave Tom a knowing wink.

I stifled the urge to roll my eyes. Instead, I pressed myself against Malcolm like the simpering college girl I wasn't. I swear my IQ dropped fifteen points.

Tom whispered something to Malcolm and waved us past the door, giving me a wink.

Down the hall and around a corner the music got louder.

"What'd he say?"

"Just guy stuff."

I stopped us and thought the words *if you want me to trust you....*

Malcolm seemed to get the message through our connection. He took a deep breath. "He said 'hit her once for me and we're square.'"

"I'm not ... This isn't a date."

Malcolm pressed me into the wall of the dark hallway; I didn't resist, keeping our cover.

"I know this isn't a date,"

He was too close to my face. I could smell his breath, warm like Italian herbs and just as appetizing. A smudge of humiliation trickled out of him. Had I hurt his feelings?

"But, that doesn't mean I'm not going to act like it is." His eyebrows raised in question.

I nodded.

"Good. Let's get a few things straight. First, take off your coat." He took his off, too, and laid them both on a table that already had a few. "Secondly ..." He ran his hands across the narrow waist of my jeans—squeezing my hips—then under my shirt to the bare flesh at my waist. He lingered all the way up to the edge of my bra, his fingertips running just under the edge.

I tried and failed to stifle a shiver when his fingers ran back down my waist. His thumbs ran under the exposed waistband of my thong. I tried not to think about him reading my enjoyment through our connection.

"Can you handle this?" he whispered.

An image of him tearing my thong down over my hips in a moment of passion flashed though my mind.

Malcolm moaned in a way I felt more than heard. I couldn't decide if it had been my image or his. His hands stilled and I pulled myself back together enough to meet his eyes. I nodded, not sure I could trust my voice.

He pressed me against the wall with the full length of his body. "Not only is this gonna work, it's gonna be fun."

He leaned away and held out his hand, waiting for me to make the decision to join him. He wouldn't drag me. I could walk out the door and he'd take me home. But if I did take his hand and follow him into that room, I now knew what I was in for.

Taking a deep breath, I pushed from the wall and took his hand, this time twining my fingers between his, ready to start the first real adventure of my life.

13

Muses work all day long and then at night get together and dance.

—Edgar Degas

We found the party in what must've been the common living area for the frat. It was a big room: On one side an open space with various seating arrangements. On the other a huge dining room with industrial-sized kitchen behind it. In the dining room, there was a guy in a neon green beanie manning a keg and a table full of liquor bottles. At one corner of the living area, a DJ was bopping, nearby bodies pulsing in time to the rhythm.

Malcolm pulled me past the dance floor towards an open window where people were smoking. He exchanged a unique handshake with a dark-haired guy and I saw another flash of green. Malcolm put his arm across my shoulders, pulled me against him, his arm bent at the elbow around my neck and kissed my temple.

He turned back to the dark-haired guy. "What ya got for me?"

The guy glanced around nervously before speaking. "Guy's name is Jerry McGovern, started here in the fall. Real weird, kept spouting off about religious crap. Told some guys he was looking for a wife, asked if they knew any 'women of virtue'. Then he changed, started sleeping with any and everyone. Never anyone serious though. He fits in pretty good now, just don't piss him off, scary shit happens."

"Like what?"

The guy looked around nervously again. "Guy took his seat in front of the TV one night and next day there was a dead cat all curled up on his pillow."

"Thanks, man." Malcolm passed him another bill.

I tried not to think about how much this was costing him. Hopefully, not more than dinner and movie.

The guy's eyes flashed around the room again. "You want my advice, stay away from this guy. I don't even meet his eyes and my room stays corpse-free. You feel me?"

"I feel you. Thanks, man." Malcolm gave him a nod, put on a college-boy swagger and pulled me into a dark corner near the dance floor. He leaned us against the wall. "Your friend Jerry shows classic signs of a sociopath." He spoke against my neck, warm puffs of air punctuating his words. "His previous address is a little town in the New Mexico desert. I'm thinking religious settlement. They often boot out grown boys until they come back with a wife or two."

His lips pressed against my skin again, warmth flooding me. Between his lips near my ear and his hands under my shirt heating the flesh about my waist, I could barely focus.

"It's bad that he's fixated on you. It is, however, good to know you're; instincts are working. We need to diffuse this guy and it sounds like he wants a 'woman of virtue'." He moved his lips right up to my ear and whispered, "Can you play dirty, Shelby?" Humor and lust poured out of him. Was that what made teasing?

I pulled my face back and looked at him square. "I was a Thespian, three years running. I can play anything you want."

"That's my girl."

A jolt of panic shot through me.

His face turned serious. "I'll be right here with you."

"That's the part I'm afraid of," I muttered.

"I'll be gentle."

"I need a drink. A strong one."

"Be right back." He slipped away, leaving me in the dark corner.

The room was getting more crowded, the music loud, but not concert or bar loud where you had to scream to tell someone you're headed to the can. I stayed in my corner and waited.

Malcolm was moving back towards me, a beer in one hand, a mixed drink in the other, when I felt Jerry's arrival.

Adrenaline and panic wracked through me like an electrical current, pushing me into vertigo and shakes.

Malcolm saw it and was at my side in a flash, not a drop spilled. He pressed me back into the corner, handing me the mixed drink, hiding me from view.

"He just walked in. You felt it?"

I nodded, taking a long drink and leaning against the wall.

"We need to give the impression we're involved and having a good time. Can you get yourself together?" He put his hand on my arm and my symptoms went down by half.

"It's better when you touch me." I took a deep breath. "I can do this," I said, more to myself than to him.

"Luv, you were born to do this."

I laughed, although maybe he was right. I am a Muse. Isn't this what we do? Dodge trouble and change the world?

I downed the rest of my drink and set my empty glass down.

Malcolm's eyebrows went up. "That had three shots in it."

"It sure did. Let's dance like we're having a good time. When he notices us, you get me another drink and I put myself in place for him to approach me. It'll give me an excuse to turn on the dirty right in front of him." My panic brought back how serious this was. There was a reason my instincts told me to run in the opposite direction when Jerry got close.

Malcolm looked beside himself with concern. "You sure, luv?"

"You're not woosing out on me are you?" I rubbed up against him.

He smiled. "Oh luv, the gloves just came off." He undid the top button of my shirt, exposing a lot more cleavage. I smiled as he moved to the lower buttons, exposing a seductive sliver of my belly. Like I said, button-up shirts just beg to be opened up.

I moved in view of Jerry and started grinding up and down Malcolm while keeping a tight grip in the front waistband of his pants. My hand touching the bare flesh there kept my panic and vertigo at a manageable level. I turned around and did some things you only see in dirty movies as the camera goes by. Malcolm, too, kept a hand on my flesh while broadcasting his enjoyment of my "acrobatics." I had a moment of self-righteous satisfaction as I realized my rigorous workouts weren't for nothing. Moving my body felt good and I had the sneaking suspicion that I looked good, too.

For ten minutes, I felt young and free—something I should've felt a long time ago. Never in my twenty-five years had I dropped so much inhibition and worry and just been ... carefree.

Malcolm made it easy, too. He was strong and confident, easy to follow and knowledgeable. I felt safe, like I hadn't in a long time.

I flipped back around and put my hand in Malcolm's pants again. I met his eyes; they were flat black, the thin rim of blue glowing in the dim light. His fingers dug into the small of my back, pulling me against him. Something raw and sexual poured out of him. I moaned from the rush of it. He grabbed my hips, grinding us together in what must have been a rather obscene show. He'd said "dirty." I didn't know he'd meant the show was gonna get real.

I put my arms around his neck, laying kisses and playfully biting his neck.

I looked into his eyes again and something snapped. Something primal and commanding. I wanted him. Right now, right here. Just like that. It was so overwhelming I almost acted on it. The feel of him through the connections in our flesh was overwhelming. I leaned in, ready to kiss him, throw myself at him, anything. For a second he came to meet me and then we were apart. He looked like I'd hit him. Just as quick, the impulse was gone. Realizing we were blowing our own cover, I stepped back toward him doing a little dance to make the moment look intentional. He let me get close, even put his hands back on me, but not like before.

"I think our friend noticed the spectacular show you've put on."

"Yeah? What was that last bit, by the way?"

"Nothing to worry about. It's time. You ready?"

I shot a glance at Jerry. He was watching us, beer in hand, stiff stance, a sneer pulling up his dirty-looking lip. Psychopath was not happy. I said a silent prayer that this would work and stepped away from Malcolm.

"Make it a triple." I flashed my teeth in a flirty smile for Jerry's benefit.

"Normally, I'd kiss a lady's hand as I walk away, but in this case ..." Malcolm gave my ass a good slap, winked and headed towards the drinks.

I tried to look like I enjoyed it, but oh did that slap hurt. That was gonna leave a mark. I made my way to the outside edge of the dance floor and stood there looking bored. Jerry took the bait and headed right for me.

14

Muses have cited everything from a bite of pure chocolate to a pile of garbage alongside the road as the inspiration for a work of art.
— "Muses," *World Look Encyclopedia*

Touching Malcolm had kept me feeling almost normal. Him gone and Jerry moving closer slammed the vertigo-inducing panic back into place.

I can do this, I reminded myself, as Jerry made his way over. I looked in Malcolm's direction, smiling when I spotted him near the drinks again.

"I didn't think I'd see you here," Jerry said.

I made a pointed effort to peel my eyes away from Malcolm and glance at Jerry.

"My boyfriend brought me, thought I could use some trouble." I gave him a coy smile before returning my gaze to Malcolm.

"Trouble?"

I looked back at him, considering. "You know," I leaned towards him like a drunken girl who just has to tell the dirty little secret. "Getting it on in public. It's such a rush. Especially if you get dirty with it."

He looked shocked and leaned away.

It was working! Even my panic eased

"You would do that? Where people might see you?"

"Might?" I let out a long annoying girl laugh.

He soaked it up and took another step back.

Malcolm chose that moment to return. He got next to me and did a couple of hip swings like he was humping my hip. I pretended to enjoy it and made the smile genuine when I saw the horror on Jerry's face. I took my drink and chugged a long swallow

"There's a dark corner over there," Malcolm said loud enough for Jerry to hear.

I made a happy noise and rubbed against Malcolm, taking another pull on my drink. The alcohol combined with my previous drink, sending warmth and wobbly through me. Or maybe it was just Malcolm. Whatever it was, I welcomed it. I was in way over my head.

"Let's do it, baby."

Malcolm wrapped an arm around my waist and walked me toward the empty dark corner. He slipped a hand down the front of my jeans, laying it flat across my belly. I sucked in a sigh of relief at his touch, the last of my panic falling away.

The corner was newly vacated, the previous occupants having moved on to a more private setting. There was a stained loveseat and a rickety end table. Malcolm took a seat in the middle of the couch and wagged his eyebrows at me. I took a deep breath and reminded myself that this was working and that I trusted Malcolm. It wasn't like we were going to do it right here on the couch, or at all for that matter. I climbed up and straddled his lap. This was a frat party; No one was going to stop us. Malcolm, gently and almost pretend-like, felt-up my chest while I downed the last of my drink and set my glass on the end table. I was buzzed and, despite my nervousness and the panic, was having a good time. I liked Malcolm, was comfortable with him. I almost wished this were a real date. Almost.

I laid kisses down his neck again, letting my hands rove all over him. "Still working?" I whispered into his ear."

"I can't decide if he looks pissed or disappointed," Malcolm said around a fake moan. "We'll know for sure when he storms out of here."

We continued to do our mock bump-and-grind on the couch for a few more minutes. Malcolm's hands were all up my shirt. He went as far as to unhook my bra, something that would have been obvious to anyone watching us. Jerry stayed and watched the show. I wasn't really going to have to have sex with Malcolm, was I?

"He's not buying it. We need to up the ante,"

I looked into his eyes. I had yet to kiss him, on the mouth that is. It just seemed too intimate for our little charade. Flesh was flesh, but a kiss?

I could blame it on the booze or the confusion of the energy passing between us. Maybe even some weird side effect of the panic, but I wanted to kiss him, and I knew the feeling was mutual.

Our eyes met and the longest five seconds of my life passed as we moved toward each other. Malcolm's hands abandoned my waist and caressed my face, encouraging me forward. Our lips met in a gentle pressure, sending tingles deep into my foundation. I shivered and pulled back, seeing my awe reflected back at me in Malcolm's defined features. I moved to kiss him again and this time it was long and soft, a moan escaped me and Malcolm wrapped his arms tight around me, crushing our lips together. I parted my lips and he caressed them with his tongue. I'd forgotten how exhilarating this was. It'd been over six years since I'd let a man get this close.

Things got hot after that and not in the composed, controlled way we'd been going about it before. Lips pushed and sucked, bodies writhed and hands found yet more intimate ways to caress. I'm not sure how much time passed before I came up for air, unable to believe that I'd let myself get so involved, that I'd let my inhibitions blow into the wind. I felt more alive than I had in a very long time. I looked into Malcolm's deep blue eyes, his lips swollen and red, both of us catching our breath as we waited to see what would happen next. Would he ask me back to his place? Would I say yes?

His eyes shifted behind me, reminding me why we were here. I'd forgotten about Jerry. Malcolm hadn't.

"He's gone," Malcolm said.

It had all been a show to him. I swung myself off Malcolm and didn't touch him again. I didn't want him feeling my humiliation. How could I have been so stupid, to let myself go like that? I can't believe I kissed him! At least I'd got rid of Jerry.

"Get me out of here, please," I said, feeling miserable.

Malcolm looked up at me from the couch, concern pulling his eyebrows together. "You okay?"

"Yeah, just glad it's over." It was partially true.

He narrowed his eyes, but didn't question me. He was gone in a flash, back seconds later with our coats. I followed him through a side door, careful not to touch him.

Out the door, Malcolm led me down a sidewalk as I struggled to re-clasp my bra. Distracted by the stupid thing, I followed him through the grass, not the sidewalk. The sidewalk was a gentle slope down a hill, but the grass had a three-foot drop-off. Five steps out the door, I fell.

barely getting my hands out in time to catch myself. My knee connected with a jagged rock. Before I even made a sound, Malcolm was lifting me from the ground and moving around the building into some light.

"You're all right. Let's get a look."

I bit my lip to keep from crying or moaning in pain. He set me on a recycle trashcan and looked at my leg. There was a blood-soaked tear in my jeans. In one swift motion, he ripped away the remaining tattered pieces of my pant leg to expose the injury.

Two pairs of pants ruined in a week. I'd go broke at this rate.

"You need stitches. I can get you fixed up at my place; then you can skip the ER."

"That's okay. I can manage. Just drop me at home." It didn't look that bad. I went to jump off the can, but he stopped me.

"I insist. I should've been closer or warned you about the drop. It's my fault. I need to do this for you." He was touching me again. I could feel his sincerity. How could I say no to that?

"All right."

"I promise to patch you up and send you on your way." He helped me off the can.

"Thank you. For everything. I couldn't have done this without you."

"It was my pleasure. A man needs to get out and feel he's alive and young once in awhile. Doing it with a pretty lady is icing on the cake." He gave me a wink. It really had been just an act to him. I was such an ass.

15

A Guardian is naturally inclined to help, care for and protect his or her Muse. Once bonded, this inclination increases. A Muse's purpose is to use his or her abilities to help others. Muses are not overly attentive to their Guardians.
—"Muses and Guardians," *World Look Encyclopedia*

Malcolm wanted to carry me to his car. He had to settle for helping me hobble.

Ten minutes later, we drove past my neighborhood near Country Club, over the hill behind it and into a newer development. After seeing his car, I shouldn't have been surprised by the neighborhood. The simple-looking place we pulled up to, however, was unexpected. It looked like any other upper-middle-class home, complete with three-car garage. Nothing overly lavish.

The garage was large, a workout area at one end, tools and storage in the middle. A serious-looking motorcycle was at the other end, next to where he parked the R8. A staircase led up to a landing where the washer and dryer sat alongside storage boxes labeled "Christmas lights" and "baseball cards." How freakishly normal.

A door at the top of the stairs led to the kitchen—clean, simple and high tech. The entire color scheme was done in black and white. He flipped on the lights and I got a look at the rest of the space. The living, dining and kitchen all combined into one big room. One side wall was nothing but floor-to-ceiling windows. At the far end, a hallway. Between was a dining table, living area with mounted television, full bar and pool table. A guy pad, but normal enough.

Malcolm dropped his keys and wallet on the island counter.

I moved to see the view. It was spectacular, the little town of Philomath in the distance distinguished by pinpricks of light. When the sun came up there'd be a perfect view of Mary's Peak, a local part of the coastal mountain range. The view started to bring up memories. I turned from the windows before they could surface.

Malcolm pulled a bottle of wine from an odd fridge that seemed designed to hold only wine bottles. I'd never seen such a thing before.

"I'm interested in an artist's opinion of my place."

"You did this yourself?"

He nodded, getting down glasses.

I walked around the space. The wood floors were bone white, the chair molding black, the upper expanse of the walls and the ceiling white. The furniture was likewise, either black or white.

"It's ... monochromatic."

He chuckled. "Fair enough."

"It's pleasing to the eye, but you need something ..."

Malcolm was pouring wine from a dark blue glass bottle. The contrast with the black and white was so pretty I got an idea.

"You need accents." I limped back to the kitchen. "Like a red throw pillow on the couch or a set of blue jars for the kitchen."

He gave me a long look. "I think you're right." He scooped me up. "Can I start with you? Something red for the kitchen?" He set me on the counter.

I blushed and he chucked my chin, handing me a glass of wine. "I'll get the first-aid kit. Don't go anywhere?"

"Be right here." I took a drink of my wine. It was fabulous.

He was gone in a flash.

Swinging my uninjured leg, I tried to relax. I'd spent the last two hours rubbing up and down the guy. We'd touched almost every square inch of each other, and I was nervous?

He doesn't want a relationship or a Muse I reminded myself. This had been a favor, a fun night for both of us. That was all. I took another long sip of wine, setting my glass down just as a gorgeous blond woman came through the front door.

Bingo.

She stopped in the entryway in her tiny spike heels, short black leather skirt and little black leather jacket with a sparkling silver top underneath. A fake orange tan and bleached blond hair completed her look.

"Well, well, well." She raised one thin, perfectly waxed eyebrow in surprise. "Where has Malcolm been keeping you?"

I could have died. Fake tan and hair aside, she was perfect, long legs and all. I felt dirty and frumpy sitting on the counter with my bloody knee. Just a stray kid Malcolm was bandaging up before sending her home to mommy. Of course, he had an immaculate creature to share himself with. She even had a manicure. My toes hadn't had paint in years, let alone my hands. I was just a charity case.

Before I could answer, Malcolm appeared, first-aid kit in hand, at the entrance to the hallway.

He was by my side in a flash. "Shelby, this is my roommate Tiffany," he said in a rush. "Tiffany, this is my friend Shelby." He didn't elaborate on my presence any further, although he did seem nervous.

Interesting.

"Whatever." Tiffany flipped her tight blond curls. "Forgot my ID, then I'm outie." She swung her hips through the house.

"Sorry," Malcolm said, once she was gone. "I thought she'd be out all night." He set a large plastic toolbox on the counter and started going through it.

"It's not like we're on a date or something." I tried to sound relaxed, giving my uninjured leg another swing, getting it back in motion.

Malcolm looked up at me, but didn't comment.

I let it go.

Malcolm rummaged through the box and got the supplies set up. Tiffany sashayed back through the kitchen on her way out. She met my eyes and a sharp jolt of surprise made me jump. Like someone came up behind me, grabbed me and said, "Boo!"

Malcolm looked up from preparing a suture. "What?"

"Nothing." A chill ran through me. Something was wrong, but not like I'd felt with Jerry. This was more ... creepy.

Malcolm wasn't buying. His hand went to my arm. "You're scared. What happened?"

"I don't know. It just hit me." I shivered.

He wrapped his jacket around my shoulders." Let's get you bandaged; then we can warm you up and send you home."

Malcolm was meticulous in his ministrations. He cleaned the area with liberal amounts of alcohol, mopping the wound with cotton pads until nothing remained but an exposed gash. It was much larger than I'd thought and certainly needed stitches.

"Where'd you learn this?" I asked as he reached for the sutures.

"Standard course at Guardian school. Had extra because of my abilities."

"In case you hurt yourself?"

"Nah, I heal too quick for this stuff. They thought I'd spend a lot of time in rescues. My Muse would've been an athlete or stunt man. Someone who needs keeping up with."

"If you don't mind my asking, why don't you have a Muse? Not that I protest. Devoting your whole life to the whims of someone else is absurd, but most Guardians seem to go with it. Why not you?"

He kept working. "I'm going to block the nerves with energy over flow. You shouldn't feel much." He put his hand on my thigh and pulled through the first stitch.

I didn't feel anything. Cool.

"I wanted to make my own path, you know?"

"I do. I feel the same way about being a Muse. What happened to what I want?"

He nodded, tying off the second stitch. "Two down, two to go."

I had so many questions. I wanted to know about his abilities, about MAGRA, how he knew Cal, about this energy transfer stuff and how he was blocking my nerves, but I just finished my wine and tried to enjoy myself like I promised myself I would. I was in a beautiful house, drinking the best wine I'd ever had with a gorgeous rich man who was tending to my injury. How much more fairy tale do you get?

"Thank you." It was the most encompassing thing I could think to say.

"It's good to use my skills. Keeps me sharp." He taped a bandage over most of my knee.

"About taking me out, ... I don't get out much, and I had a good time."

He straightened up and met my eyes, pushing the first-aid box aside. He put his hands on the counter on either side of me and leaned in. "I had fun, too."

I leaned in and just like that, we were kissing again, long and soft. His hands stayed on the counter and my brain had a panic moment. Was I kissing him or was he kissing me? He doesn't want a Muse. I don't want a boyfriend. Do I? I pulled my lips away and he leaned in to find them. Yep, he was kissing me, too. His hands went to my face, my neck, twined through my hair. The chilling sensation returned.

It didn't creep in either. One moment I was fine, heat rolling into the corners of my body, as I contemplated reaching toward the button of his jeans. The next, I was dunked in ice. I pulled away, gasping.

"What?" He grabbed my hands.

"I don't know. It just got cold." I shivered.

Malcolm looked around. "It's not cold in here." He put an arm around me and rubbed my shoulder.

"It happened earlier, but it came and went so fast I forgot." My teeth were almost chattering.

Malcolm looked around the room again. "I don't like this; you're reacting to something. You should stay here tonight. I'll take you home in the morning."

I raised an eyebrow at him. "If you want me in bed, the least you can do is be honest about it."

"I do want you in bed, but not like this. You can stay in the guest room. You'll be safe here until I get you back to Cal tomorrow. I don't want you spending the night alone."

Another shiver went through me and I started to get scared. What was wrong with me? "All right, let's do it. I could use a blanket."

He helped me off the counter, across his vast living space and down the hall into a spare bedroom. It was also furnished in the monochromatic motif.

Malcolm set me on the bed and wrapped an extra blanket around me. "I'll get you something to sleep in." Five seconds later he was back, matching black sweats in hand.

"Wow. How fast are you?" I stood up to change.

He turned his back to give me privacy. He'd had his hands under my clothing all night, not much mystery left. I was also strangely comfortable around him. Like seeing him in my house, it just felt right. He could have watched.

"My top speed was 271 miles an hour, but I doubt I'm that fast anymore."

I finished pulling the sweatpants on and tried to imagine that. "Really?"

He turned and, seeing the look on my face, started backpedaling. "In a straight line. I'm a lot slower around turns."

I opened my mouth to ask how fast and another shiver wracked through me.

"Your lips are turning blue." He moved to the thermostat, beeping the keypad to the maximum. He helped me out of my blouse without looking away from my eyes and pulled the sweatshirt over my head. He made a production out of tucking me in bed, pulling extra blankets from the closet. He sat on the bed and rubbed my shoulder.

"Do you know what's wrong with me?" I shivered again.

"Muses are unique creatures, sensitive to the forces in the universe. They feel and express manifestations the rest of us can't even imagine. In a way, they—you—are far more unique and powerful than Guardians will ever be.

"Some power within the cosmos is directing at you or through you and you're having a physical manifestation of it. In my studies as a Guardian, we were taught of such things. The manifestations were said to be rare if we did our jobs right. I imagine you're just a new force within the universe and things are trying to find a balance. You should be fine by morning. No Muse has ever died from universal-directed energy, just made uncomfortable."

Uncomfortable, I was.

"Your lips aren't even blue anymore." He ran a finger across them. "You should sleep." He got up to leave, but something inside me called out.

"Stay with me," I blurted. "You can sleep here, keep me warm."

Malcolm turned back, looking tired "I can't make love to you tonight. Not like this."

"I know. I just don't wanna be alone. I'm always alone." I said the last in a small voice. I trusted Malcolm and I'd opened up my deepest darkest secret to him, made myself vulnerable. How he reacted would say a million things.

He looked uncertain for a moment and then his face transformed. "I can do that, but you have to do something for me."

"What?"

"Promise to trust me. No matter what Cal or anybody tells you about me. I've made mistakes in my life, but I'm a good person. I don't want my past dimming your light. It's so beautiful, the way you look at me." He ran his hand down the side of my face. "I wouldn't change it for anything."

I think I was falling in love. I couldn't decide if it was wonderful, horrible or just plain dangerous. Looking into Malcolm's eyes, I knew this was a promise I could keep. "I promise."

He was gone. Back ten seconds later wearing nothing but pajama bottoms and sliding into bed next to me.

"You know you'll be warmer if we share skin." His breath even smelled minty. He had time to brush his teeth?

"Okay," I said around another shiver. I peeled off the sweatshirt and Malcolm wrapped himself around me from behind. I instantly felt warmer.

Malcolm settled in next to me. "No bad dreams now, luv."

A contented feeling of rightness swept through me and I drifted off to sleep. Not alone for the first time in far too long.

16

The Muses love the Morning.

—Thomas Fuller

I woke up to the sun on my face, snuggled in next to Malcolm, content. The silk sheets were amazing, add the man and stick a fork in me—I'm done. Malcolm stirred. I opened my eyes and looked into his ocean blue ones. "Hi," I said.

"Hi."

I know it's cliché, but what do you say to a man after you wake up in bed with him in his own guest bedroom after not having sex with him, after a night of mock dirty dancing to throw possible sociopaths of your scent? I'd have to ask Diane later, but I was pretty sure "Hi" was it.

"Shivers gone?"

I dug my toes deeper under his feet and nodded.

"Good, cause I was thinking ..." He stretched out from under the covers revealing a perfect strip of curly blond chest hair. "Now that we've slept together, we should get to know each other better." He smiled. "I don't even know your favorite color or flower. Do you like chocolate? These are things a guy should know."

They were all "present" questions. I couldn't help but smile. Unfortunately, there was a bigger issue to address than what color roses to send me after a fight.

"Shouldn't we discuss the Muse/Guardian thing first?" Sometimes I hated being practical.

"It's pretty simple. Cal is going to guard you and I'm going to date you." He leaned in and gave me a slow kiss so warm and sweet it wiped my mind of every thought.

It took me a minute to remember what we were talking about. "A guy approached me in the cafeteria yesterday and Cal made him wear my vinaigrette. I doubt he'll take kindly to us dating."

"So we don't tell him. At least not for a while. He doesn't control you, luv, and I can handle myself when he finds out."

"Why not just tell him up front?"

"He'll make it hard for us to see each other. I think we'd both like to know where this is going before it becomes something we have to fight for."

Fair enough. "My favorite color is red, carnations are my favorite flower and, yes. I do like chocolate. White or milk, none of that nasty dark stuff."

He hopped out of bed. "What about breakfast? Eggs? Sausage? No, I got it, pancakes. Blueberry ones."

He was right. "What? How did you ...?" I couldn't even speak.

"They're my favorite too." He jumped back onto the bed and brushed another kiss across my lips. "Can't seem to stop kissing you."

We shared another long press of lips, and then he jumped off the bed again. He opened a door I'd thought was another closet. It was a bathroom. Nice.

"There should be an extra toothbrush in the drawer. I'll get breakfast started." He was gone.

I flopped out of bed into the bathroom. Sore from my antics the night before, I would've loved to climb into the beautiful tile and glass walled-in shower, but it would defeat the purpose to put dirty clothes back on. Plus, I didn't have time. I had to get the kids and get home before Cal realized I was gone.

I freshened up and padded out to Malcolm's living area. His long wall of windows faced west so it wasn't too bright in the black-and-white room. Malcolm was in the kitchen sporting wet hair, new pajama pants and a black T-shirt. He'd had time to shower? I'd run my fingers through my hair and mopped the runoff mascara from my face.

I took a seat at the island counter.

"You know the secret to perfect blueberry pancakes?" He started pouring batter into a skillet.

I shook my head. I'd always wanted to know how restaurants got the blueberries evenly spaced, but like so many things, I'd never had time to find out.

"Come here and I'll show you."

Malcolm pulled me between him and the stove. "You have to drop the blueberries in when the cakes are already in the skillet." He dropped a few into the first pancake and handed me the bowl of berries. I continued to drop them in while he pulled down plates, got out syrup and butter, glasses and juice. He set the table at an efficient speed considering he didn't use his super speed to do it. He made it back just in time to flip the first two cakes. He finished setting the table complete with cloth napkins and came back to pull the pancakes out of the skillet. He poured two more and let me plop the blueberries into them. When those finished, he set two pancakes on each plate and we dug in.

Malcolm set his napkin in his lap and proceeded to cut perfect squares of pancake. He dipped them in syrup and placed them in his mouth without a single drip. Impressive.

"Tell me about yourself," he said.

"You remember I have kids?" I cut my pancakes into shoddy looking pieces and dripped syrup back onto my plate. He didn't seem to notice.

"Cal's right? I can't picture that. You must tell."

"Not much to tell. Met Cal in high school, thought I loved him, was naive and got pregnant, had a baby, got married, managed to get pregnant again, and then he took off. Told everyone he was going into the Army and just disappeared. I didn't hear from him until last week when he showed up announcing I was a Muse and he's my Guardian."

"Hmmm."

"Hmmm what?"

"Cal's a healer; they don't guard artist types." He took another perfectly square bite. "He must have called in some big favors to get assigned to you."

"I'd say he had to move a mountain, the way he's acting."

"He must really care about you."

I shook my head since my mouth was full of pancake. I swallowed. "He did it for the kids. Said he couldn't stand another man playing daddy to them."

"I've never heard of a Guardian having kids with someone he wasn't guarding. There's no precedent for it. That must be why they made the allowance."

I shrugged. "So what kind of Guardian should guard an artistic Muse?"

He thought for a moment as he chewed. "An intuitive or telepathic one. Artistic types can get pretty neurotic. It can take a telepath to keep up with them."

I didn't let the neurotic comment bother me. Plenty of artists went weird. Kali is a telepathic Guardian. That's why she was sent to me....

"Tell me about your kids. I look forward to meeting them."

He cut off another perfect square of cake and inserted it into his mouth without dripping.

"Do you always talk and act so formal? I thought you were just polite before."

He rolled his eyes and stuffed a huge oddly cut bite of pancake into his mouth. He made a display of chewing it with his mouth half open and noisily swallowing it down.

"I spent most of my childhood in an English boarding school. One of the teachers was a right old bastard and insisted our English be perfect. I spent the better part of my teens trying to do away with the English accent I acquired."

"Is that where the `luv' came from?"

He nodded, "Your kids?" He took another bite that was far too large.

"Chloe just turned eight and is in second grade. She's sweet, easygoing and sings everywhere she goes. Julian is a little more complicated." I took a long drink of juice, trying to think of a way to elaborate without making him sound like a monster. Then I remembered Malcolm was a Guardian and would know what I was talking about. "Julian has trouble with secondary authority figures. Cal is helping him. I imagine it will be better soon."

Malcolm made an affirmative noise around his juice. "You should have Cal get him into one of the pre-Guardian acclimation camps. How old is he?"

"Six next month"

"He's just the right age then. Guardian children don't start full time at the academies until age 12, but in the meantime, they should go to pre-Guardian camp four times a year. It teaches them to cope with what they are. Gives them a sense of belonging, like they're not alone. That's a big deal when you're a little kid who's different than everyone else."

He had a point. "You think it would help?"

"It's the ones that don't go that have problems."

"Like what?"

"The few that I've met? Superiority complexes, sociopathic behavior, psychological problems like that. It's how they learn cope as a child. It's why they started the camps. Imagine knowing you're different, powerful and special. Not being around others like you could turn your head."

I felt myself gulp. Julian was going to Guardian camp.

"Cal can tell you more about it. Probably already planning to."

I nodded and set my fork down. I'd finished my pancakes, and all this talk about my kids reminded me that I needed to get back to them.

"Ready to go already?" He wiped his mouth and set his napkin on the table.

"Have to get back before Cal realizes I'm gone."

"Your jeans were trashed Keep the sweats. Get your stuff together and meet me back here in five?" As if he needed a whole five minutes.

"Sure."

I followed him across the living area, not letting my gaze stray out the windows. Back in the bedroom, I gathered up my stuff, slipped on my shoes and trudged back out to the kitchen. Malcolm wasn't there yet, but

Tiffany was pouring herself a cup of coffee, still in her clothes from the night before.

"Well hello. Little miss skinned knees stayed the night. Did Malcolm kiss it and make it all better?"

Having to fend for myself and look out for my own mental welfare since I was five has taught me how to read people and not let them get to me.

I smiled and took on a conspirator's tone. "He did and let me tell you, that tongue can do amazing things." I winked for good measure.

Her mouth fell open. Evidently, she wasn't expecting my candor.

I smiled another sly smile and then Malcolm was behind me, sliding a hand around my waist, planting a kiss on my temple.

"Ready, luv?"

I made a happy affirmative noise and took his hand as we headed out to the garage.

17

At the age of eighteen, Guardians are allowed to choose their own occupations for the next seven years. Most Guardians work for MAGRA in various capacities. Some are assigned to watch a potential Muse. A few choose advanced training in preparation for guarding a high-profile Muse. Guardians also may choose to travel or attend college. Once a Guardian reaches twenty-five, he or she must return to MAGRA for assignment. To refuse is considered treason. Unattached Guardians are shunned by Guardian society.
— "Guardians," *World Look Encyclopedia*

"I should explain about Tiffany," Malcolm said, pulling out of his driveway.

"Could be a good idea."

"She's an old friend. Just staying with me till she gets back on her feet."

"By old friend you mean old flame?" I tried to keep my voice neutral.

"We did see each other, but that was a long time ago."

"She's a non-traditional Guardian, too?"

He shot me a look that confirmed my suspicion.

"Just figured you'd only date someone like you. Or a Muse." I added as an afterthought.

"I see."

"I just want to hear you say it. Are we looking at something long-term or is this just for fun, to piss off Cal or something?"

He laughed, a deep rich sound that filled my chest and made me feel lighter.

"I'm, indeed, looking for something long-term with you. The added benefit of pissing off Cal aside. That is if you're looking for something long-term as well?"

I hesitated. I shouldn't have, but I did. It had been a long time since I'd had a relationship, and I had the kids to think of. Not to mention he was rich and handsome and all those other intimidating things. How could we ever have a balanced relationship? I'd never be able to give him near what he could give me.

"Let's take it one day at a time."

"You've had a lot of changes lately."

"Yes I have," I said to the window. I had to pick up the kids, shower and introduce my kids to their long-lost father. Then I had to spend the evening with a man I detested, allow him to touch me for our chi balancing and somehow manage to hide my stitched-up knee and sore muscles. No easy feat when he can read my body like a CAT scan, telling me when I'm ovulating and if my electrolytes are off balance.

Malcolm's hand on mine pulled me back.

"You were glaring at your reflection."

"Sorry, just have a lot on my mind."

"Anything I can do?"

I blew out a sigh and squeezed his hand. "Tell me how we're keeping this from Cal." "Easy. We sneak, and we do it in plain sight using your usual habits. Misdirection."

"So, tomorrow morning I talk Cal into watching the kids so I can have my run and you just happen to meet me?"

"Exactly."

"He said he can smell you on me."

"Did he?" Malcolm laughed again. "I can take care of that."

I wanted to ask how but had a more pressing question. "Why does Cal hate you so much?"

Malcolm looked thoughtful. "We were friends once, best friends. When I decided not to work for the Authority, he couldn't accept it and left. I haven't talked to him in over ten years."

"It's so terrible to want more with your life?"

"The way we're brought up, it's equal to treason. I've been shunned, if you will."

"I'm sorry. I know what that's like."

"Do you?"

"I do, but we'll have to save that for another day." We'd arrived at my house, and I was itching to get out of the car. I opened the door and hesitated. "Do I get your phone number or something?"

He smiled. "Well, I already have yours. Let me see your phone."

I handed it over and watched his fingers blur across the keys. This was the second time in as many days a man had put his number in my phone. I hoped I wasn't starting a trend. I scrolled through the entries when he handed it back. He'd entered himself as "Luv." This made me smile and lean back to give him a long kiss goodbye.

"Around ten on the path around the park over there?"

"Mmhmm." I was lightheaded from the kiss.

"If you don't find me, it's because Cal or someone is watching you."

"Okay." I got out of the car. He waited for me to get through the front door before pulling away.

Locking the door, I went to shower. I got clean as fast as I could, not neglecting to shave my legs. I put a fresh bandage on my knee and stuffed my clothes from the night before into the washer. Didn't want Cal noticing anything off. Feeling refreshed and somehow more alive than I had in years, I set off to get the kids.

Diane and Johnas live in one of his parents' nicer rentals. It's a house in a good neighborhood, just on the smaller side. They're both working on their master's degrees and haven't had kids yet. The idea of them doing so is somewhat scary. Not that they'll be bad parents, but Johnas is 6 foot 6 and well over 280 lbs of Native American muscle. Diane is about 5 foot 1 and a 100 lbs. soaking wet, not to mention pale with red hair. They're both gorgeous, but I can't help but wonder what their kids will look like.

Diane answered the door looking harassed. Julian is normally good for her, but with all the changes lately, he was probably acting up. "Julian?"

She nodded. "Julian."

"I'm here to rescue you."

"Thank God. What took you so long?"

"I got held up."

"Oh my God, you slept with him!"

"Shhhh! No!" I pushed through her front door.

"Honey, you're glowing like a ripe peach in the sun. You got something."

"I got a boyfriend."

"Nu-uh."

"Ya-huh."

"Told ya this would work. Now he can guard you and Cal can crawl back into whatever hole he's been hiding in all these years."

"Malcolm doesn't want to guard me and even if he did, he'd never work for MAGRA."

"Whatever, I'm excited anyway. You've needed some for far too long."

"Just keep it down. I'm not telling Cal or the kids yet."

"Why not?" We moved into her living room.

I flopped on the couch. "He and Cal don't get along. Speaking of which, Cal doesn't know I went out last night and I need to get back before he realizes I'm not there now."

"Since when does my Shel answer to anyone, especially the backstabbing Cal?"

"He didn't give me a choice, Di. He threatened to handcuff us together on a permanent basis, like when I'm showering and sleeping, if I didn't agree to be more ... accommodating.

"Shit."

"Yeah."

"That's damn sexy."

"Had a feeling you'd say that."

"So you stayed the night, but you didn't sleep with him?"

"You know me better than that."

Diane opened her mouth to respond, but Chloe ran shrieking into the room. Her long dark hair was braided into matching plaits, accentuating the high cheekbones and heavy lips she'd inherited from Cal's Native American ancestors. Combine that with my big long-lashed eyes and she was quite striking.

Johnas was growling and stomping after her, Julian on his back egging him on. Chloe leapt into my lap, pretending to be afraid as Johnas loomed into the room like a dark cousin of Frankenstein's monster.

"Mommy, make him stop." Chloe hid her face behind my still damp hair.

"I can't. Only Auntie Diane can stop him. She has the magic word." I whispered the last bit.

Chloe climbed into Diane's lap. Johnas let out a loud roar and staggered forward. Julian giggled with delight.

"Make him stop, Auntie Diane. Please."

Diane waved her arms and said some nonsense words.

Johnas instantly froze in place Julian kicked his sides like Johnas was a pony and made a whining noise, before sliding off his back in disappointment.

"You did it," Chloe said in awe.

"I told you she has the magic."

Chloe looked at Diane. "But you said Mommy has the magic."

I felt my eyes go wide and my pulse jump into my throat.

Diane turned bright red.

"Chloe, get you stuff together? Help your brother?"

Chloe is not a kid who needs telling twice. "Okay, Mommy." She slid out of Diane's lap, took Julian by the hand and pulled him back down the hallway.

"I'll go help." Johnas gave Diane wide eyes and followed them out.

I wheeled on Diane. "How could you? Do you really think it's your place to tell them? In a couple hours I have to tell them about Cal. Don't I have enough on my plate?"

"I didn't say you were an M-u-s-e." She spelled it. "I just said you were special and could help people. That's all."

I glared at her.

"They know something's up. They wouldn't stop talking about their new uncle and how he's gonna make their dad come back. Chloe said you're different, too, that you don't talk to them much and you're acting funny. Sounds like you're distracted. I was defending you, trying to help her understand you have a job now that keeps you busy. That you're not neglecting them because you're unhappy with them. I know she seems like an easygoing girl, but she's more perceptive than you give her credit for."

Diane was right. In the wake of all this, I'd neglected the kids. Making sure they get three squares and baths is a lot less than I normally do with them. I had to do better, especially with a man coming into my life. The kids come first, even before me. I couldn't forget or back burner them. It went against everything I believed in as a parent.

"You're right; I don't know what's got into me lately."

"You'll be all right and you'll do the right thing. You don't know any other way."

I hugged her. I was so overwhelmed the last thing I needed was a boyfriend, especially one I had to sneak around with. *But Malcolm feels so right. He brings out the twenty-five-year-old in me. Someone I never thought I'd meet.* I had to see where this would take us. If I got in over my head, I'd just jump ship and swim back to shore I just wished things could be that easy with Cal, speaking of which ...

"I gotta go." I pulled out of our hug.

"Yes dear, you always do."

"Don't I know it."

Diane and Johnas helped me get the kids in the car. Diane hugged me one last time, reminding me to take it one step at a time and to make sure I got some. Interesting priorities.

I got home and breathed in the peace. I'd done it. Had a whole night out and enjoyed myself. Cal hadn't found out. I was getting away with it. No, I was living my life. I wasn't some teenager evading her parents. I was a grownup and how I lived my life was my business. I could go out anytime I wanted and from now on, I would. Cal wouldn't make me afraid to live my life. If he handcuffed himself to me as punishment, well, I'd just make it punishment for him. This line of thinking gave me an idea that just might work.

In the meantime, I had homework to do, a house to clean, lunch and dinner to make and kids to spend extra time with before I shattered their universe.

18

The Muse gave the Greeks genius and the art of the
well-tuned phrase.

—Horace

Cal arrived promptly at four. Under his usual trench
coat was a pair of double-pleated slacks and a plaid shirt
that brought out the gold flecks is his eyes. He was trying
to impress us. *Great.*

I stopped him in the entryway, Chloe and Julian still in
their rooms.

"Let's get a few things straight," I said.

Cal looked annoyed, which just pissed me off.

"*I* am their parent. *You* are a stranger. Daddy or not,
you don't know us and, until you do, *I* call the shots. I say
what, I say who and when. You disrespect that in any way
and handcuffs or not I will make life very unpleasant for
you."

He gulped, and I had to work really hard not to smile.

"*I'm* going to tell the kids. *You* may answer questions
and tell them things, but only details I approve of. This
has weeks of tantrums and late-night drama written all
over it and I want to minimize the fallout."

"They're resilient kids, Shel; they'll be all right."

"That is exactly what I'm talking about. You don't know that. You don't know them. I'll tell you what they can handle."

Cal put his hand on my shoulder and I resisted the urge to shrug it off. "You've done an amazing job with them. You're a good mom. I'll let you call the shots. We're in this together now, on the same team. I'm sorry I couldn't give you that before."

I did shrug him off. "Don't be nice to me. I'm not sure I can take it."

He frowned.

"Tell them where you've been and why. Tell them about yourself, too. Just keep it PG and don't exaggerate. Julian is impressionable. Finding out his Dad is a superhero is going to be huge for him. I'll be fielding phone calls from the other parents for months. One more reason for them to dislike me." I muttered the last bit to myself, but Cal heard.

"They don't like you?"

I resisted the urge to roll my eyes. "Cal, I'm twenty-five and have an eight-year-old. It doesn't take a calculator to do the math. I don't exactly fit into the clique of late thirties, early forties, highly educated moms that are the majority around here. I'm a bit of an enigma and not the kind that everybody wants to buddy up to because it's interesting. Single teen mom: I must look like the epitome of white trash to them."

While I talked, I didn't look at Cal. I couldn't. It hurt too much. He'd promised me things once and if he'd fulfilled those promises, I probably wouldn't feel the way I did now. I was tired. Tired of being alone, tired of being an outcast, tired of not having what everyone else seemed to have.

He pulled my chin up. "I'm so sorry. This is my fault. I promise things will be better from now on."

I pulled away from him. "Don't promise me things. Let's just do this so I can get on with my life." I called the kids down.

"What, now?"

"You wanna spend time with them, right?"

"Yeah,"

"Wouldn't you like to do that as their daddy?" I whispered the last word as the kids came tromping down the stairs.

"Uncle Cal, what're you doing here?"

Cal looked terrified. *Good. He should be.* He was about to become a father. Only eight years late, could be worse.

I took the kids into the living room and sat them on the couch.

"I gotta tell you guys something important, okay?" Had to give them a little warning, didn't I? I gave Cal one last glance where he was standing between the entryway and living room leaning against the wall. This was his last chance to bolt. Please bolt. I don't want to do this. I don't want things to change. A few stupid things aside, I was happy. Finally, after all these years, I'd gotten over him. Of course, that was when he chose to pop back in.

He didn't bolt. He gave a nod.

Here goes nothing. "Uncle Cal is your dad. He's been away training for an important job, but he's back now and wants to get to know you."

That was it. There was nothing more to say until it sank in, until it registered. The suspense was awful. Nothing happened and then slowly their faces changed. They looked at Cal, then me, and then back at Cal. It was eerily synchronous.

Finally, I couldn't take it anymore. "I'm sure you have questions for your Dad. If you need me I'll be in the kitchen." I got up and stood next to Cal. "I think it'd be safe for you to take my chair, Dad." I punched his shoulder and went to make dinner.

It went better than I thought it would. The kids were young enough they didn't have any real concept of sex or marriage or even time for that matter. Julian, who'd already spent some time with Cal, jumped right in and started peppering him with questions. Chloe was more reserved. I caught her eye when I peeked in a bit later and she looked almost ... knowing. Fair enough, she'd realized something was up before this. Otherwise she looked unsure, maybe scared. She didn't talk much but answered questions Cal or an excited Julian asked her. I'd say she was weary. That's my girl, careful of whom she trusts.

They talked for a half hour while I started the spaghetti. I set everything out for them to make the salad and went back to the living room. Julian was in Cal's lap, Chloe still on the couch, but smiling. As much as I wanted this to be difficult for Cal, I didn't want that for the kids. The better it went now, the better they'd continue acclimating to the change. Why couldn't he have waited eight more years until they were both angry teenagers?

Cal helped the kids make salad and we ate. He watched me put the kids to bed. A bath for Julian, a shower for Chloe. He watched me towel dry her long hair, apply conditioner and comb through it. If he kept her on his own, he'd need to know how to do it. As I combed her hair, I explained you start at the ends and work your way up. Chloe's hair is to her bottom, so it's a long process. He at least faked interest.

After a story and hugs, even from Cal, the kids were tucked in. The whole process had taken an hour. An hour of every day since I was sixteen had been devoted just to putting the kids to bed. I didn't mind, really, but it made my bitterness at Cal that much worse.

When I came out of my room in pajamas, Cal was standing in Julian's doorway watching him.

"I came to see him after he was born."

I settled in on the other side of the doorway.

"Kali helped me. It was the first week you were home from the hospital. She snuck me in while you were sleeping. I got to hold him." He looked at me. "I've seen you a few times over the years. I stayed hidden because I didn't want to upset you. I couldn't stay and there was no way I could explain that to you, but I've always cared."

He met my eyes, and I looked away.

"You don't need to sneak around again. Even then, I would've let you see them. I may not've been happy about it, but I would've. Barring that you don't do anything really bad in the future, I always will." I met his eyes again. I'd avoided mentioning the part where he said he'd always cared. I was trying to take it as he'd always cared about all of us, but I'd seen the look in his eyes. There was passion there. Passion I'd known and loved. Why did I have to know him so well? If he'd been a fling or someone I barely knew, this would be so much easier. Damn it.

"Thank you," he said. "I promise I won't lie to you again."

I pushed off from the wall. "Don't promise me things, Cal. Don't make vows or give your word. Can you just agree to that?"

He nodded, and I walked away.

A few minutes later, I was at the sink, Cal standing there with a dishtowel waiting for direction. I was filling the dishwasher and he looked silly standing there, towel in hand, with his oversized body and dressy clothes. I glanced out the window over the sink, trying to hide my snicker, and what I saw sent my heart to my throat.

My kitchen window looks into the backyard and standing under my maple tree, bold as you please, was Tiffany. She was looking right at me, dressed in black, her bleached platinum hair pulled into a ponytail. Her dull grey eyes pulled into the scowl of her face. The shock of seeing her there was bad enough, but the violent wave of panic and vertigo that hit me right afterward was staggering.

I gripped the counter and tried to keep my breathing even. If Cal realized something was wrong, he'd touch me, discover my cut-up knee and the jig would be up. If I told him Tiffany was out there, I'd have to explain how I knew her and still, the jig would be up.

I put a few more dishes in the dishwasher and glanced out the window again. She was gone. The vertigo eased and my heart slowed down. I finished filling the dishwasher, started it and washed the extras, handing them to Cal to dry and put away. He was none the wiser, but I was in trouble. Tiffany was dangerous and she'd set her sights on me.

19

The 'Muse' is not an artistic mystery, but a mathematical equation. The gift are those ideas you think of as you drift to sleep. The giver is that one you think of when you first awake.

— Roman Payne

My house is a tri-level, built in the '70s when the style was popular. The main level has the kitchen, living room and dining area. Up a short flight of stairs are three bedrooms and a full bath. From the main level, down a short flight of stairs, are a bonus or family room and a utility room with toilet. There's also a door to the backyard and one to the garage. My only television is in the family room. I don't have cable. I hate commercials, but the kids and I watch movies.

Cal followed me downstairs. I willed myself to relax. Tiffany wouldn't bother me with Cal here. I didn't even know what she wanted ... yet. I would not be afraid. Hadn't Malcolm said my alarm system could go off prematurely? She was just trying to intimidate me ... get me away from Malcolm. Her envy had tripped my alarm. That was all.

Cal started to sit next to me.

"Could we talk first?" I blurted.

"Sure." He stopped mid-sit and moved over.

I straightened up, adjusted myself to a more comfortable position. I wasn't nervous, no way.

"I understand you need to guard me and we need to do these energy-balancing things, but I'm not comfortable with you reading how much gas is in my bowels or if my birth control is working."

"You don't take birth control."

"I know and that's what I'm talking about. A girl needs her secrets. Especially from her ex-husband."

"I'm your Guardian. We shouldn't have secrets."

"Do I get anything to myself? You can read every hiccup in my body and Kali can hear every fleeting thought in my head. Can't you turn it off, just be here and not read me like a novel?"

He contemplated. "I can, but I like making sure you're all right."

"How about a compromise then? If I have any complaints or you have specific concerns, I let you look. Otherwise, we just be normal together."

I held my breath while he thought.

"You know I could just not give you a choice?"

It was his turn to play the power card. He and I were looking for balance, pulling back and forth to see who'd give in, where we'd draw the lines in the sand. He'd let me have my way with the kids. I could give him this. Plus, he was right.

"I know you can, but I'm hoping you're a better man than that. I need my privacy. At least till I get used to this." It was the "just give me time" card. It'd worked before. Would it work now?

"I can't make any promises—sometimes things overflow and spill out—but I won't read you without your permission, as far as I can help it."

I waited for him to meet my eyes. "Thank you. That means a lot to me." And it did. Even if there'd been no stitches and no Malcolm. His letting me have this simply because I asked for it would be enough. I blew out a nervous breath and leaned back on the couch. "You wanna watch a movie?"

"Sure."

"I've got the new *Die Hard*. Kali was gonna watch it with me, but ..."

"That'd be great."

When I turned back from putting the movie in, Cal was at the end of the couch with his shirt off. I slowly sat in the middle of the couch and inched my way over, trying not to think about how much bigger and more muscular his chest was than it used to be. He put his arm up and I moved under it until we were touching. He lowered his arm and there we were.

I tried to relax into him as the movie started. I could feel the gentle trickle of energy passing into me. With it came snippets of Cal's mood. He was content but hesitant; or was he nervous? He also had that emotion I couldn't identify in Malcolm. It felt of so many things, I couldn't place it. The movie played, but I just listened to Cal's emotions, trying to identify them. Not thirty minutes later, I drifted to sleep with Cal's emotions pulsing against me like the soothing rhythm of his heart.

I was back on the dance floor at the fraternity. Malcolm behind me, us grinding against each other to the music. My hands were around the back of his neck, enough buttons of my shirt undone to display a full swath of my stomach and hips. Malcolm moved his long, broad hand down the length of my belly, his fingers slipping under the edge of my jeans. My breath came out in a moan. I wanted him to move lower. Never mind the crowd, all the people watching. I wanted him to touch me, needed him to. He found me. I gasped, turned my head to kiss him. Only it wasn't Malcolm's lips I found. They were Cal's. I pulled back, but he moved deeper. Suddenly, I didn't care that it was Cal. I kissed him, an urgent demand that screamed for more. His other arm wrapped around me, pulling me against him, grinding us harder, deeper. Cal remembered what I liked. He knew how to do it.

I sat bolt upright in bed. My bed. The clock read just after nine in the morning. I could hear voices and cooking sounds in the kitchen. Cal and the kids were making breakfast. He'd let me sleep in. He must've carried me to bed. At least I was fully dressed this time. By the look of my bed and his shoes next to it, he'd slept with me again. It was just a dream. A very real, very intense dream.

I lay back down and waited for my heart rate and breathing to return to normal. Had I just had a wet dream? I didn't know women had those. I'd ask Diane. She'd know. She was encyclopedia erotica. When she started talking about this and that thing she and Johnas tried the other night, I did anything possible to drown out her voice. Didn't she realize I hadn't gotten any in seven years? Talk about torture.

In the dream, I'd been sure it was Malcolm behind me. Why'd it change to Cal? I certainly didn't want Cal that way. Malcolm maybe, but not Cal. The dream must've pulled from memories I had of Cal. I had no memories like that with Malcolm. More disturbing was why I'd let

Cal do it, even in a dream. Why didn't I stop him when I realized he wasn't Malcolm? I didn't have an answer for that and it ate at me.

I decided to buy myself some extra time to compose myself by taking a quick shower. It sounded like they needed some time on breakfast anyway.

Done with my shower, I dried off, wrapped a towel around myself and padded back to my room. I'd made the assumption Cal was in the kitchen with the kids. I was wrong. He was sitting on the bed in fresh clothes. It was only now I saw the duffle bag tucked into the closet. *Moving in much?*

"Naked here." I pulled the towel more tightly around myself.

He rolled his eyes. As if he hadn't seen it all and then some.

I didn't know what to do. I just stood there.

He flashed his eyes to the door.

I took the hint and closed it.

"What're your plans today?"

To leave you here with the kids while I sneak off to see my boyfriend. "Just a run, housework and homework. Why? You gotta be somewhere?" I snickered. We both knew I was his full-time job.

"You need help with the kids?" He did just want to spend time with them. This was going to be easier than I thought.

"It'd be great if you'd watch them while I run."

He thought about it. "All right. Then I'll keep them distracted so you can work."

I couldn't believe it was that easy. He genuinely wanted to hang out here and couldn't see past it. *Win for me.*

"Sounds good." I moved to the dresser and pulled out a pair of underwear. Cal stared into the closet while I pulled them on, along with a sports bra. Seriously, why did I care anymore? He could watch and it probably wouldn't faze either of us. That's what I thought until I looked up from pulling on my running pants and caught him watching me. The look on his face flashed me back to my dream and a full shiver ran through me.

"What?" He got off the bed and walked towards me.

Something in me called out ... pulled me toward him. I took a step forward and then stopped myself.

I forced my head to clear, took a step back. "Nothing, just my hair on my back gave me a shiver."

He bought it.

I squeezed past him to get a shirt from the closet.

He watched me. *Creepy much?*

"Going for a long one today. Should be back in an hour or so." *Liar, liar, pants on fire.* And were they ever. I pulled on my socks and running shoes, trying to ignore about twenty things running through my body. What was with me today?

"Don't worry about a thing. I'll even save you some food."

My very own househusband. Why wasn't I feeling guilty? Oh yeah, he'd broken my heart, left me to raise two kids by myself and was now attempting to crash my life. If anyone had guilt, it was him. And unless I was mistaken; it was showing.

20

A Muse's profession is based on the genetic abilities of the individual. Guarding a Muse is a full-time occupation because each Guardian is supported financially by his or her Muse. MAGRA assists financially when necessary. Guardians who do not guard a Muse choose occupations that use their preternatural strength, speed, healing, intuition, telepathy and invisibility.
　　—"Muses and Guardians," *World Look Encyclopedia*

I waited at the half-way point which happened to be on a little footbridge over three feet of creek. I didn't wait long. Malcolm came around the corner dressed for the occasion in a black running suit. He pulled me into his arms, our lips meeting in a kiss. I pulled him closer and an intense rush of lust spread through me. A rush so intense every nerve in my body reacted, blood pooling low in places that hadn't seen attention in far too long.

I pulled from the kiss, ready to go back to his place quick, so we'd have enough time, but I stopped myself from telling him that. He was so beautiful, his chest heaving from the intensity of our kiss. Had I asked, he would've scooped me up and taken off running. But I wanted more with Malcolm, not just a fling, and I didn't want to rush. I couldn't afford to be wrong. I needed more than hormones to tell me this was the right thing.

Then again, there's merit in just plain getting laid.... I shook myself. What would he think of me if I did that? What if I asked him to take me to his place and he said no? I'd die of humiliation.

I pulled him close again and ran my hand across his face, over his lips.

"Missed you," he said, "had the naughtiest dream last night." His voice was deeper than usual, gruff with suppressed emotion that I could feel but still not identify. I needed to ask one of these guys what it was, but I was a chicken. What if it was something terrible, like amusement? Again, I'd die of humiliation.

"Gonna tell me about it?"

"If I told you, I might be tempted to act on it."

"Another time then?"

He pulled me tight against him. "Looking forward to it."

For our first official date, we walked around the park. The trail is about two miles. We covered the distance in about forty minutes. We talked. He told me about his businesses: an investment firm, a real estate firm, a couple companies that run large manufacturing lines. He told me how he'd started moving some businesses back to the United States in an attempt to help the economy.

He was well-off. There was no question, but it wasn't important to him. He was born with money, but he'd had years where he was forced to fend for himself. He knew the value of hard work and what it meant to go without. Earning his Ph.D. and accomplishing what went with that had shaped him, not the money.

Being an orphan raised in a home where I wasn't welcome taught me the value of some things and the over-rated novelty of others. It had made me pretty unmaterialistic. Malcolm was the same. He'd had everything, then nothing, only to have everything again. That could really put life in perspective for you.

We talked about me, too; my kids, my work, I told him about Diane and Johnas, about being an orphan, a bit about my sister and brother. He asked me what happened to my parents, and I said they died in a car accident. I left out the part about the Guardian who refused to save them. I don't know why. It didn't seem like the right time to tell him. I didn't want him feeling like I was only interested in him because of his perspective on Guardians

"So that's what you and Cal had in common? You're both orphans?" Malcolm asked as I mused over not mentioning the Guardian bit.

It was true. Cal's mother abandoned him at birth. There was no record of his father. He'd been raised in a slew of foster homes and orphanages until the Hammonds found him during his teen years. They'd never adopted him, but when he became an adult, he took their name. After our divorce, I kept it out of respect for his foster parents and everything they'd done for me. I also gave it to both the kids. By keeping it, we all stayed Hammonds

"Never thought of it that way, but you're right; we were both orphans. We didn't feel so alone when we were together."

Malcolm squeezed my hand. "You feel totally alone, don't you?"

I looked into his eyes and said in my most serious voice, "I am alone. There're people that love me, but I have no one but myself. I've always made my own way and I've accepted it."

This is who I am. He could either accept it, too or he couldn't.

"Do you want to be alone?"

"I've relied on people before; it didn't end well."

"You didn't answer the question."

"Sometimes I think it's easier, but I don't *want* to be alone. I'm just not sure I'll ever trust like that again."

"Why?"

It was such a simple question and it had such a simple answer. "Because everyone I have ever relied on has left me."

I felt more confusion come from him. "But, you just told me about Diane and Johnas. Did they leave you?"

"They're the closest thing I have to family, but it's not the same. They'd do anything for me, but they're not family, so there are things I wouldn't ask."

We just walked for a while. That weird emotion I couldn't identify and something sad was all I could feel from him. Finally he spoke.

"It's a bit early in the game, but I hope someday you'll trust me. Even if it's just as a friend." He smiled and I relaxed. Amazing how he could do that to me.

My baggage reached far and wide, not exactly first-date material.

"So Tiffany? Is she like family for you, now that your dad is gone?" This question served the dual purpose of feeling out their relationship and changing the subject. Not to mention I was still a little freaked out over seeing her in my yard.

"Tiffany is ... from a different era in my life and is just passing through."

"So you don't trust her, either?"

"She's ..." Anxiety washed in through our connection. How'd he keep that from me before?

"So, what you're saying is that I shouldn't trust her?"

He stopped and pulled me around to look at him, his forehead wrinkling in concern. "What'd she do? Did she threaten you?"

I tried to squelch the fear I was feeling. Then again the fear could be directed at him and his reaction so I let it show on my face. "Why? Should I be afraid of her?"

"No, it's just ..."

Wow, Tiffany really had him lost for words today.

"If she approaches you, says anything at all, tell me right away."

I don't take orders. I let go of his hand and walked away. If he thought he could just tell me what to do, he had another thing coming.

Within a second, he was in front of me again.

"What happened?" He looked confused.

Just this once I'd tell him. "I don't take orders." I crossed my arms over my chest. "If you need someone to boss around, find yourself another girl."

He did that ridiculously cute thing little kids or dogs do sometimes where they cock their head to the side. "I wasn't ordering you; I was making a request."

"Didn't sound like one."

He put his hands on my shoulders. "Shelby, I'm sorry. I didn't mean for it to come out that way. Tiffany's just not someone you want to mess with. Okay?"

He was so sincere.

"Okay."

"See you tomorrow for lunch?"

"Where's your office?"

"English building, third floor, room 312."

"Twelve-ish?"

"I'll bring the grub."

When he uses slang words, it's harder to hide the English accent. Now that I knew what to listen for, the accent was pretty evident.

He looked frustrated and pulled me into a long kiss to cover it up. We said goodbye and I jogged away, determined to get good and sweaty. I'd told Cal I was going on a hard run. I intended to make good on it.

I was halfway home when I noticed someone on the trail in front of me. A woman was standing in the middle of the track. I was going to squeeze by and keep going until I realized it was Tiffany.

I've learned to hold my own over the years both mentally and physically by way of self-defense classes and some low-level martial arts. It takes a lot to intimidate me. I stopped a few feet in front of her. She was wearing a super-short pair of jogging shorts with a matching zippered jacket, her hair in a ponytail. She was curveless, like a pole. The more I looked at her, the more she looked like a Barbie-doll reject.

She just stared at me. I had no idea of her abilities. She could've hypnotized me or shot lasers from her eyes that fried me to a crisp, but I was betting she didn't want to hurt me. She just wanted to scare me off. I could see it in her face, her posture. *Fell on hard times, my ass.*

I'm nothing if not civil and despite my sometimes pessimistic view on things, I try to give people the benefit of the doubt.

"Malcolm just went that way. I bet you could still catch him if you hurry."

"Came to see you, actually."

I just looked at her. *Out with it already, beanpole.*

"Malcolm's a complicated man. He's not the sit-home-and-be husband type. Save yourself the anguish and end it now."

"I'm a big girl; I think I can handle it."

"Why put yourself through that? Haven't you been through enough?"

That threw me. How'd she know anything about me?

First rule when dealing with a bully is not to be intimidated.

"You want him for yourself." I crossed my arms over my chest.

"Something like that."

"I'm not playing games. If he wanted you, he'd be with you. Don't be a sore loser." I stalked past her and started to jog again.

"I could make things hard for you. I bet Cal doesn't know about your little rendezvous."

That stopped me. I gave her a long look. "I fail to see how this is his or your business."

"Cal doesn't like to be double crossed. He has quite the temper, if I remember right."

Really now, do all Guardians know each other? I was starting to feel out of the loop here.

"Some things are worth the risk." I gave her a knowing look.

She knew if I told Malcolm she was threatening me, it'd be over. Just talking to me was a gamble. I was calling her bluff.

"Think it over, Ms. Hammond. I'd hate to see your life get any harder than it already is."

I shook my head and jogged away. How pathetic. No wonder she hadn't made Malcolm's cut.

I wasn't backing down and I wasn't telling Malcolm. I wouldn't give her the satisfaction of knowing she'd got to me. Running to the big bad Guardian at the first sign of trouble isn't my style anyway.

21

At the age of five, Guardians attend camps at their local Guardian academies. The experience teaches them control of and responsibility for their abilities. Guardians who do not receive instruction as children frequently develop psychological maladies. Megalomania and obsessive-compulsive or manic disorders are common. In rare cases, untutored Guardians have been diagnosed with antisocial personality disorder.

—"Guardians," *World Look Encyclopedia*

Cal was waiting in the entryway. Shit.

"I'm assuming you didn't do this on purpose."

I refused to look guilty. "Do what?" I said, breathless from my run.

"You were out without protection."

"Oh." I wouldn't be able to see Malcolm on a run again but was working on a better idea, anyway.

He puffed up his chest and moved towards me. "This won't be happening again."

Cal was always funny and happy before. This menacing persona was strange.

"I'll be more careful in the future."

He gave me another long look. "You should eat some protein so you don't burn muscle for energy." He walked toward the dining room, that same hard edge in his steps.

I followed. The table was set for one. Scrambled eggs, sausage, wheaty-looking toast, fresh fruit and some green juice was spread over my little table.

"Did some shopping. The eggs are free range, the sausage from organically raised pigs, the bread organic sprouted whole-grain wheat and the fruit organic. The juice has a whole serving of vegetables including wheat grass, which is just good for your blood and tissues and stuff." He said this really fast, like he was nervous. I tried not to smirk.

"I'd like you and the kids to eat better. More organic, all natural, high fiber."

This actually made sense. Cal's a healer. He can read everything inside a person's body. Nutrition is part of how well bodies run. Of course it's important to him that we eat well.

The food didn't look that odd. If nothing tasted like cardboard and if he didn't confiscate my jellybean stash, I could try this.

"Did the kids eat?"

"Yeah." He pulled out my chair for me. "They had the same thing and liked it."

He was actually sweating. Nervous much?

"Cal? I can get my own chair."

"Oh." He let go and stepped away.

I sat down and he watched as I tried each dish It was all good. I nodded my approval at him.

He beamed. "Wait till you try the organic, fair-traded coffee." He went to the kitchen and came back with a mug of dark brew, some brown-looking sugar and a carton of organic half-and-half. "It's all organic."

He was so excited and nervous it was cute, bringing back memories of the floppy teenage boy who'd fumbled with my bra clasp for the first time. The memory, in contrast to the man standing in front of me, made me smile. Somehow, we'd become grownups.

The coffee was better than what I normally had. I took my second drink and realized it'd been a few days since I'd coffee at all. Spending the night with a Guardian and getting an energy download did more for me than coffee ever could. I always woke up feeling great.

I took a few more bites and Cal, seeing I wasn't going to protest the food, sat down. "Wanna talk to you about something."

This ought to be good. "What's up?"

"About Julian. I know I don't know him that well, but I do know about being a Guardian and I think this could really help him."

Ah, Guardian camp. "I'm listening," I said around a drink of the green stuff. It wasn't half-bad.

"When Guardians are identified as children, they're invited to attend camps. It teaches them to cope with how they're feeling."

"Sounds interesting." The last bite of sausage went into my mouth. I'd finished the eggs and one of the slices of toast, too.

"The thing is," Cal said in a rush, "The sooner we get Julian into one of these camps the better off he's gonna be. He should've already been to two by now and ... there's one starting tomorrow."

I choked, mid-drink, green juice pouring out my nose. I groped for a napkin and Cal passed me one, looking stricken.

"You all right?"

"Fine." I mopped juice from my face and blew my nose. I'd about given up on not embarrassing myself in front of Cal. "You just surprised me. He's only five. We just found out about you and about him maybe being a Guardian, too. This is a lot for one week. I don't know, Cal."

Malcolm and I'd talked about this and I'd thought it was a good idea, but so soon? I had so many questions. A mother doesn't just let her baby run off to some camp without all the info.

"So what do they do at these camps? Where is it? For how long?"

Cal tensed again. "Mostly they just spend time learning about themselves and other Guardians. At Julian's age, they play games and get to know the other kids. They have classes that teach them about what they are, why they feel different and how to cope with it. I promise you, he'll come back a different boy."

I gave him a negative look.

"At least different at school," he amended quickly.

I didn't want a different boy, but a better-behaved boy at school would be okay.

"Where's this place?"

"The closest Guardian academy in Olympia, Washington, about a four-hour drive. He'd be there for a week, leaving tomorrow and coming back next Monday. I wouldn't push you on this, but they only do the camp every three months."

Three months would see a lot more phone calls from Mrs. Brooks. Perhaps even a suspension. He really wasn't doing well at school.

"How will he get up there?"

"If I put in the call tonight, the bus will stop here en route to pick up other kids."

"Have you talked to Julian about this? Does he even want to go?"

"Thought I'd talk to you first."

I stared at my empty plate. "A week's a long time."

"Seven days is needed. They're retraining him how to think about adults. I don't want him to go away either, but it's necessary.

That got me. I looked up at him.

His face softened. "I just got here. I've said a hundred words to the kid and now he's leaving. You don't think I'll miss him, too?"

He touched my hand. Understanding flowed from him. He cared about Julian and would miss him.

We talked a few more minutes. I wanted to know who'd be taking care of Julian, what would happen if he had a nightmare or needed help getting dressed, that kind of thing. He was, after all, only five. He'd be six in a few short weeks, but today he was still my little five-year-old.

Cal had an answer for everything. He assured me Guardian kids are made of tougher stuff, that they all go to these camps at age five and they all do fine.

In the end, I was out of questions and convinced.

"You know this is right. I can feel it from you."

I nodded and looked away. The intensity of his chocolate brown eyes had burned into my mind. I had to blink a few times to make the image clear. He'd always had that effect on me.

I pulled myself together and called Julian.

He sauntered into the room, looking annoyed that he'd been pulled away from whatever he was doing.

"Your dad has something to talk to you about." I got up from the table.

Cal shot me a confused look.

"Tell him about it. If he wants to go, it's fine with me."

Julian would eventually go this school to full time. Malcolm had given his recommendation and, since I knew nothing about this Guardian stuff, I was letting them have it. This would be Cal's shot. If it went well, he'd earn some points. If it didn't? Well ... we'd see.

I had no doubt Julian would want to go. Sure enough, once Cal explained, Julian wouldn't stop hopping up and down in excitement.

Cal made the necessary calls, helped Julian pack and stayed long enough answer all his questions so he'd finally sleep.

Once the kids were in bed, I kicked Cal out. I needed my space back, my downtime. I didn't like how he'd started moving in, bringing changes of clothes and buying groceries. He'd tried to leave a toothbrush and some hippy toothpaste in my drawer, but I'd thrown a fit and he'd tucked them back in his bag. If he thought he was moving in here, ever, he had better think again.

I spent the rest of my peaceful Cal-free evening reading for Professor Malcolm's English class and finishing a botany worksheet. It was slow going. I couldn't stop thinking about Tiffany's threat, about what Cal would do if he knew about Malcolm and me and about Julian spending more than one night away from home for the first time.

When I finally lay down in bed, I texted Malcolm. Told him I was thinking about him and wished him sweet dreams.

He called me.

I answered and relaxed at the deep smoothness of his voice. "Luv?"

"Mmmmhmm," I said, quite content.

"It's late. Busy day?"

"Some snobby teacher assigned boring reading about pioneers or something."

"That jerk. I'm gonna have a talk with him. You shouldn't be up half the night doing homework. You're a Muse; you need your rest."

"Got that right." I snuggled a little deeper in the bed. "It was a great day though. The only thing that could make it better is if you were here right now."

"Don't tempt me, luv. I could be there in a flash."

"Naw, I gotta sleep. Julian's gonna be up at the ass-crack of dawn all excited for Guardian camp."

"Did you just say 'the ass-crack of dawn'?"

"It's one of those terms we mommies use when kids get us up before we get enough sleep.."

"Noted. So Julian's going to Guardian camp? When?"

"Tomorrow."

"Wow. Cal moves quick." He had no idea.

"It's gonna help, right?"

"Absolutely, luv."

"Good." I yawned.

"You should sleep. Just wanted to hear your voice."

"It was nice to hear yours, too."

"Good night, luv. No bad dreams."

"You, too."

22

Intentional invisibility is a basic skill for Guardians. The ability is often employed at meetings and appearances when the presence of a bodyguard would be counter-productive for the Muse. A Guardian becomes visible if someone actively seeks him or her.

—"Guardians," *World Look Encyclopedia*

I stayed with Cal and Julian until the bus came to get him. I hugged him goodbye, forcing myself to let go. It was hard to believe a week ago I hadn't known he was more than my little boy or that Cal or I were more than parents. Crazy how fast our world had changed. A week ago, Julian didn't even have a dad; now he had a superhero dad and was off to superhero camp. This was probably the best week of his life and the weirdest of mine.

Julian hopped up the steps of the bus, found a seat next to the first little boy he spotted and started talking excitedly. He didn't even wave goodbye.

I'd made the right decision, or so I kept telling myself as I headed off to class.

It was Monday so I only had botany. Cal was in the wind.. I hadn't seen him since Julian's pick up. After his mistake yesterday with my run, I knew he wasn't far away, but I had a plan to give him the slip.

I left botany and headed for the work-out center. Cal didn't appear, but somehow I knew he was with me.

Once in the athletic center, I cut through the women's locker room and came out the other side near the back door. I knew if I hurried, I could get clear of Cal's watchful eye and make it in time to have lunch with Malcolm.

Down three buildings and around a corner I bent down to tie my shoe. Standing up again, I called out for Cal. I wanted it to look like I'd stopped for a reason. I waited a full minute and he didn't appear. It would've been smart to ask Cal how he can follow me undetected; too late now.

Down two more buildings and I was at the English building. Up three flights of stairs and around a corner, I found Malcolm's office. I was ten minutes early, but somehow I knew he was in there. Somehow, I also knew Cal hadn't followed me.

I knocked. Just another student with a question for her professor.

Malcolm opened the door wearing a pair of khaki slacks and black button-up shirt. No tie. The black made his eyes look brighter, deeper. "Ms. Hammond, is there something I can do for you?"

It was such a good act, I almost bought it. Then I realized, since I was a student and he was a professor, we could both get in trouble if anyone found out about our relationship. Not to mention the act was a good cover in case Cal caught up to me.

"Just a question about the reading."

"Of course." He opened the door wider and I stepped past him. He scanned the hallway. Satisfied we weren't being watched, he closed the door behind me.

The next thing I knew, I was up against the door with my legs wrapped around Malcolm. He was so fast and magically gentle, his kisses so long and gentle that I barely realized I'd moved.

His hands went to my face, my hair, down my arms, over and under my thighs. He used the added leverage to pull me closer and grind against me. That got a moan out of me. He pulled back and shushed me, letting me slide to the floor with an mischievous smile on his face.

If Cal had caught up with me, he would've shown himself during that little scene. We were in the clear.

We ate a lunch of take-out sushi. Malcolm got me to try some wasabi, and my nose didn't burn off. We talked about Julian leaving, about my classes and about how I gave Cal the slip. That brought us full circle, and I decided to bring up the whole professor/student thing. As if we didn't already have the whole Muse/Guardian thing going against us.

"So, how does this work with the university if we get caught together?"

Malcolm stuffed a whole sushi roll in his mouth, puff-cheeked as he chewed. I had a feeling he chose this meal because we wouldn't need formal table manners. Didn't want me to thinking he was a snob. How cute. He swallowed. "If we manage to keep this from Cal, the university will be none the wiser. Plus, this is a temporary gig. I'll be gone at the end of the term and won't return until you're finished here. Fair enough?"

I kissed him. "Fair enough."

Before I knew it, it was one o'clock and I had to go. Cal was probably losing his mind. I had a story planned for where I'd been, but he'd still be threatening me with the handcuffs. If we did this again, I'd have to think of a new plan.

Halfway to the art studio, I could finally breathe. The last thing I needed was Cal catching me coming out the English building and putting it all together.

I was at the back door to the studio when someone grabbed me and slammed me against the brick wall by the door.

Cal's sharp features pressed into my face. "Where the hell were you?" He was yelling in my face like a drill sergeant intimidating a new recruit.

He pressed me into the wall so hard I couldn't breathe. "In the cafeteria, getting some lunch."

His face relaxed and he let off a bit. "You never came out of the bathroom at the athletic center. I was sure something happened to you." He stepped back.

I faked dawning comprehension. "I went out the back way cause it's in the direction of the cafeteria. It didn't occur to me you might lose me." I was a bad liar, but Cal bought it. He took another step back, and I took another breath in.

"It's my fault. I'm sorry. Won't happen again. Please, go ahead." He gestured toward the door. I couldn't believe I was getting off this easy.

"Really?"

He nodded.

I hesitated. "How do you do this stealthy thing anyway? Maybe if I know how you do it, I can make sure you're with me in the future?" I was a bad little girl, collecting information to use against the enemy.

"It's easy really; all Guardians can do it. If you're not looking for me, you can't see me."

My mouth fell open. I'd never once glanced around to see if he was with me. I'd assumed he was around and either been bitter about it or chosen to ignore him. No wonder Malcolm could tell when Cal wasn't with me. "I'll remember that," I managed to say as I opened the door to the studio in a daze. Really? It was that easy? I stopped, let the door close and turned back to Cal. "What else can you do? Just so I know."

He smiled a familiar boyish smile. "Well." He nervously cleared his throat. "You've seen the healing and the reading thing."

I nodded.

"I'm also pretty indestructible. I can heal others so it's not a far stretch that I can heal myself pretty dang fast."

"Wait. So, you're like bullet proof?"

He smiled that smile again. "Yeah."

Damn. I gave myself a mental shake. "What else?"

"Not much really; all Guardians are stronger than normal and a bit faster."

"The stealth thing, all Guardians can do that?"

"Most."

"Anything else?"

"I can manipulate body chemicals." He looked uncomfortable all of the sudden.

I felt my eyes narrow. "Like what?"

"Like if you were depressed, I could get your brain to release more serotonin or if your blood sugar was high I could get you to release insulin. Stuff like that."

"So if I couldn't sleep, you could make my body release sleepy-time chemicals?"

He nodded, looking nervous.

Why was I so afraid of Cal? He was the one afraid of me. I was acting like a squeamish girl afraid of a little spider that was just trying to flee for its life. Except this spider was afraid I wouldn't let him in ... into my life with his kids. I almost felt bad. Almost.

"You made me fall asleep the other night so you could stay over, didn't you?"

He looked at the ground and nodded.

I shook my head and did a little pace back and forth. "This isn't working, Cal. I thought you wanted me to trust you."

"I do. You're just making it so damn hard ... hard to protect you, hard to see the kids, hard to be in a room with you!" He punched the brick wall behind him. His fist made a dent and brick dust fluttered to the ground. His hand was unscathed.

Instead of being cowed, my temper flared. "What the hell were you expecting? You show up, crash my life, invade my house and move in on my kids. You strut around like you're the big man and know everything. When do you share information with me? I've had to hear everything from ..." I stopped myself just in time. I'd almost said Malcolm. My mind flew around for a suitable replacement. "The internet," I finished lamely. "I'm fucking scared Cal, and you're not doing a damn thing to make this easier or to prepare me for what's gonna happen next."

Cal looked shocked. Hadn't he thought of this? Doesn't Guardian camp have a class in Muse Sensitivity 101? He leaned against the wall. "I'm sorry, Shel. You're right. I'll work on it."

"Whatever. I have work to do." I let the studio door slam behind me. What a pushover.

23

Pheromones are released during bonding between a Muse and his or her Guardian. These chemicals create intense sexual attraction that encourages an emotional bond and long-term commitment. A bonded Muse and Guardian is considered a mated pair.

—"Muses and Guardians," *World Look Encyclopedia*

I didn't get much done on my piece. Just wasn't feeling it. I spent some time highlighting and expanding the root structure, but that was it. I left the studio after only a half hour and went home. I paced between my entryway and kitchen, pissed Cal was actually affecting my ability to work.

I texted him, told him he could pack it in. He'd be by at nine for our balancing thing, but I wanted free of him for a while. He'd been parked at the curb outside my house. He texted back, *K,* and drove away.

I couldn't stop thinking about Cal's presumptions over how things should be between us. Did he think I should blindly follow him, trusting he knew best? Did he know me at all or was he remembering the scared little teenager

I'd been? The one without family, who knew nothing about the world, who needed her hand held. Well, I wasn't that girl anymore. I paced some more until the walls started to press in on me. I needed out. I called Malcolm.

"My luv, to what do I owe the pleasure?" There was more than a hint of accent and it made me smile.

"Gonna visit Isabella. Wanna come?" I had a few hours before Chloe got home.

"Now? Where's Cal?"

"Told him I was in for the day; he'll be back tonight."

"I was just leaving campus. Be there in five?"

"Perfect."

We hung up and I pulled myself together, fluffing my hair in the entryway mirror.

I stopped.

I looked different.

My skin was clear and brighter, my hair shinier. I felt taller somehow and just seemed to look ... good.

Malcolm knocked and I let him in.

"What?" He must have noticed the dazed look on my face.

"Do I look different to you?" I looked back in the mirror, trying to see exactly what had changed.

Malcolm wrapped himself around me from behind, slid all my hair to one side and started kissing my neck. "Didn't Cal tell you? There're perks to being a Muse."

"He neglected to mention it." I added this to the list of things Cal was keeping from me.

He kissed down to my shoulder, "Your physical presence improves; your skin gets a healthy glow, no more pimples, wrinkles or stretch marks."

That I couldn't believe. I pulled up my shirt to check and ran my hand over my belly, turning to the side to check the angle.

They were gone.

The zig-zagging of stretch marks on my fair skin from two babies were gone just like that. Freaky.

Malcolm ran his hand over the exposed skin, kissing back up my neck. He smiled at me in the mirror, flashing those amazing blue eyes. He kissed his way up to my temple and held me, watching us in the mirror.

"No wrinkles? How will I age?"

"You won't. Not past thirty-five."

"What happens then?"

"You stay that way forever."

I turned into him. "Did you just tell me I'm gonna live forever?"

"As long as you're not killed."

"Like a car accident or a bullet?"

"Mmhmm." He went back to nuzzling my neck. "Did I mention you smell amazing? That's another perk." His hand crept under my shirt. "But the thing women enjoy most?" His fingers ran over the fabric of my bra. "Musedom does something amazing for their breasts."

I nearly scoffed. Mine were surely beyond repair.

"They never sag or point at the floor, even after a dozen babies."

Mine already did that. Had they changed? I couldn't strip in front of Malcolm. We were close, but not that close, not yet.

He turned me back to the mirror and his fingers brushed around my back towards my bra clasp. "Want to find out if it's true for you, too?"

I pulled my arms across my chest, covering myself. What if they weren't nice again? He'd see how sad they were. Then again, twenty minutes ago I hadn't known my body was changing at all. He'd have seen them soon anyway.

He undid the clasp and let the back fall open, moving his hands to my waist. He waited, watching my eyes in the mirror. "You're nervous."

I nodded. "A man hasn't seen me naked in six years. Even my gyno is a woman."

"You don't have to show me. I can give you a moment." Always the gentleman, he started to pull away.

"Wait, just give me a sec."

He stopped, hands still on my waist. "Can I try something?"

I nodded, taking in a shuddering breath.

Behind me, he pulled off his jacket and shirt revealing a perfectly chiseled chest, like you'd find on some A-list actor in a billion-dollar film. I could see every muscle: abs, arms, pecs and neck. It was unreal, and I was only looking at his reflection. He ran his hands up my back pulling my thermal up to my shoulders and wrapping around me again, pressing our flesh together. It was the most skin we'd shared since that first night together.

He closed his eyes and seemed to concentrate.

Energy hit me like a tsunami breaking over a city, filling every street and path, forcing its way through. It filled every pore, lit up every nerve. Every hair on my body rose at attention. I collapsed against him. Just touching felt good, made me shiver. I found my feet again and turned in his arms, pulling my shirt off as I went. Suddenly, I wasn't able to get my bra off fast enough. I pressed my bare chest against his, my head against his shoulder, and just breathed, listening to his heart. It was beyond anything I'd ever felt before. I wanted this moment, this feeling, to last forever. After I caught my breath and the energy reached a subtle pitch, I found my voice. "What'd you do?"

"Remember what I told you about nerve endings? When more of them touch, we can transfer more energy." He breathed into my hair.

"This is just energy?"

"It's life. Plucked from the air. Your home is particularly full of it."

Life. My home was full of life. Mold spores and giggling children. I felt it, too. Like an aura in the air, it was refreshing and light, dancing with its own magic.

"Is that what gives you power ... abilities?"

"You too, luv."

"I don't have any of that."

He pulled my chin up, looking into my eyes. "You have more power than I do."

I searched his eyes. "How's that possible?"

"I'll show you." He bent to pick up his shirt.

It was colder without him pressed against me, but the energy stayed with me. Not leaving me weak and tired like I expected. Cool.

I turned to get my clothes back on and saw my bare chest in the mirror. Not only were my breasts perfect again, perky and pointing in the appropriate direction, but they were stretch mark free and perfectly balanced. I stared at them, a lost part of my youth returned to me like a lost teddy bear or piece of jewelry I thought I'd never see again. It was amazing and it was just life, plucked from the air.

24

A Muse's creation and the perception of that creation is fluid. A work of fine art, writing, music, dance or architecture transforms to fit the needs of the recipient. Works created by a Muse may be perceived differently by different people.

— "Muses," *World Look Encyclopedia*

Entering Isabella's was a feast for the senses, the smell amazing: baked bread, wildflowers and coffee all mingled into a scent you could actually taste.

The painting I'd sold Isabella was hanging to the right of the register, lit and centered between brick pillars. Only it was different somehow. When I got right in front, I saw subtle changes only I, the artist, would notice.

"It's different. Did she change it? Did she have someone else do it?" I couldn't believe it. Why change it after she paid me all that money? I would've done what she wanted for no extra charge.

Malcolm slid an arm around my waist and whispered in my ear "No one changed it, luv. It's part of your ability. When you gave the painting to her, it changed into what she needed it to be. To help her become what she needed to be."

All I could do was stare at him incredulously.

"Look around."

I did. The whole ambiance of the shop had changed. Vases of wildflowers were spread about, plenty of people populating the cushy chairs and little tables. The light seemed dimmer, and a peaceful low-level hum emanated from the patrons. The air buzzed with positive energy. Isabella walked amongst the patrons in a little red housedress and black flats, her smooth black hair pulled into an elegant knot at the base of her neck. She looked better than I remembered as she moved about the tables serving espresso and straightening vases.

"It's so different," I whispered mostly to myself.

"That's not the half of it, luv." Malcolm whispered back.

Isabella spotted us and the most luminous smile spread across her face. If I didn't know better, I'd have wondered why some beautiful woman was smiling at me. She looked at least ten years younger and ... happy.

"Shelby, darling, I was hoping you'd visit me before I left town." Isabella's thick Italian accent wrapped me in a hug just as her arms did.

"You look amazing; your place looks amazing. What happened?"

Isabella and Malcolm exchanged a long look.

"She doesn't know?" Isabella asked.

"This is her first."

"We shall have a chat then. My apartment is the appropriate place."

It seemed a year ago Malcolm had carried me, convulsing, up the steps to Isabella's apartment. He'd put his hand on my face and made me believe I was a Muse.

That incident had raised more questions than it answered. I had a feeling this time would be the same.

Isabella's apartment was different than before with a vibrant, alive air similar to the cafe downstairs. I stared, trying to figure out what else was so different. It was something palpable.

"Shelby?" Malcolm said from the sofa, "Isabella wants to tell you what you've done for her."

I blinked at him and just stood there, my body catching up with my mind. I'd done this? I didn't fully comprehend everything that had happened here. How could I have done it?

I sat down next to Malcolm, putting my hand in his lap. The feeling in the air was overwhelming, buzzing around me like it had something to say.

He put his arm across my shoulders and the buzzing lessened.

I looked at Isabella in the chair across from us. "I don't understand how I did any of this or how you could know I did."

"Tell her about your husband," Malcolm said to her.

An anguished expression crossed her face. She swallowed what must have been tears, took a deep breath and began. "You remember the story about my mother dying when I was little?

I nodded.

"My father and I came to the United States when I was a teenager, tried to build a new life. When I was a college student here in Corvallis, I met the most wonderful man. We were both only twenty and fell madly in love. We married and while I toiled at finishing my business degree, he showed great promise in the field of botany. He was so good with plants they grew faster, larger and healthier under his care. Roses especially seemed to blossom under his touch.

"Sounds amazing."

"It was and, as you can imagine, he was destined to become a Muse. On the eve of his twenty-fifth birthday, a woman appeared in the greenhouse where we were working late on a project. She identified herself as a Guardian and told him what he was. At first we were ecstatic about what this would mean for him ... for us ... but then we learned the other things that go along with being a Muse."

Her eyes flashed to Malcolm and then back to me.

"As you've already found out, darling, it's not easy being a Muse and his case was no exception. He was forever torn between his obligations as a husband and father and those of being a Muse. We found a balance, though, and had many happy years together. That is ... until the accident." She wiped a tear from her face. "Two years ago, my husband, Albert, and his Guardian, Alandis, were killed. Their private jet had an engine failure and the plane crashed. They went out on a job and just never came home. Just like that, he was gone." She paused for a moment, emotions obviously overtaking her, but when she looked up again, she was smiling. "I never thought I'd get over it. Albert was everything to me.

My father died over a decade ago and my only daughter is a full Guardian now. She rarely has time for a phone call, let alone a visit. I'd gotten so depressed I was considering suicide. Your sketching in the cafe that day gave me hope. I'd given up on finding a painting for that space. Somehow, I knew you could do it, and it gave me something to hold onto. If there was a painting for that space, perhaps there was something for me to live for after all.

"For weeks I waited in anticipation. When you finally pulled the paper back, I knew. I knew it happened for a reason. I didn't know you were a Muse, but it makes so much sense now." She took both my hands in hers. "You can do amazing things, darling. Don't ever doubt yourself." She went to her desk, pulled out an envelope and showed it to me.

It was a round-trip ticket to Italy.

"The painting brought back memories of Tuscany and my family there. I had aunts and uncles, handfuls of cousins. I got in touch with them and I'm going to visit. My cousin has a daughter who wants to come back with me to help with the cafe. I'm so excited! I can't wait to leave, only three days till my flight." She took the ticket back and returned it to her desk.

Malcolm leaned into my ear. "Do you see it now?" he whispered.

I turned to him. "I breathed life into her, into the cafe."

Malcolm closed his fingers around an invisible something in the air. He put the something in my palm and closed my fingers around it. "Life, plucked from the air."

25

Each of the arts whose office is to refine, purify, adorn, embellish and grace life is under the patronage of a Muse, no god being found worthy to preside over them.

—Ralph Waldo Emerson

I'd been quiet the whole way home. Just taking it all in, trying to comprehend exactly what I'd done, how I'd done it and if it'd really been me who'd done it.

Parked outside my house, I finally looked at Malcolm. "I didn't do all that. It's not possible. All I did was give her a painting."

"Define a Muse for me, luv."

I blinked in surprise. "You mean the goddesses that inspired art or literature in Greek mythology?"

"Those would be the ones. Didn't you every wonder where the legends came from? Legends of women who could merely be looked upon and inspire art, change, and according to some legends even prosperity."

I stared passed Malcolm in a daze as the truth hit me. "They were simply the inspiration, the stimulation that got others to change or create. They never actually did the changing themselves." The next thought came in like a wave, breaking over my mind, leaving behind the truth of what I was and how I could help people. "People have to change themselves. I only help them find what needs changing and how to do it."

Touching people and influencing their thoughts or motivations was one thing. I could control that, but doing so much without even realizing it was beyond my comprehension.

Minutes passed and I didn't say anything.

"You all right, luv?" He stroked my hand and I felt energy ... life ... wash into me.

"So you pull the life out of the air and it gives you your power and abilities?"

He nodded.

"Then you channel it into me and I inspire people with it?"

He nodded again, watching me.

I went quiet, still trying to comprehend the implications of what I'd done. I'd changed Isabella's life. I may have changed the life of her cousin's daughter who was coming to help with the cafe. How many other people would see that painting and be changed or inspired in some way?

"You're a Muse, a vessel. It's what you were born, created and intended to do, just like Guardians were intended to help and protect you while you do it."

"I don't understand what Guardians get in return?"

"Aren't children enough? We can't reproduce without you. We'd die out and so would you without us."

I let that sink in. Ordinary parents devoted their lives for a lot less than survival of the species. I leaned back in the plush seat of Malcolm's multimillion-dollar Audi and blew out a sigh. "I guess I really am a Muse."

Malcolm squeezed my hand and smiled.

"Why won't Cal tell me this stuff?"

"Cal and I used to be friends. I'd like to think I know him pretty well, but I can't imagine why he's not helping you with this." He shook his head. "I'd like to give him a good punch. He's making things harder on you."

"Last thing I need is the two of you fighting. I'll deal with it. I have to go; Chloe'll be home any minute." I reached for the door handle but Malcolm held onto my hand, stopping me. I turned to look at him.

"You don't have to do everything alone, Shelby. I can help. I want to help."

"I know, but this I can handle. How 'bout I call you when Chloe gets her period? Think you can help me with that?"

Malcolm's face went through the most hilarious set of expressions for about five seconds.

I burst out laughing.

He grimaced. "Not sure what I was expecting, but it wasn't that."

"Gotta take the good with the bad." I started to get out of the car, but Malcolm grabbed me, pulling me across the seat into his lap.

"I'd love to help teach your daughter about her menstrual cycles." He looked serious, determined.

I didn't know what to say. I'd been joking for the shock value. Trying to derail him from his focus on helping me. Unsure how to respond, I just kissed him.

So much for Malcolm not being a family man.

An hour later, I was helping Chloe with her homework when Cal burst through the door like a winded rhinoceros.

"You! Outside! Now!" he bellowed, every vein and cord in his face and neck straining against his skin.

I blinked at him, betting Tiffany had made good on her threat. As much as I wanted to refuse such a rudely barked order, I didn't wanna make a scene in front of Chloe.

I told her I'd be right back and followed Cal outside. Despite my calm exterior, my heart beat wildly in my chest, adrenaline pumping through my veins. Please not the handcuffs. I could take anything but that.

Kali was on my porch. I hadn't seen her since the night of my one bottle of wine and ridiculous drunkenness. I hadn't forgotten about her, but it was safe to say she'd become the least of my worries.

We stared at each other, her light blue eyes holding my gaze like a modern-day Mona Lisa. It took some effort to pull myself out of her stare. When I finally did, she spoke.

"It's true. You're dating him."

I'd forgotten she could read minds. I needed to stop thinking of her as just my Kali and remember she's a Guardian with abilities.

Cal growled and stalked down the steps, around the edge of the garage. Every few seconds he'd come back into view. He was pacing. It's one of those things we have in common.

"Shel, Malcolm's dangerous. He's—"

"Whatever it is, I don't care. He's saved my life more times than both of you combined and I really like him. I don't care what's in his past. I'm thinking about his future. We all have things we'd rather forget." I looked at Cal, and he flinched. "Yeah, we all have demons. And I'd just as soon forget all of them. I don't live in the past, remember?"

Kali gave me a long look. What was she seeing in my head? I watched her face, but she betrayed nothing. I thought about trying to block her out. Perhaps thinking the same word repeatedly would keep her from hearing anything she shouldn't, but I decided I had nothing to hide. I was proud of my relationship with Malcolm. Hell, I was happy. For the first time in years—maybe ever—I was happy.

Her betrayal aside, I loved Kali. Under normal circumstances, I'd be bursting to share with her. Now was my chance. I opened my mind, let play the memories of Malcolm and me together. Him saving me at the cafe and again in the alley, a few choice scenes from our night at the fraternity, the scene of us together in front of the mirror and finally the image of him plucking life from the air and closing my hand around it.

At last, Kali's face softened. "Cal."

He glided smoothly up the steps, his temper finally under control.

Kali began, "It's true, he's changed. He's not a danger to them. I've seen it."

Cal opened his mouth to protest, but she cut him off.

"She's happy, Cal. Let her have it; you owe her that much."

"Why do I have to keep paying for something I had no choice about?"

"You had a choice. You could've stayed, just been her husband. They would've assigned her another Guardian, but you would've gotten to stay with her."

"You know what would've happened. I couldn't live with that." He sounded so defeated.

"Your choice. You left and she moved on. You're gonna have to live with that. She's with Malcolm now."

They'd been talking like I wasn't there, but I didn't care. This was the information I'd been starving for, information Cal wouldn't give me.

He swallowed hard. "Why Malcolm? Of all people, why him?"

"Can you think of someone better? You know he'll take care of her. You need to accept she's not the girl you left behind.."

Cal looked searchingly at me, begging me with his eyes, as if I could change the past and the choices he'd made.

I just stared back.

"Be back at nine." He crossed the street, got in his SUV and drove away.

I refused to feel bad.

Then it hit me. Did he just find out I was dating Malcolm and was okay with it? I looked at Kali not daring to believe it.

"Believe it. You're your own woman now. He'll get over it." She'd read my mind.

"Thank you. He's been ... difficult."

"He worked hard to get here. He's had to go through training and do things that changed him. Give him time. He's in there. He's just overwhelmed with being back. He's not in the Guardian world anymore. This thing with Malcolm ..." She shook her head and started to speak.

"Don't, Kali. I know Malcolm has a past and I don't care.

She nodded knowingly.

"Cal said if I spent too much time with Malcolm, he'd become my Guardian. Is that really how it works?"

"Sort of, but I think you and Cal are past that. It should be fine. Malcolm doesn't seem to wanna guard you, anyway."

I nodded.

We stood in silence while I tried to process everything that just happened, everything I just learned.

"He really—"

"That's between you and Cal, and I'm not getting in the middle of it."

"But you said ..."

She let out a long sigh. "I think subconsciously he was thinking you'd just be waiting for him, that he'd explain everything and you'd forgive him and things would go back how they were before. Whether or not that's what he really wants, I'm not sure. Either way he needed to see that didn't happen so he could start making a new, conscious plan."

"You read all that in his head?"

"I just know him."

"You and every other Guardian," I muttered.

"Shel?"

"Yeah?" I met her hypnotic gaze again.

"For what it's worth, I am sorry. I never wanted to lie to you, but it was necessary."

"Why didn't you just tell me?"

"Sometimes people we think will be Muses turn twenty-five and nothing happens."

That floored me. "You mean everything is going along fine and then they just have no abilities?

She nodded. " Most often it's the ones who figure it out or are told that don't change."

I started to say I wish that had happened to me, but meeting Malcolm and learning all this was kind of cool. Like an adventure or something.

"Shel?" Kali pulled me from my thoughts again. "I want you to understand. People who think they're going to be a Muse and then aren't, it does something to them.

Some don't recover. We couldn't risk telling you and having that happen. Do you understand? It wasn't that we wanted to keep it from you. We had to, for the sake of your sanity."

I slowly nodded, trying to comprehend it all. I'd only had one Muse class today, but more information than was healthy had come at me.

"I hope someday you'll forgive me and we can be friends again."

I was dazed and just looked at her.

"Are you okay?"

"Yeah, I think I just need some food. I should get dinner started." I turned and started back through the door.

"If you don't feel better after you eat, call one of us, okay?"

"Okay." I closed the door behind me and leaned against it. I'd like to say having so many people care about me was nice, but mostly it felt strange. I didn't know what to do with the feelings and emotions that accompanied it. I didn't know what to say to sentimental comments about wanting to get along. Those things just didn't happen to me.

I went to make dinner still feeling dazed, wondering if having all these people in my life would last.

Chloe and I ate an early dinner. I felt a bit better. Afterwards we gathered all the garbage for pick up, and I went to take the cans to the curb.

Tiffany was waiting behind the neighbor's bush.

"How was your meeting with Cal?"

I was tired, both mentally and physically and not in the mood for her drama. "It was great. We had a long talk, sang Kumbaya and went our separate ways." It was snarky, but like I cared?

She looked stunned. "He's not gonna make you stop seeing Malcolm is he?"

"Evidently I'm a big girl now and can date whoever I want."

She shook her head.

"Look, Tiffany, I'm tired and quite frankly tired of this game. Just tell me what you want, so I can tell you I won't do it and we can both get on with our lives."

She sneered. "You have no idea who you're messing with. This isn't about what I want. It's about what *he* wants and *he* wants you gone and Malcolm back in the fold. This is the last time I'm gonna ask you. Either agree not to see him again or things *will* get ugly."

Maybe it was all the changes in my life, all the people who suddenly cared about me or maybe I was falling in love with Malcolm, but I was done. Done being bullied, done being told what I should and would do. I started laughing. "Whoever you and *he* are, you're just gonna have to get over it. I just don't care anymore. What Malcolm does is up to him. Unless he breaks it off with me, I'm staying. I've got too much shit on my plate to worry about what one bleached-blonde, orange fake-tanned, flat-chested beanpole thinks about it."

Her mouth fell open. Ten seconds passed where she didn't say anything. I was about to walk away when she spoke. "You will regret this."

"Honey, I got knocked up when I was sixteen, married to the world's biggest liar when I was seventeen, got knocked up again when I was eighteen, divorced when I was nineteen and have managed to build myself a new life without so much as a mother to cry to, let alone help me. I don't have regrets. I cope. I make plans. I trudge on, and I sure as fuck don't take threats from envious ex-girlfriends."

She was livid. Her face beet red, her fists clenched. She turned on her heel and clomped off in a pair of insanely high heels. Good riddance.

I felt better after that. Evidently, I just needed to yell at someone. I decided not to tell Malcolm about our little encounters. I was confident she'd back off and I didn't want to create any drama for him. The last thing I needed was that bitch driving a wedge between us.

Chloe and I had a girl's night. We watched a movie and ate popcorn. I read her the girly book Julian always complains about and left her sleeping on her princess pillow.

Ten minutes later Cal knocked. We didn't speak. I set the timer for two hours and we went down to the couch. He watched four episodes of *Sex and the City* with me. Yes, I'd chosen them to torment him. When the timer went off, he left. Still not a word. I'd figured he'd try talking about the whole Muse/Guardian thing, maybe talk about Malcolm or something, but he never even cleared his throat.

The last thing I did before falling asleep was text Malcolm.

I have news.

What?

It's a surprise. My house. Tomorrow night. Nine o'clock. Knock softly.

I won't sleep with anticipation.

Me either.

26

Spend time every day listening to what your Muse is
trying to tell you.

—Saint Bartholomew

I should've known shit was about to hit the fan, but
how could I? I was just a naive little Muse....

The next day I got Chloe to school, ran, and made it
to Malcolm's class. Every time I glanced up at him, I had
to hide a smile. He really made me that happy. At one
point, I looked around for Cal, but didn't find him. In
fact, I hadn't seen him all day. I left class with everyone
else, went down to the lobby and waited. Cal didn't
appear. I was about to call him when Tiffany came
around the corner, an oversized purse in tow.

"Got something you'll want to see." She walked into
the women's bathroom.

I reluctantly followed, a bad feeling chewing at my gut.

Tiffany locked the door behind us and leaned against
it. "You just couldn't play nice. I didn't want to do this,
but you leave me no choice." She reached into her bag
and pulled out a little stuffed monkey. Only it wasn't just
any stuffed monkey, it was Julian's, his favorite, the one

he sleeps with every night. Just the fact that it was here and not 400 miles away with him at camp sent me into a wave of panic. He'd be so upset when he couldn't find it. I'd watched him pack it in his backpack before he left. How did she get it?

What happened next made it click.

Tiffany reached into her bag again and pulled out Olivia, Chloe's favorite doll.

The bottom fell out of my stomach.

"Where are they?" My voice was barely a whisper.

"Who? Your kids? They're where you think they are, but these little guys," she jostled the toys, "are to show you how very easily I can get to them."

"No."

"No, what?"

"No, I don't want you near them. I'll do whatever you want, just leave them alone." It killed me to say it, but what choice did I have? My pride wasn't worth this. Nothing could happen to my kids. I'd die first. Giving up a man I hardly knew wasn't even a trade-off. If I'd thought for even a second she'd threaten my kids, I would've chosen my words and my boyfriend more carefully.

She smiled, her mouth pulling into a grinchy U. "I knew you could be reasonable."

I felt myself swallow and waited. She'd tell me what she wanted, I'd do it, and then I'd permanently attach myself to Cal's arm. I was in over my head. I realized that now.

She took a step towards me, moving into my bubble, making me more uncomfortable.

"You're going, right now, to Malcolm's office and breaking things off with him. Then you're going to meet me on the first level of the stadium parking garage in about," she checked her phone, "three hours." She squeezed the toys hard enough that parts of them bulged. "If you tell anyone—the police, Malcolm, Cal or any other Guardians—what I've said, they won't be able to hide you or your children from my wrath."

I looked straight into the black pits of her eyes and believed her. I was nauseated and the world had tipped about fifteen degrees. If I touched her, I'd probably die of a horror-induced heart attack.

"Understand?"

I hadn't spoken yet, still processing all the possible scenarios: I could die, but as long as the kids were safe, they'd be all right. They had Cal now. I could tell Cal or Malcolm or even the police. There was the possibility she was full of it and we could hide. But if there was even a slim possibility she was telling the truth, I couldn't take the chance on the kids. She'd already proven she could get to them without anyone being the wiser.

Sealing my own doom, I nodded slowly and with careful emphasis.

She smiled that terrible smile again and just like that, we had an agreement.

27

The Muse is born in pain, thrives on it and loves to inflict it.

—Warren Criswell

Telling Malcolm it was over was insignificant in the plan to save my kids, but was still one of the hardest things I'd ever do.

I'd become attached to Malcolm. I loved his company, his smile, how alive and amazing he made me feel. When he was around, I felt young and beautiful. Like a woman, not just a frumpy mommy.

So when Tiffany held open the bathroom door saying, "Malcolm awaits," I felt full of lead. My feet would barely move and the world kept tipping on its side.

Somehow, I made it up three flights of stairs to Malcolm's office. I found myself staring at the little plaque on his door that read "English Department." He hadn't been teaching long enough for them to customize his office. Now I'd never know if he stuck around long enough for them to do that.

I stood outside his door waiting for inspiration. What could I say? He'd want a reason and he'd try talking me out of it.

The one thing I knew for sure was he couldn't touch me. If he touched me, the "I just don't want to date anyone" charade I was planning wouldn't work. He'd sense my fear and anxiety, my heartbreak.

That was it. I got an idea that just might work. One that would convince him it was over. I'd have to break the first and only promise I'd ever made him, but if something happened to my kids, would it matter?

I planned my story, took a deep breath and knocked.

The first glimpse of his face registered surprise, but quickly changed to that wide perfect smile that left me weak in the knees.

I didn't smile back. "Professor Dixon, can I talk to you?"

He looked worried. "Of course."

I stepped through the door willing my knees not to buckle, my nerves to hold true.

I have to do this. I have to save my kids, I said to myself over again as he shut the door behind me. He stepped into me, wrapping an arm around my waist, a hand going to my face.

"What's the matter, luv?" I watched his eyes as the feelings hit him, as he felt my sadness and fear.

His beautiful face changed from concern to alarm. His eyes narrowed in confusion when I still didn't say anything.

"What happened?" His voice so low and soft. He was afraid. He'd jumped to the conclusion I thought he would.

"Cal told me." I kept my voice flat, emotionless.

He let go of me, took a step back. His eyes registered regret; for just a split second I saw a frown. Sadness.

"You have to understand." His voice was so strained, so desperate.

I swallowed tears.

"I was a different person then. I didn't know what I wanted. I thought I was doing the right thing, what was best for the Guardians, the Muses, for humanity. I was wrong. I realize that now. Don't you see? It was you that helped me, you that brought me back?" He stepped forward again, put a hand on my face. "I love you."

I couldn't swallow my tears anymore and one rolled down my cheek. I wanted to say I loved him too. I wanted to wrap my arms around him and tell him everything, but I couldn't. It took everything I had to step away from his warm strong arms.

"I can't."

His hand fell slowly to his side in one of those drawn-out moments that stays with you. One of those moments that, years later, you think back on and wonder if you could have stopped it. You wonder how different things could have been if you'd tried. If you'd just made a different choice, but there wasn't another choice. The kids came first. Always. A second tear rolled down my cheek.

I reached for the door. I had to get out, away from him, to breathe, to plan my next move. I turned the handle.

"You promised." His voice was flat, hollow, broken. I knew the emotion behind it so well. "You promised you wouldn't believe it, that it wouldn't matter."

I was a wuss. I didn't turn around. "Goodbye, Malcolm."

The last thing I heard was his deep voice hoarse with emotion. "Luv."

I closed the door and walked away.

I made it to my car before I burst into full sobs. I pulled myself together and looked around for Cal. He hadn't been with me all day. Where was he? I was tempted to call him and ask, but I didn't want to draw attention to the fact I knew he wasn't with me. I had two-and-half hours to get Chloe safe and get back to meet Tiffany. Julian was out of my reach. Why had I been dumb enough to let him out of my sight? All I could do was hope he was protected enough at the school until Cal could get to him.

Cal would take care of them. I'd accepted and made peace with it. I could regret giving him such a hard time before, but like I told Tiffany, I don't have regrets. I just move forward plowing through the mess in front of me, trying to find a safe path again. I wouldn't make it to the safe path this time, but I'd get close enough to set the kids back on it before I drowned in the mess.

The staff at Chloe's school was suspicious when I picked her up in the middle of the day. I probably should've given a reason, but she's my kid, damn it. I could take her out of school anytime I wanted.

I got on the highway and headed west. I needed a place to hide her. A place no one would look for her, but still with someone I trusted. There was only one person I knew like that and she lived thirty minutes out of town in Kings Valley.

We were halfway there when Chloe spoke from the backseat. "Don't be scared, Mommy. It's gonna be okay. That lady's gonna hurt you, but you'll be all right."

I looked at Chloe in the rearview mirror. I'd packed her a bag before picking her up. She was playing with her dolls, humming a little song.

"What'd you say, Chloe?"

She looked up at me in the mirror. "That lady with the blonde hair and the mean face. She's gonna hurt you, but you'll be okay. I saw you. You're happy." She went back to humming.

"Where'd you see me, sweetie?

"In my mind."

"Like in a dream?"

"No, just in my mind. She hurts your hand, but Daddy and the blond man get her."

"Get her?"

"Mmmhmm."

Perhaps she'd seen Tiffany in our yard, but how would she know about a blond man? Maybe Cal warned her to tell him if she saw me with a blond man. It wasn't possible she knew so much.

"You mean like they put her in jail?"

"No."

"What do they do, honey?"

"I don't know. They just get her."

I tried to get more out of her, but she didn't seem concerned. She giggled at me and said not to worry so much. I let it rest. Getting her worked up wouldn't help either of us. Getting her safe and me back to town was enough to worry about.

Chloe's confidence and relaxed state made me feel better. She's an easygoing girl who would cope well with whatever came her way. With or without me, she'd be all right. Unlike when I had my accident, she and Julian had Cal now. He'd take care of them. He always had. Whether I knew it or not, he was there for us, watching over us. I suppressed the urge to call him, text him, anything! I wanted to tell him I was sorry I was so hard on him and that I forgave him. It's amazing how, when you get to the end, you see things so clearly.

I didn't call him. Facing Malcolm had been too much. I couldn't do it again. It would make this too real and I might change my mind. I might get stupid and tell him everything. He might talk me out of my plan. I couldn't take the chance.

Less than two hours before I had to meet Tiffany, I pulled up to little house on a big piece of land surrounded by trees. A woman in her mid-sixties looked out through the window. Our eyes met and she disappeared behind the curtains again. I waited, holding my breath, to see if she'd come out and talk to me. It was a whole minute before she finally opened the door and stepped onto the porch. I told Chloe to stay in the car and went to meet the woman.

She watched me approach, not happy to see me. "Had a feeling you'd show up here one day."

"It's not what you think."

"You're not the first. What makes you think I'll help you and not the others?"

"I'm not abandoning her so I can go drink and party. She's in danger."

"The police and social services aren't going to hurt her. Do the right and grown-up thing: Go turn yourselves in." She turned to walk back into the house.

I was afraid she'd assume something like this, but how much could I tell her and make sure she and Chloe stayed safe?

"I'm a Muse, Carol. Some bad Guardians are threatening my kids. I need to hide her until this blows over. No one will look for her here.

She stopped with her hand on the door. "I knew you were special, but a Muse?" She contemplated. "Prove it."

I only knew one way to do that. "Give me your hand."

She slowly turned around, pure awe in her face. She'd thought I was bluffing. She held out her hand, trusting.

I took it and waited. I'd learned it's harder to read emotions from normal people, but if they were feeling something directed at me, I could pick it up. I hoped.

"You're disappointed, sad. You're surprised, too, and ..." She was feeling the emotion I kept reading from Malcolm and Cal, only different. That's when it clicked. It was love. Only the love she felt for me was different, smoother somehow.

I dropped her hand and swallowed more tears. "You love me like a daughter." I swallowed again. Carol had been one of the women who worked in the daycare at my high school. She took care of Chloe while I was in classes. She'd also been my friend. I'd visited her here at her house countless times. She'd always been there for me. When I finished school, it was natural for me to move on. I'd stopped visiting. I saw now she'd been hurt by that. She'd called a few times and I'd thought she was just checking on me when really ... she missed me.

"It's true. You are a Muse."

"Carol, I'm sorry, but I need your help and I have to know now. Can you take her?"

She hesitated only a moment. "Of course, but I thought you had two now."

"He's out of state. I'm hoping he'll be okay until this blows over."

"Hoping? That doesn't sound like you, Shelby."

She was right. I plan everything, obsessing over every detail. For once, I just didn't know and it was killing me.

"I know!" I snapped. "I don't know what's gonna happen. Can you just keep her and a low profile for a few days? I need to know she's safe. They won't look for her here."

Carol nodded and I whirled back to the car. With as much patience as I could muster, I got Chloe out of the car and in a show of Herculean strength, I didn't cry. Not in front of my girl.

I hugged her more tightly than I should have, trying not to remind myself this would probably be the last time I saw her. Cal would find her eventually. She'd be all right.

"I'll see you Friday, Mommy. We're gonna get ice cream."

That's when I lost it. I turned around just in time to hide my tears. Back at my car, I looked at Carol. I hadn't told her when I'd be back, but she trusted me. How I wished I was worthy of it.

I made it back to town with ten minutes to spare.

The parking garage was full, but I spotted Tiffany. She was leaning against a black Miata. The black didn't suit her. It brought out the orange in her skin, making her look more fake and just plain wrong. Black was Malcolm's color. She was an imposter in it.

It was mid-class, traffic in the garage minimal. I parked a few cars down and headed over to her. She smiled that grinchy U again. There was a jolt from behind me and the lights went out.

28

Who knows where inspiration comes from. Perhaps it arises from desperation. Perhaps it comes from the flukes of the universe, the kindness of the Muses.

—Amy Tan

Consciousness is a slow process. First, just noises, then my eyes slowly opened. Discomfort registered and I remembered I had limbs and had to breathe.

I took in a sharp breath and pulled my head up, the world slowly coming into focus. Tiffany was a few feet in front of me. I found myself handcuffed and strapped to a chair with bungee cords. It was a rolling office-type chair, my ankles cuffed awkwardly to the base of it. It wasn't painful, yet.

I was in a garage or shop. The walls cement. No windows, but a door to the right. A table scattered with duct tape, more handcuffs, more bungee cords, a stun gun and a little black zippered pouch.

"Sleep well?" Tiffany sounded bored.

I didn't reply and she didn't seem to mind. She didn't strike me as the type who liked to play with her food anyway. In fact, she seemed annoyed by the whole situation. She just wanted me gone. All this was extra work. Why oh why couldn't I just have taken the hint and walked away from Malcolm? Looking back now, I can't see myself making a different decision, but that was kind of moot since here we were.

She didn't say anything so I decided to ask.

"What's your plan?"

She didn't raise an eyebrow or even look speculative. "A friend of yours is coming to get you."

A friend of mine? A number of faces flitted through my head, but I knew I wasn't gonna be that lucky. So who was it? The answer walked through the door and, for the first time in my life, I considered taking on regrets.

Jerry, my favorite sociopathic stalker, came in the door with a sick sweet smile.

My heart shot into my throat, sweat broke out everywhere. The memory of him dragging me down that alley, the horrible things coming out of his mind all resurfaced.

She was giving me to him? Of course. He'd cart me off to whatever "religious compound" he was from and she'd never have to deal with me again. Wouldn't even get her hands dirty killing me. I picked a spot on the wall to stare at. Jerry's a predator, fueled by fear. If I ran, he'd chase. If I stared him down, it would be a challenge. If I bit, he'd bite back. Passive, indifferent, that's what I needed to be.

"We'll look, my purty's awake." All hints he might have an accent were gone; it was full-blown hillbilly now. Where'd this guy come from?

Out the corner of my eye, I saw Tiffany roll her eyes. She looked at Jerry. "What time will they be here?"

"Said they'd be 'round 'bout noon. Long drive where they're comin' from."

I repressed a shiver as images of what the "place they were comin' from" would be like. A dusty, barren street of dilapidated houses. Nothing like the green, fertile richness of Corvallis with its colorful summers, mild winters and plenty of rainfall to cleanse the air. Images of broken women in prairie clothes standing on porches surrounded by too many children, all with dirty, desperate faces flashed before me. It was something out of a news report about polygamist communities. I shrugged the shiver off and cemented my resolve. I could handle that; I bet I could even help those people, those women, give them something to work towards, hope for. I focused back on my spot on the wall and watched them with my peripherals. This was the choice I'd made to save my children. I would go along with it. I had no other choice.

"Be back in the morning." Tiffany looked right at me. "Someone has to go console Malcolm. Don't have too much fun with her," she said to Jerry. She winked at me and walked out the door with a smug smile on her face.

Bitch.

I tried not to think what "consoling Malcolm" would look like. I couldn't imagine his hands on her, whispering, "luv" in her ear.

I shook myself. I had bigger problems right now. I was tied up and alone with a sociopath. I'd be lucky to survive the night. He seemed to want me alive though. For now.

I took a good look at him out my peripherals. He was wearing slacks with cowboy boots and a white button-up shirt. I'd forgotten how rat-like he was with his beady little eyes and big nose, his skin and hair washed of any color. Even without the psycho thing, he'd be icky.

He sat in Tiffany's chair and for a whole minute just looked at me. Like a man sizing up a steak he was about to eat. He touched my cheek, ran his finger down my neck.

"Sure gonna miss yur purty face."

I didn't feel anything from him. Thank God.

"She says we're gotta break you before we leave or you'll just shrivel up and die. I didn't know you was a Muse. What's that like?"

I didn't answer, just stared at my happy spot.

He leaned into me, thin lips brushing my ear, "We're gonna be together forever. You're gonna have to talk to me sometime. Gonna be a long night, just you and me. We can do it easy or hard. Either way, I'll get some noise out of you tonight."

I blinked, resisting the urge to swallow. Poker face for me. A million things that would get some "noise" out of me ran through my head and I decided some neutral, not afraid, not cocky, conversation could be in my favor. The "break" me comment was a bit too scary to address, best start with logistics.

"Where're you taking me?"

"There now, not so hard. But I asked you a question first." He leaned back in his chair and waited.

"I don't remember what you asked."

A sharp pain ripped across my face, my head thrown to the side.

He'd slapped me.

"You'll do better to remember what I ask and what I tell you now."

I would not cry.

"Tell me what it's like being a Muse, my pretty."

The pain in my face was beyond distracting, but I answered as quickly as I could. "I've only been one a few days. It's different."

He seemed to relax again. "Different how?"

I thought fast. I didn't wanna give any Muse secrets away, but I had to say something. "People treat me differently. They're nicer, seem to wanna be around me." And it was true, as I looked back on the last week or so there was the guy in the cafeteria who came and sat down with me, the guy at the grocery store who ended up being a cop and other people in general like the guys at the party. I'd had more attention in the last two weeks than in the whole year before that. Not to mention Jerry here and his obscene obsession with me.

Jerry seemed to think, his eyes narrowing. "Good thing that's going away. Don't want people thinking too much about my wife."

It was my turn to look long and hard at Jerry. I pulled up all the courage I had and tried to appeal to any humanity he had, any logic. "Don't you want a wife who loves you, who wants to be with you?" Without flinching, I braced for another hit. It didn't come.

"Love is learned and earned. You'll love me eventually and there's no truer love than the kind that's from respect.

He was talking about fear. Fear is learned, respect earned. Love was ... Well I didn't know much about love. I'd thought I loved Cal, knew I loved my kids, but that's natural. I was pretty sure I loved Malcolm and that had been pretty natural, too, something that accumulated and was suddenly there. Malcolm had perhaps earned my respect, but my love, that was something entirely different.

I thought of Malcolm, of his warm smile and deep eyes. I'd never feel that way about Jerry. "I'll never love you. I may fear you. I may even respect you for some twisted reason, but I'll never ..." There was another smack. Same cheek, same exact spot. I let the pain burn across my face and settle down again. It was starting to swell, my jaw more difficult to move.

I found my happy spot on the wall and peeked at Jerry with my peripherals. He was watching me again. I was starting to think I wasn't what he thought I'd be.

Suddenly, he got up and moved to the table. He picked up the stun gun and tossed it from hand to hand. "These things are fun. Never used one afore, but it proved itself quite rightly." He dropped the stun gun on the table with a thud and picked up the zippered pouch.

He pulled out a little vial and held it up for inspection, giving it a little shake. "Tiffany got me some sleepy juice for you. Said you might be a bit feisty. Told her I like 'em that way." He smiled, showing crooked, plaque-covered teeth.

I couldn't repress a shiver. I didn't want this guy poking me with anything. A syringe filled with God-only-knew-what was high on the list.

"I like this electric gun, though. Gave you a good hit last time. You were out for hours, this time just give you a little one. Should keep you out till I get back with supper."

He crossed to me and before I could open my mouth to protest, he'd hit me with it.

29

It's only very recently that women have succeeded in entering those professions which, as Muses, they typified for the Greeks.

—Miriam Beard

I came around to the smell of food. Just a mild hint of biscuits and gravy on the air. Enough to make my stomach rumble. What times was it? When was the last time I'd eaten? I had no concept of time in the little cement room. Tiffany grabbed me at two in the afternoon. If it was seven, I'd been missing five hours. Cal was looking for me by now, but he didn't know about Tiffany or Jerry. I doubt he'll find me. If Malcolm stretched his imagination, he'd figure it was Jerry, but Tiffany was working her alibi. I didn't have much hope of rescue and, realistically, I didn't want to be. This is what I had to do to keep my kids safe. I didn't want to go with Jerry, but living the rest of my life knowing my kids were safe, would be worth it, or so I was gonna keep telling myself.

I opened my eyes to Jerry staring at me again, looking pleased with himself.

"Supper time."

He picked up a syrofoam container and plastic fork. Inside were pathetic looking biscuits and gravy. The kind you get from a convenience store prepackaged and frozen only to be thawed out to sit in a warmer for hours before a customer buys them. Not yum.

Jerry set the container in his lap pulling my chair towards him until his knees held mine between them. There was enough clothing between us that I didn't get any feelings off him. Thank God. He forked up a dainty bite and moved it towards my mouth, an understandable gesture since I was still handcuffed and strapped to the stupid chair.

I couldn't decide if I should open my mouth and accept the bite or resist. I hesitated, meeting Jerry's eyes.

He saw the question in my eyes.

"I wanna take care of you, want you happy. It's fine I promise." He moved the bite toward my mouth again.

I don't know how, but I knew he was being honest. The problem being his versions of taking care of me and making me happy were probably twisted so far up in his brain they were probably what I called misery and torture.

I opened my mouth and my jaw screamed. The cheekbone under my eye blared the loudest. Probably fractured. I winced and opened my mouth as wide as I could around the pain and swelling.

Jerry noticed. "See what happens when you don't play nice. If you'd just been a good little girl and done what I say, it wouldn't hurt. Now, have a bite."

I opened my mouth and took the bite. It tasted freezer burnt and cheap like it was, but otherwise fine.

He fed me a few more bites. Then he dripped gravy on his finger. He looked down at the drip and back to my face, the light of idea flaring behind his eyes. This couldn't be good.

"Get that for me, hon?" He held the dripping finger to my lips.

I kept them closed. There was no way I was licking or sucking anything off him. I was willing to go with him to keep my kids safe, but that was it.

"Come on now, soon we'll be honeymooning and you'll be begging me for things. I do love that mouth of yours. Just a taste."

Eww, eww, eww! I turned my head to the side. So not interested, buddy.

He didn't like that. He threw my container of food against the wall and grabbed my face.

I cried out in pain.

He pulled my face forward and I followed, afraid he'd rip my jaw off. He held my face and looked into my eyes. His were wide black holes. A big blaring sign announcing, *No light enters here and none escapes!*

Jerry pushed his finger into my face still holding my jaw. "Suck it off."

I swallowed down the lump that was forming in my throat and tentatively licked the gravy off his finger. He pushed his finger into my mouth. I fought the overwhelming urge to bite it off.

Mouths and fingers have many nerve endings and after the initial second of contact, I got a flood of his feelings towards me. Dark and sexual, so much longing, longing to hurt, to conquer. I closed my eyes to block out the vertigo and pain.

It all hurt. My face, my ego, my soul. The darkness that was Jerry flooded my very being. Then something clicked in place. A rush of energy poured into me, no longer a trickle, now a river of rushing dark energy that filled me up. A longing for pain—to inflict it—mixed grotesquely with something sexual and took on a life of its own. A monster formed inside me and took over.

I leaned into Jerry and sucked hungrily at his finger, gazing longingly at him.

The look on his face was no longer one of desire and longing, it was fear. I liked that. I chewed playfully on his finger and pulled it all into my mouth, sucking impatiently at it, wanting more.

He ripped his finger from my mouth, pushing me away.

I watched him, willing him to come back and untie me so I could get at all of him. It was the monster, the dark energy fighting for control. I could see her fully now, like another personality within me that had seized control when my defenses were low.

"Untie me. I'll make your fantasies real," I heard myself say as I struggled against the bindings and handcuffs. That wasn't me talking. I fought to push the dark girl aside, get her out of me, anything!

Jerry looked me over carefully. The only fear he held was self-preservation and I'd been sucking his energy. He may not have realized it consciously, but somewhere inside he knew I was a threat. What would happen if I pulled too much energy? Would he pass out? Die? I didn't even know. The monster inside me didn't care. She wanted more. More energy meant more power. Power to build herself.

Jerry moved towards me. Got down on my level and looked into my eyes, far enough away she couldn't touch him.

She/I leaned forward, looking alluringly at him. Ick!

"Why the change of heart?" he asked coolly.

"I can feel your power," she said.

"You want me?"

"Yes," she hissed in a voice that couldn't be mine.

I watched it happen this time: Jerry slowly pulled back his hand in a threat.

She just smiled.

His hand flew.

She cried out in pleasure. I registered pain as he hit across my cheek in the same spot as before.

He pulled back his hand again, a smile on his face.

Something in my head snapped back. She was pushed aside and I flinched, crying out for him to stop.

He did. "That's what I thought. Don't tempt me again. I won't take the time to test your resolve."

I quickly nodded. I had to keep *her* from surfacing again.

He went back to his seat, picked up his own box of biscuits and gravy and ate. My food lay forgotten, smashed against the opposite wall.

I quietly breathed through the pain in my face and tried to digest what had just happened to me.

I'd pulled in his energy, his dark cruel energy. It manifested as a personality with his desires. I could still feel her in the back of mind, waiting to resurface. I focused and pushed her down. She seemed to retreat and go quiet. With a little fit of panic, I wondered if she'd ever leave or if she was in me forever. Not a happy thought.

"Tell me about you," Jerry said.

I was mentally exhausted, physically beaten and still hungry. "I like art," I said, feeling broken.

"Won't be doing that anymore, not after tomorrow." He winked at me in a way that screamed *Psycho*! "What else?"

I thought for a moment. There wasn't much else. I had kids, I kept house, I went to school and I painted. Those things are hardly hobbies. "I like cars; driving is fun." My voice was more monotone than I'd intended. Was I really that defeated?

He leaned forward with his food. "There aren't cars where we're going. Plus, driving is not very ladylike. You should leave it to the men." He took a big bite of food, chewing with his mouth open, his breath whistling in though his nose. "What else?"

I remembered that I liked to run, workout, take martial arts. He wouldn't like those answers either. I wanted to say I don't know, but had a feeling that answer might earn me another slap.

"Don't you do anything girly, like knit or bake?"

I shrugged.

"Well," he paused to lick the last of the gravy out of his container. It was disgusting to watch and I looked away. "I guess you're just gonna have to learn some new hobbies ain't ya?"

I didn't say anything and that seemed to suit him.

He got up and whistled as he gave me a wide berth and walked behind me. A light went on and I heard a door close. There must have been a bathroom behind me. Sure enough about ten minutes later, there was a flush and he emerged followed by the waft of his stink.

"Your turn, honey," he said undoing the bungee cord around my chest. He was letting me go to the bathroom?

My brain had just started calculating some kind of escape when he wrapped the bungee cord around my neck pulling it tight like a noose. I choked and gasped, my face feeling like it would burst.

"You try anything and I'll knock your lights out with this here tip of my boot." I looked down; they were cowboy style, tipped in metal. I'd have thought silver, but Jerry wasn't that classy.

Holding the strap around my neck tight, he undid one of my cuffs, pulled it to the other hand and cuffed them together. He then uncuffed the other hand and double-cuffed me together. Overkill much? He did the same with my feet, undid a few more bungee cords and finally I could stand. There were real prison-style cuffs around my ankles so I could walk or at least shuffle to the bathroom.

Jerry walked me to the bathroom, a tight pull on the bungee cord around my neck. Once in the bathroom, he let the long end of cord fall down my back and reached for the button of my jeans. I instinctively pulled back and he hit me again. At least it was on the other side this time, but his aim was off. He hit my chin more than anything.

It took a second to register, but when it did, I cried out in pain. It felt like the whole side of my face had shattered. The main nerves for your face run up through your chin. He'd hit one or maybe all of them.

I tried to swallow as tears rolled down my face. I couldn't stop them anymore. I hurt too much and I was breaking. Why fight? I'd resigned myself to this and I couldn't change it. Even if I did get away from him, then what? I couldn't go home. If Tiffany found out, she'd hurt my kids. Still, though, I couldn't resign myself to Jerry. If I got away from him, killed him, would Tiffany just kill me? That would be better than living the rest of my life with Jerry. Could I take the chance she wouldn't hurt my kids? Looking at Jerry and feeling pain shoot through my face again, I started to think it might be worth the risk.

He unbuttoned my pants and pulled them down along with my underwear, his fingers lingering along my thighs. This was easily the most humiliating moment of my life and it was about to get a lot worse. He grabbed the end of the bungee cord again and used it to pull me down to sit on the toilet. Was he going to order me to pee and, if I didn't, beat me up more?

"Could you at least turn around or something?" I said to the floor. I had to try.

He opened the door but didn't leave and didn't look away from me. "I thought you liked an audience?" It was a stab at the display Malcolm and I put on at the fraternity. I can't believe I thought it would never bite me in the ass.

I bit my lip and tried to pee so I could be out of this mortifying situation already. A whole long minute passed and I finally willed myself to go. Luckily, my bladder was full to begin with. Finished, I took the initiative and made use of the toilet paper. He watched.

When I stood up again he grabbed me and pressed me into the wall opposite the toilet, my jeans and underwear still around my knees.

"I been arguing with Miss Tiffany about you for a couple days now." His hands moved over my exposed hips and thighs. His hands were rough and not gentle, but it wasn't enough, I couldn't pull energy or get a reading. Finally, he dug his fingers into my ass and pulled me against him, forcing his knees between mine and running his other hand over my bruised face. "She says you're a Muse and we gotta do something to you or you won't last a week with me. I don't like what she has in mind. You're face is so pretty, I'm not sure I can let her do it." He moved in to kiss me and the dark thing inside me purred with delight. If he kissed me or touched me anymore than he was, I could pull energy from him. It would feed her, but what would it do to him? If I pulled enough, would it weaken him? Kill him? He can't pull it out of the air like Cal and Malcolm can.

The dark girl in my head came up with a plan that I hoped I could live with. Very reluctantly, I let her take control.

"Tell me what she has planned and I'll give you something you want," she said as she ground her/my hips against him. I could feel his excitement through his jeans. This was dangerous. He was already too close.

She loved it. The game, the toying with him. She thrived on it.

"Tiffany said not to tell you; that's part of how it works."

"Please?" She moved her mouth dangerously close to his. Just a little further.

He took the bait and latched onto her mouth. I say her mouth because my mouth would never allow such a thing.

He kissed her hard, pressing us against the wall, grinding harder. She lifted my/her knees and wrapped them around him as best she could, still restricted by the jeans around our knees and the cuffs around our ankles. She reveled in the feeling, the control she thought she had over him. Feminine wiles at their worst. Then I reminded her what we were after and she greedily started to pull. She kissed him harder and rubbed herself against him as much as she could, all the while pulling harder for more energy.

I could feel the energy pour in again. She bathed in it, pressing harder. His hand came up and squeezed our breast, the other hand moving towards the button of his jeans. She let out a happy moan accompanied by the biggest pull yet.

He pulled away gasping.

"What're you doing to me?" He lost his balance and sat down hard on the toilet.

She smiled sweetly at him.

That's enough I said to her inside my head. *We had a deal.*

She wrapped herself up in the energy we'd pulled and retreated to her corner of my mind. I'd made a deal to let her come out again at later dates and times. I hoped I wouldn't be regretting that promise.

Jerry staggered to the sink and took long drinks of water from the faucet. "What did you do to me?" he said again.

I stood against the wall where he'd left me and watched, gauging his strength before I made a move. I waited too long. The next thing I knew I was sliding to the floor and he was yelling at me to tell him what I'd done.

He'd punched me in the side of the head, probably as hard as he could and hard enough to slam my head into the wall and make lights pop in my vision. He kicked me in the leg with his metal-toed boot.

I swung my cuffed-together arms and pulled his legs from under him. He fell on his ass. I got to my feet and kicked at his groin. I only made partial contact but didn't wait around to try again. I bolted for the door that leads outside. It was only twelve feet from the bathroom. Had I not been shackled at the ankles, pants around my knees, I would've made it.

Halfway to the door, he grabbed me and I stumbled. Falling to the ground, he kicked me again. My ribs, my head, anywhere he could. It was five kicks before I stopped screaming and trying to get away; it was another five kicks before he stopped kicking me and staggered to the table.

I watched, unable to make myself move, as he loaded up a syringe and half-limped back to me. He looked for a vein in my arm. I tried to pull away and he hit me. He found a vein, pushed in the plunger and, within a minute, the world went dark again.

30

Illustrious acts high raptures do infuse, And every conqueror creates a Muse.

—Edmund Waller

Something woke me. Nothing tangible, just a feeling. Only one eye would open, and it had a hard time focusing. I was back in the chair, strapped the way I was before. Jerry'd also strapped my head with duct tape.

I was still groggy from the meds. Kind of glad for that, the pain would be a lot worse when they wore off. I already hurt everywhere. My ribs were bruised, if not fractured,, my face and arms bruised something terrible. My pants were back up, even buttoned, but my legs hurt so much I didn't know if I could walk.

I was still taking stock of myself, testing my bindings when Tiffany walked through the door.

She looked comfortable in a pair of matching sweats and sneakers, her hair a neat ponytail. She spotted me and stopped in her tracks. Was I that bad?

She took the chair in front of me, setting a couple paper bags and a cup of coffee on the table

Jerry was stretched out on a cot in the corner, snoring.

"Long night?" she said.

I just looked at her with my one good eye.

"Went jogging with Malcolm this morning." She stretched her arms in the air. "Not that we needed the workout after last night."

I'd have given a lot to punch her one good. Instead, I just looked away. I was beaten. I was getting out of her way. Did she have to rub it in?

I needed a subject change. "Where'd you find Jerry?"

"Following you. He'd been trying to nab you for weeks."

"Weeks?"

She leaned forward. "Didn't those boys tell you anything? People are drawn to you. They know you can help them. It's when the crazies come out to play it gets interesting." She threw a glance at Jerry. He was definitely in the "crazies" category. "Certainly making my job easier, though." She got up and kicked him awake.

He grumbled and stalked to the bathroom. Tiffany went to the table and opened one of the sacks. To my horror, she pulled out a bottle of hydrochloric acid.

She had to be kidding.

"Did you know it's possible to un-become a Muse?"

Another shocked look was all I had.

She started gently removing the duct tape from my head, careful of my hair.

"It's just such a painful process, no one would go through it on purpose." She removed the rest of the tape, waded it up and tossed it onto the table. "It takes such a traumatic event the Muse can't recover. They have a complete loss of self. You see, a lot of being a Muse is in the person themselves. You could say it's hardwired into their personality, their spirit, their life force."

That made sense, but I didn't like where it was leading.

She leaned into my ear. "We're going to break your spirit, Shelby, strip you of what makes you ... you. You won't be a Muse any more, and Jerry can take you home to be his little wife."

I felt sick. "You're gonna leave my kids alone, right? Forever?"

She gave me a long look, pursing her thin lips. "Your daughter, yes. Your son won't know the difference."

"What do you mean?"

"I shouldn't tell you, but if I do, perhaps it'll put your mind at ease." She threw a glance at the bathroom door. We hadn't heard a flush yet. "The Muse/Guardian system is broken. We have the power and we squander it trying to help the pathetic normals, bowing to and reassuring their governments. We should be in control. We should have the power."

She was quiet for too long, glancing around, breathing fast.

I had to focus, my heart pounding in my ears, my adrenaline pumping.

"The Guardians need to realize this and take a stand. They need to relearn what it means to be a Guardian and it's best to start by retraining the little ones. There are only two Guardian schools on the West Coast. If we eliminate one, all the little kiddies will go to the other. We have people in place to start the re-education process. It's unfortunate, but your son will be at the school when we eliminate it. The date has been set for months; there's nothing I can do to stop in now." She actually shrugged.

"What do you mean eliminate?" I was straining against the cuffs and bindings. "What are you gonna do to my son?" I was yelling now. She'd made me give up the love of my life, my children. Now she was going to burn me with acid and send me to live out the rest of my life as a broken shell, abused by a sociopath. All that and my kids weren't even going to be safe? The deal was off. I was getting out of here and, before I left, God help me if I didn't take her and Jerry down.

"It's just a bomb, strategically placed under the mess hall during breakfast. It'll be quick and clean. He won't suffer."

If that was supposed to be comforting, she had a lot to learn. "When? When are you doing this?"

"Don't fight it, Shelby. It'll just make it harder."

"Tell me when. I need to know when."

Tears were running down my face. She gave me that look, the same one she had when she walked in the door and saw how beaten I was. Was it sympathy?

She shrugged. "Day after tomorrow, at breakfast." She looked at her watch. "Forty-eight hours from now."

"This wasn't our deal. You said you'd leave them alone."

"I don't think I ever actually said that."

Jerry walked out of the bathroom, looking haggard.

He took the coffee and the other paper sack over to the cot, where he scarfed down a greasy breakfast sandwich. He was about to mutilate me with acid and he could eat?

At least Tiffany looked a little pale as she pulled on a pair of gloves and situated the acid on the table.

"Don't do this, Tiffany. Let me go. I won't bother Malcolm again. I swear on my children, I won't."

Her hand shook as she adjusted the bottle on the table again. "It's out of my hands. The order's come down. You must be eliminated." She picked up the bottle and undid the lid. "You ready to do this already?" she barked at Jerry.

I started to struggle against the straps. They were going to pour it on me? All Jerry's comments about my pretty face suddenly made sense. I started to panic. This could blind me; it would disfigure me for sure.

"I'm coming." He started to get up.

"Tiffany, please don't." I begged.

"It's for the good of the world, for the good of humanity. I have to." She started to pour. Only it wasn't my face, it was my hand, my right hand. The one I use to paint and draw. They were taking away my ability to create, the gift that made me a Muse.

The pain was beyond anything, like having someone hold a lighter to your skin and just letting it burn until your flesh turned black and flaked away. Then they just kept holding it there until the next layer did the same.

Any dignity I may have had left was gone. I screamed. I cried. I begged them to stop. At one point, I thought I'd black out from the pain, but I didn't. The dark girl hiding in the corner of my mind poked her head out and smiled at me before heading back to her hole.

Finally, I was able to stop screaming and open my eyes. I, by no means, stopped moaning or writhing against the bonds that held me, but I could focus enough to see what was going on around me. I shot a glance at my hand. Just a quick one. I had to see, like watching a train wreck, I just had to know. The flash I got showed my flesh hadn't so much burned as melted. All my fingers seemed to be intact, but whether or not they worked remained to be seen. About half the flesh from the back of my hand was gone. Tiffany's aim was bad; the handcuff had been hit, too. She hit the part where the links connect. I was pretty sure if I moved just right the cuff would fall apart. I wasn't excited about moving my hand and decided to wait for the right moment.

The smell of charred flesh was so thick they'd opened the door. Tiffany was outside leaning against the wall. Did she feel bad? Had the look and smell from my mutilation made her vomit? One could only hope.

Jerry, however, was standing in front of me with the gloves on. He looked excited, but somehow apprehensive. "You coming back in for this, Miss Tiffany?"

She didn't answer, just came in, shut the door behind her and sat down on the cot.

Jerry turned back to me. "I just throw it in her face?" he asked, shifting from foot to foot in his excitement.

"Tell her to close her eyes or she could go blind."

"Please don't," I begged Jerry.

"You have to or this won't work," Tiffany told him flatly. "Otherwise she'll be dead by the end of the week. Tell her, her new name first. It'll help with the trauma. Never call her the old name again." She was looking away, trying not to see.

This was it, now or never. I prepared my arm muscles to rip through the cuff and attack both of them, to fight my way out of here and back to my children, to save Julian. His little face swam in my vision, releasing all those mommy chemicals that make old grannies lift cars off trapped people.

I was ready, muscles tensed.

Jerry leaned down to my lips. "Just one last kiss from the prettiest girl in the world?" He phrased it like a question, but before I could respond, he was kissing me and this was my chance.

I kissed back, hard and fierce. Sucking his lower lip into my mouth, I pulled his energy as hard and fast as I could. I sucked and sucked, not thinking about what I was doing or how horrible he tasted. I kissed and sucked as long and hard as I could, willing him with my mind, body and all the powers at my disposal to stay, to kiss me, to kiss me until he died.

He didn't. He started to pull away and that was when I struck. I bit into his lip, as hard and fast as I could.

He reared up, screaming. Blood running down his chin. It'd been a quick bite, the last thing I wanted was his flesh or blood in me, bad enough I had more of that dark energy swirling through me. I pushed it down into the dark girl's pit and shivered.

Jerry was screaming as he stomped towards the bathroom. "You stupid bitch. I'm gonna burn your eyes out and spend the next fifty years tripping you and laughing about it!"

Tiffany didn't even see if he was all right. She retreated outside again.

This was my chance.

Being careful not to move my fingers, I pulled up on the handcuff and sure enough, it fell apart, freeing my injured hand. A few feet away on the table, I could see the cuff keys. I reached out and used my forearm to pull my chair closer to the table. I then used my free injured hand to reach for the keys. After some intensive manipulation, I snagged them around my little finger. I moved my right hand over to meet my left and dropped the key into that hand. I then tucked my injured hand against my stomach where it was going to stay.

Tiffany was nowhere to be seen. Jerry was still in the bathroom, yelling all the horrible things he would do to me. Threats I was sure he'd make good on if he ever had the chance.

Realizing I had only moments before someone realized I was loose, I maneuvered the key around in my hand, somehow got it into the hole and gave it a turn. The cuff came loose and my hands were free. I went for my ankle cuffs and, with an aching body, was finally able to stand unencumbered. Now for the real battle.

I started with Jerry. The door to the bathroom was open and Jerry was looking in the mirror, surveying the damage to his still bleeding lip. I got a running start, aiming with my good arm for the back of his head. He didn't see me coming until the last second. We connected and his forehead smashed into the mirror, shattering it. Not hesitating, I threw all my weight into his shoulder and knocked him to the floor. Just once, I kicked him in the groin as hard as I could. This time I made full contact. He yelled, clutching himself in pain. I looked around for something to finish the job.

His fall had knocked the seat off the toilet. I picked it up with my good hand and hesitated. Could I really kill another human being?

He was pressed into the corner where he'd had me against the wall with the bungee cord around my neck. He was holding himself, face covered in blood, looking up at me like he couldn't believe it.

I raised the toilet seat, ready to send him back to whatever hell he crawled out of, when my nerve failed. My arm holding the seat fell and I turned away from him. I caught my reflection in the shattered mirror and for a moment wondered who I was looking at.

Most of my face was blue and purple, swollen beyond recognition. One eye so damaged it was barely recognizable, the other just a sliver. I was hunched over in pain, my injured hand held tightly to my stomach. He'd done this to me, wanted me this way. He'd even said I was pretty like this. He'd kissed this face.

My feet came out from under me. I fell back hard, hitting my head on the wall, chin slamming into my chest. I was jerked around and suddenly Jerry's hands were around my neck. He was throwing more threats at me, calling me names as I struggled to get away from him. The bathroom was small, though, and I'd hooked my legs awkwardly around pipes under the sink. One of my hands was useless, the other pushing against Jerry's bloody face. It wasn't enough. I couldn't get air, and my face felt like it was going to explode again.

The dark girl surfaced. This time I didn't fight her. She came and Jerry saw the difference. Something in my face or something in the way I felt under his hands must have changed because he slowly pulled away. Like someone backing away from a tiger, hoping if they do it slowly enough they won't be attacked.

Watching me, he backed into the corner of the bathroom, back near the toilet. I realized he was afraid. I'd not seen him afraid before.

The dark girl was in control and I let her be. Whatever she was doing was working. She reached down and picked up the toilet seat I'd dropped.

Jerry just watched her in a trance. The last thing I saw in his eyes was peace. He didn't even flinch as she brought the seat down to connect with his skull. He was calm and still as his life ended, his shell becoming nothing but a broken smear.

When the job was done, *she* simply floated back into her dark hole with a satisfied smile. That left me standing alone in the bathroom barely able to stand, holding a bloodied toilet seat. I dropped it to the floor, staggered from the bathroom and went looking for Tiffany.

31

Our most basic common link is that we all inhabit this planet. We all breathe the same air. We all cherish our children's future. And we are all mortal.
—John F. Kennedy

Outside, the sun hit me full in the face. Two weeks of nothing but rain and gloom, and now that I'm beaten and broken, there's sun? I ignored that irony and looked around for Tiffany. I tried to stay on my feet, but my adrenaline was ebbing and the real pain was coming back. My blood-soaked hand was shaking and soon my knees would follow. I had to move.

A gravel parking lot surrounded by trees spread out before me. There was one vehicle, a beat-up old Ford Taurus—Jerry's car. Tiffany was nowhere in sight.

I took one step down the cement stairs and tripped, falling down three steps to land in a heap on the hard-packed gravel. I looked up at my prison, an office attached to a bigger warehouse.

I was exhausted and in so much pain. I could only hope that if Tiffany appeared, I'd be able to defend myself. I had a feeling she was long gone, though. Just one of those things I somehow knew.

I started crawling across the parking lot, figuring it had to let out at a road sometime. From there, I could get help. It was slow-going with only one arm to pull myself along.

I was halfway across when I heard a car coming up the road. I tried and failed to stand, ending up in a heap again. The car got closer and I recognized the sound of the engine. I'd know that engine anywhere. It was Malcolm's diesel supercar.

The car came to a screeching stop and, before I could blink, I was in Malcolm's arms, being lifted from the ground.

"Oh God, luv, don't die on me, please." His voice was so deep and husky I could barely understand him. Was he crying?

I tried to tell him I was all right, but the words wouldn't come and my eyelids were getting heavy.

In the distance, I heard his deep voice again. "Cal, where are you? I have her. She needs you, now." He was taking me to Cal. I'd be all right. "Meet me outside" was the last thing I heard, and we were moving.

I wish I could've been more coherent for the ride. It was unlike anything I'd ever experienced. He was running with me between trees, across roads and around corners so fast I couldn't focus on anything we passed. Twenty seconds later we stopped.

"Dear God in heaven, is that really her?" Cal's voice. A warm hand pressed against my neck, all my pain vanishing.

"Is she gonna be all right?"

"Most of her,"

I opened my one good eye and looked at Cal. "Julian," I started to say.

"He's all right, Shel. He's at Guardian camp, remember?"

I tried to shake my head, but they weren't paying attention.

"Let's get her inside." Cal put another hand to my face.

We were moving again, and I felt myself start to fade. He was putting me to sleep, but I had to tell him about Julian. How long would it take me to heal? How long before he'd let me wake again?

"Cal ... Julian," I tried to say, but the lights went out and I slipped into oblivion.

I sat bolt upright in my bed. I could tell it was early morning by the sun pouring in through the window. Cal was asleep next to me and I realized I wasn't wearing much, just underwear. My burned hand was splinted and wrapped. It didn't hurt and neither did the rest of me. I was healed. I pulled on some clothes one-handed, not sure I should use the damaged hand yet. The bra was a trick, but I felt better with it on.

Sufficiently dressed in sweats and a T-shirt, I tried to wake Cal. I needed his help to get Julian. I didn't even know where the school was. I shouldn't have let him go in the first place. Why had I been so stupid? As I moved around the bed to wake Cal, I swore I'd never put Julian or Chloe at risk again.

I called Cal's name a few times and shook his shoulder. He didn't even stir. Shit. I checked the pulse in his neck. It was beating at a steady pace. What was wrong with him? I spent another minute trying to wake him, calling his name louder and louder, shaking him as hard as I dared. I was about to call an ambulance when Kali came in, followed by Malcolm and a man I'd never seen before.

The unfamiliar face was ultra pale with white hair, his eyes a light grey. He couldn't have been older than thirty. He was built on the small side and no taller than Kali's five-foot-eight. He was wearing pale blue jeans, a white pullover and all-white Adidas. If you didn't look carefully, you might miss him all together.

"What day is it? Who's that?" I said, feeling myself tense. I'd been beaten and nearly broken. Strangers were not in my comfort zone.

Kali exchanged a glance with the light stranger. He nodded and she moved next to him, taking his hand and twining her fingers between his in that intimate gesture Malcolm was so fond of.

"It's Thursday. You slept almost a full twenty-four hours."

I had time. It was morning. I still had twenty-four hours to get to Julian. I let out a breath. Now if I could just get someone to take me to him or tell me where he was. Maybe I could look it up on the Internet.

Kali interrupted my thoughts. "Shelby, did you hear me?"

I looked up and blinked at her, trying to focus.

"I said this is my husband, Andre. Andre, this is Shelby."

He didn't reach out to shake my hand. "It's nice to finally meet you, Shelby. I've heard a lot about you."

"Funny, I've never heard of you." I looked back at Kali, her golden hair shiny in the pale morning light.

"I've wanted to introduce you for a long time, but I couldn't until I knew who was coming to guard you. Andre won't have anything to do with the Authority. We had to make sure whoever came was trustworthy before we told you."

I looked at her trying to absorb. "Cal's trustworthy?"

She nodded, stepping in closer to Andre.

I shook my head and tried to let it go.

"We have to save Julian. What's wrong with Cal?"

"What's wrong with Julian?" Kali asked as Malcolm moved to check Cal. He was wearing his usual jeans and black T-shirt with running shoes. He looked tired, dark circles under his eyes and a bit of a hunch to his normally perfect posture. He almost looked sick. I gave him a sad smile. When all this was over we needed to talk, but it would have to wait. Julian came first.

He touched Cal's shoulder, shook him a bit. "Cal, you idiot," he muttered. "He needs to bond, and soon. Then he should be all right." Malcolm had a with a very careful expression on his face. I didn't like it.

Kali nodded. "In a minute. I wanna hear about Julian."

I pulled myself back from the two men in my life and looked at Kali. There must have been something in my face because she came forward and laid a hand on my shoulder.

"Everything's okay now. You're safe. They can't hurt you anymore. Tell us what's wrong with Julian."

I gave myself a shake and willed myself to start talking. Then I couldn't stop. The words poured out on their own, starting at the beginning. Everything from the moment I'd first seen Tiffany on the running trail, her threats, and why I didn't tell anyone. I thought it would've made things worse, that I could handle it on my own, I told them. In a way, I had, but it had still been stupid of me.

"You should've told me," Malcolm said. "I could've made her go away. I could've kept you all safe."

I guess we were having this talk now after all.

"Could you really? And at what cost? Running? Living in fear for the rest of our lives? They're children. They deserve to play outside, to run and not be afraid."

Malcolm met my eyes. "They deserve a mother more."

I looked away. "Children can live without a mother."

A sound escaped both him and Kali, but neither pushed the issue.

"What happened next?" Kali asked.

I met Malcolm's eyes. "I broke up with Malcolm."

"She made you?"

I nodded.

"Cal didn't tell you what I used to be?"

I shook my head.

"You still wanna be with me?"

I nodded.

"Even though everything you went through was because you were with me?"

"It was my choice. I'd make it again," I said in a small voice.

Malcolm visibly relaxed, some tension draining out of him which somehow pulled some out of me. I relaxed just a little. The next thing I knew, he was hugging me. It caught me off guard, but it felt so good to be touching him again. He pulled my face up to look at him.

"Don't ever do that again. The truth. Always."

I nodded. If I couldn't give him this, then we had nothing. We had to have trust, understanding, to build a relationship.

"Finish your story, Shel. You said we have to save Julian ... Cal is fading by the minute."

"Cal's fading?"

"You've not bonded with him already?"

"I don't even know what that means."

Kali studied my face and looked carefully at Malcolm before speaking, "Cal needs to bond with his Muse in order to regain some strength. It's not difficult, but it takes awhile. I want to hear about Julian so we can make a plan while you do that."

I just stared at her, my mind gone blank again.

"It's gonna be all right. Focus. Finish your story. You can collapse later."

I swallowed and nodded. Malcolm wrapped his arms around me from behind and held me against him. I couldn't believe how good it felt to be near him again. Like a piece of me had been missing. I found the strength to move forward, to take a breath and continue the story, to relive the nightmare.

"After that, I grabbed Chloe and stashed her."

"Where?" Kali and Malcolm said at the same moment.

I didn't answer, just told about getting stun-gunned in the parking garage.

"Shelby, where's Chloe?"

"She's safe."

"You're not answering the question." Kali sounded annoyed.

"And I'm not going to. When this is over, I'll tell you. You can even come with me to get her, but until then the secret stays safe with me."

"You don't trust us." Andre spoke for the first time.

"It's not that. I've just seen how these people operate and I wouldn't put it past them to do something terrible to one or all of us to get the information. If only I know, they'll never know and she'll be safe.

To my great surprise, Malcolm squeezed me and said he understood.

Kali didn't look happy but let it go.

I continued with the story, telling how I was tied down and what Jerry wanted with me. I left out the part about pulling energy from Jerry and about the dark girl. As I mentally skipped over it, I heard Kali's voice in my head. *We'll come back to that. I wanna know more later.*

I gave her a little nod and went on with my story.

Finally, I got past the first bathroom scene, the beating and the injection. I told about Tiffany burning my hand with acid.

I couldn't see Malcolm's face, but as I told about the acid, his arms tensed around me. Kali's eyes kept flicking up to his face.

"They were trying to break you so you wouldn't need a Guardian anymore, so Jerry could take you and you wouldn't go crazy and die," Kali said, glancing again at Malcolm. She looked back at me. "If Tiffany knew you at all, she'd realize it wouldn't work on you. Not like that anyway. Your personality, your essence is too strong. It just would've killed you."

"Somehow I find that comforting." I snuggled closer into Malcolm, pulling his arms tighter around me. "I'd rather die than be a broken shadow of what I once was."

"That's what Tiffany didn't know about you, that you'd rather die."

We were quiet for a moment and I remembered Cal and Julian. We had to get through this.

I pushed through the story, knowing time was of the essence. I told about biting Jerry and about Tiffany disappearing. I felt myself go hollow as I told how I killed him.

Andre whistled. "A toilet seat? What a way to go."

I gave him an intense, blank look. "It was better than he deserved."

Andre gave a curt nod, and I felt more than saw him pull away. I'd killed a man, and he'd tried to make a joke. Jerry may have been a sadistic bastard who'd spend his life tormenting everyone he came across, but I'd still killed another human being. I couldn't joke about it.

I ended by telling how I dragged myself across the parking lot. I looked up at Malcolm. "How'd you know where to find me?"

"I called in a favor and had the GPS on Tiffany's car hacked. She'd been acting strange and I had a feeling she was up to something. I had no idea I'd find you though." He almost sounded ... ashamed.

I turned to look at him. "She made it sound like you were back together, once I was out of the picture.

He met my eyes full on. "Before yesterday, I would've said she and I would never be together again, but now ..." He took a deep breath and let it out slowly. "She'll be lucky if I leave her alive, maimed and broken."

Out the corner of my eye, I saw Kali nodding her agreement. Good to know they had my back.

"What about Julian, Shel? You haven't said anything about him, yet."

She was right. I couldn't believe I was so focused on getting to the end of the story that I'd left out the most important part.

I told them what Tiffany said about blowing up the school so the next generation of Guardians would go to the other school and be programmed the way Tiffany's boss wanted them to be.

When I finished, everyone was quiet. Malcolm stepped away from me, trailing his fingers in mine as he went. Kali moved to look out the window. Malcolm looked down at Cal. Andre stayed where he was, watching me.

"The bomb shelter," Kali said.

Malcolm made an affirmative noise.

"The tunnel," Andre added.

The three of them looked at each other, Kali nodding back and forth between them.

I watched in fascination as the three of them had a silent conversation, no doubt Kali relaying information telepathically.

Finally, Kali moved towards the door. "We've got a plan, but we're going to need Cal." She looked at Malcolm.

"I'll take care of it," he said.

She gave him a nod, and Andre followed her out.

32

The ability to "pull energy" from sources both animate and inanimate is among those that can appear in Muses who undergo severe trauma shortly after their twenty-fifth birthday. Accessing energy in this way provides a Muse and his or her Guardian with additional energy for crises. Muses can read the emotions of their animate sources, an enhanced perception critical to their survival during the process. Psychosis can occur if a Muse does not release excess energy into his or her Guardian or another human.

—"Muses," *World Look Encyclopedia*

Malcolm stared out the window for a while before looking at me with a sad, resigned look I couldn't read. I wanted to touch him to feel what he was thinking, but he probably had a reason for keeping it from me. I let him have his space. I'd want mine.

He looked back out the window. "You remember Isabella saying the relationship between a Muse and their Guardian is intimate?"

"Yes."

"You're about to find out what that means." He looked at me then. "I'm surprised you didn't ask sooner."

I thought about it. "There were so many things happening, I guess I just couldn't handle another one."

He nodded. "I thought it was because you'd bonded already. If I'd known ..." He almost sounded angry, but when he looked at me, there was hope in his eyes. Then, like flicking a switch, his demeanor changed, his arms wrapped around me, lips meeting mine. He kissed me long and urgently, leaving us both breathless. He put a hand on my face and what he was feeling poured into me.

He loved me, cared for me, wanted me all to himself. Then there was sadness.

"What is it?"

"I just want you do know whatever happens in the next half hour, I'll still feel this way about you." He caressed my cheek.

I nodded, and he slowly pulled away. I could feel in his lingering touch how much it cost him to pull away. What was going on?

"There's a balance between Muses and Guardians. Muses need Guardians to stay alive. Guardians need Muses to keep their species going. Muses need the protection of Guardians, and Guardians understand the important work Muses do and how it helps the world." He looked at Cal and back at me. "You need each other. The way a married couple might need each other to make raising kids and life in general just easier. Married couples need to keep their bond alive and so do Muses and Guardians."

Malcolm was back at the window, looking away from me again. He looked tired, maybe sick.

"What're you trying to say, Malcolm?"

"When you bond with Cal, you'll want to have sex with him."

It took me a minute to absorb that. "Why?"

He looked at me and smirked, a half smile that was so familiar and yet so out of place on his face. "That's just how it works. It ties you closer together. As human beings, we care much more for our romantic partners than we ever would for someone we were just assigned to. It's natural."

"You said I'll *want* to. You didn't say I'd *have* to."

"You don't have to, but believe me, you'll want to. It's almost impossible not to."

I looked over at Cal in the bed. I'd loved him for a long time. I'd married him, had children with him. Given him all of me, planned my future with him and been sure of our place in the world together. Then he'd left me without even an explanation and, while his reasoning may have been just, it didn't change what happened to me. How he'd shattered my world and how long it had taken me to rebuild it.

I could never give him that again. I wasn't sure I could give it to anyone, even Malcolm. Cal would get his chance with his kids. I could trust him to protect my body, but my heart was off limits and so was the rest of me that would or could connect with him in any way.

"If I don't do this, what'll happen to Cal?"

Malcolm looked me straight in the eyes. "He'll die."

I blew out a breath and sat down on the bed. There was no way I could put myself in that position but I couldn't let him die either.

"I need more information. How does this work?"

He sat next to me. "When Cal heals you or gives you energy, it's like transferring life force into you. While he takes most of it out of the air, some of his own ends up in the path. He can't restore this energy fast enough to keep up with the rate you take it. You're gonna need to think of something you like or preferably love about Cal. Let the feeling fill you up. Then you touch him and let that feeling flow into him. Your unique life force will go with it, replacing what he lost when he healed you and maintaining your balance. It should restore him within moments, but—"

"Then I'm gonna want him."

"And he's gonna want you."

I let out a long frustrated noise and started pacing. "How am I supposed to do this? I don't love him. Why didn't he tell me about this?"

Malcolm shook his head. "I don't know his thoughts, but Cal was probably hoping it would happen naturally and he wouldn't have to explain. That you'd just think you had feelings for him again and things would go back how they were before he left."

I stopped and my mouth fell open. "That jerk!" I kicked the bed a few times. "Now I *really* don't want to help him."

"Every minute we delay is another minute before we get to Julian," he said in that grave voice of his.

He was right. I got up and started to pace. Stupid Cal. If he had just told me all this, any of this, none of this would have happened. There had to be a way out of bonding with Cal.

"Isabella's husband was a Muse. How'd they get around this bonding mess?"

"I don't know for sure, but some couples manage it by staying with their significant other during the bonding. The presence of that someone can be enough to keep things from going too far. In other relationships, it becomes almost a threesome, an 'if you can't beat 'em, join em' mentality. If you think it will help, I'll stay with you, but we must hurry."

I paced some more, my aggravation growing. I crossed in front of the lamp on my dresser and it went out with a pop. I jumped and let out a little scream. When my vision adjusted to the dark, Malcolm was sitting very still on my bed, watching me.

"Shel?"

"Yeah?"

"What happens when you touch me?"

"What do you mean?"

"What do you feel?"

"I don't know ... your emotions, your feelings. Sometimes it's like I can sense what you're thinking. Not hear it, just kind of know."

"What about other people? Has this happened with anyone else?"

"Yeah ..."

"Wow," Malcolm said, but somehow it sounded more like *fuck*.

"What now?"

"Later. We need to help Cal and Julian now. Where's a new light bulb?"

"Dining room, third drawer down."

He was back in less than ten seconds, the new light bulb casting the room in bright light. I could get used to his speed. I really could.

"It's time, Shel. We can't delay anymore. Do you want me to stay with you?"

I thought of Julian and nodded, allowing myself to be steered towards Cal. I could do this, not just because I had to save Julian, but because I couldn't leave Cal like this. Looking at him, I could see how much color he'd lost in the last twenty minutes. He needed help, and I was the only one who could do it. Wasn't I?

"Wait, can anyone else help him? Does it have to be me? You Guardians pull life out of the air. Can't you transfer some into him?"

Malcolm sighed. "If it were that easy, don't you think we'd just do that? You think I want to *see* you desire him? See him want you, too, and wonder if I should leave and let you two have at it?" He pulled my face up until we were almost kissing. "I'd give anything for it not to be this way, but if you don't do this, Cal will die. It has to be a Muse and you're the only one here. Okay?"

"Okay."

Malcolm sat with me on the edge of the bed and we pulled the blanket off Cal. His skin was so pale it almost looked blue. He was warm, but not near as warm as he should've been. My heart went out. I had to help him, no matter the cost. Seeing him like this made me panic. He couldn't die.

I swallowed the edge of alarm. "What do I do?"

Malcolm sat behind me and rested his hands on my arms. "Pick a place with lots of nerves and rest your hand. The more skin touching the better, but your one good hand should be enough."

I ran my hand over him trying to pick a spot that didn't make me too uncomfortable. I decided on his chest, just below his neck in the collarbone region. "All right, now what?"

Malcolm moved in behind me, a leg on either side until I was all but in his lap, his chest against my back. I relaxed a bit. His presence would keep me from doing something I'd regret, right?

"Think of something you like about him. Even something you used to like about him. Perhaps a happy memory like your wedding or first date. Anything you think will work." Malcolm's voice was so deep and soft in my ear it soothed me as I searched for a memory.

It was hard to find one about Cal. I'd locked that entire phase of my life in a trunk in the attic of my mind, never to be looked at again. I spent a minute trying to pry open that trunk. My first glimpse of what lay inside made me pull away from Cal and rub my own arms. Like a spider web had stuck to me and I had to get it off.

It wasn't that my time with Cal had been horrible. It was the opposite. Our time together had been wonderful. After years living with my aunt as an outcast, feeling unloved and alone, Cal had been the sun, the warmth in the world and the first person who'd ever really cared about me. We fit together so well I thought we'd be together forever. When he'd left so abruptly and without explanation, it was like he'd died. Someone else I loved had died. I felt as though I wasn't meant to be loved and, after a horrific mourning period, I'd accepted my fate to be alone. I'd stuffed everything that was Cal into that proverbial trunk, locked it, climbed out of the attic and locked that door, too. I couldn't make myself go back in there. I just couldn't.

Malcolm hugged me to him. "You're shaking."

"No memories of Cal. I can't." It took everything I had not to sob.

"Okay, okay." He hugged me a little tighter and I let myself be comforted. It was all just too much, Julian and Jerry, my life changing so fast and completely. I had to lean on someone for a moment. I had to.

He didn't even give me a minute to recover before he dived back in. "How about a more recent memory, one not tied so closely to you. Something with the kids? A happy moment with the kids."

I took a deep breath, willed myself to be steady and thought, "There might be one."

"Go into that memory Remember where you were, what the lighting was like, the smells. Remember Cal, remember your kids, remember how it made you feel."

I laid my hand on Cal again and closed my eyes, letting my thoughts take me away.

I was standing in my entryway next to Johnas. Diane and Kali were there, too. It was that first night Cal was back, my birthday. The night everything changed. Cal was standing in front of us, and Julian and Chloe had wandered in to see the new arrival. I remembered the look on Cal's face when he'd first seen Julian. Awe and regret in the same expression. It had surprised me.

When Julian was born, I was proud of how beautiful he was, how strong and healthy, how he looked so much like Cal. Cal had only been gone a few months and I couldn't help but think if Cal could see him, he'd be proud of his son. He'd think he was beautiful, too. Cal missing that moment ... the thought of him missing all the moments that would follow had made me cry. I'd been sad about all the moments he missed with Chloe, but it was different with Julian, different when it was his son, our son.

When Cal finally met Julian, when I saw that look on Cal's face and realized he did think Julian was beautiful, that moment had filled me with something. Joy. Joy that Cal had finally met his son and that he saw enough beauty in him to be sad he'd missed the first precious years of his life.

Sitting on my bed with Cal near death in front of me and Malcolm behind me, I realized that I did love Cal and that I always would no matter how much I might hate him, too. I realized that I wanted him in our lives. Not as my husband, but so I knew he was well and happy. Sometimes you just need to see or hear from someone to feel content, like a friend that meant so much to you once before life separated you. Sometimes you just need that letter or email to know all is right in world because that person is still out there alive and well.

I let those feelings fill me up: the fulfillment of seeing Cal with his son ... realizing there was a place for Cal in my life and realizing I wanted him in that place.

I visualized that feeling moving out through my hand into Cal. I imagined it filling him up, bringing back his color and breathing life back into him. And just like that, it did.

Malcolm's breath caught as Cal's color returned. The circles under his eyes disappeared, and his skin grew hot under my hand. I started to pull away, but Malcolm held my hand to Cal's chest.

"He was nearly gone, luv. Wait till he's looking at you."

Cal took a great breath and then another. His eyes slowly opened. They were the perfect chocolate brown I remembered and made me smile. He smiled back.

I turned to Malcolm. "Thank you. For helping me. I couldn't have done it without you. I couldn't have even survived the last few weeks without you." I leaned in to kiss him, and as our lips touched, it was like the floodgates opened. I felt the energy, the life force I'd been pushing into Cal redirect itself and move into Malcolm. Sitting there with my hand pressed against Cal, Malcolm's hands pressed against mine as I kissed Malcolm the energy circled through me into Cal and back into Malcolm. It was the most exquisite feeling, like I was full and happy, like everything was as it should be. All the nerves in my body lit up, like they were being itched in that unscratchable way. In that way that you can never make happen, but when you do, you'd purr if you could.

As if that amazing pleasure in every nerve wasn't enough, the places Cal or Malcolm were touching me felt a hundred times better. I suddenly realized what those moments with Cal and Malcolm meant. Those moments when all I could think was how I wanted them touching me. That moment in the bedroom with Cal, a moment at the frat party with Malcolm and another with him in front of the mirror. They were the beginnings of a bond. This was like that only a hundred times stronger and so overwhelming. Those moments I could control. This moment I didn't want to control.

All I could think was that I needed them touching me, all of me. That this was right, and I could never get enough of either of them.

I was kissing Malcolm, and Cal was there, too. Malcolm kissed my neck, his huge hands moving under my shirt. Cal's hand stretched flat across my stomach. Malcolm's hands were there, too, and they were pulling off my shirt, both of them together. This should've terrified me, pulled me back to reality, but it didn't. I wanted them to undress me, and I wanted to undress them. Cal was already in just boxers, so I reached for Malcolm's shirt and off it came. I couldn't stop moving my hand on his chest. Every little touch felt amazing, much better than should ever be allowed.

Malcolm's sapphire eyes pulled me in and I kissed him again, letting my hand explore as much of him as I could reach.

Cal's hands trailed along my back, his lips following behind. I pulled from Malcolm, meeting Cal's smoldering gaze. He kissed me, soft and lingering. Just barely a brush of lips. It was that kiss that stopped me. There was something about it. Something so wonderful I couldn't pull in any air. It was like there just wasn't any. There was nothing but the feel of his lips against mine. The feel of those big warm hands wrapped around me. It was the feel of home, of familiarity and rightness. Even after all these years my body, my soul still recognized him.

I pulled back from the kiss and he did, too, a look of wonderment on his face that surely matched the one on mine.

Malcolm's hands against my skin stopped, too.

"What happened?" I said, completely breathless.

Kali's voice came from the doorway. "You bonded to both of them."

33

MAGRA considers a Muse with two Guardians to be a danger to humanity. Before the ascendance of MAGRA, Muses occasionally bonded with more than one Guardian. Such a powerful triad possessed exaggerated abilities that had the potential to help humanity. In most cases, triads used their power for selfish gain. In rare cases, a Muse has bonded with three Guardians. MAGRA eliminates such alliances by killing the two Guardians and using the Muse as a subject of experimentation.

—"Muses and Guardians," *World Look Encyclopedia*

Several things happened at once. Malcolm disappeared from my side. There was a noise from Kali and suddenly she was on the floor at the foot of the bed. The door shut, Malcolm in front of it. Cal got up too and moved around the bed towards Kali. They didn't look happy with her and I was suddenly afraid for her.

Adrenaline chased away the last of the amazing tingles as I moved between Kali and the boys. I didn't know what was going on, but I didn't like the look on Cal's or Malcolm's face.

"Shelly-belly, move away from her," Cal said, putting himself between Kali and the window.

What was going on?

"Come on, you guys, I'm not gonna tell. I'm married to Andre for God's sake." Kali was still on the floor, so afraid she was trembling.

"Being with Andre won't earn you a death sentence," Malcolm said in a voice so flat, it didn't sound like him at all.

Kali gulped and started to say something, but I interrupted.

"Somebody tell me what's going on."

All eyes flicked to me as if they hadn't realized I was still here. Amazing, since I was only a foot away from Kali, who was the current center of attention.

Both Cal's and Malcolm's expressions tightened when they turned back to Kali.

She rushed to answer me. "They think I'm going to tell the Authority you've bonded to both of them."

"And that's important because ..."

All three sets of eyes looked at me again.

Malcolm answered that one. "If the Authority finds out you've bonded to both of us they'll take you away, make you into a laboratory experiment. Cal and I will be lucky to escape a death sentence" His gaze flicked back to Kali.

She shrank against the footboard. "I wouldn't tell them."

"We can't take that chance," said Malcolm, glancing at Cal.

A decision was being made, the look in Malcolm's eyes matching the one in Cal's.

I couldn't believe what I was hearing. "Just like that, you'd kill her?"

"You don't understand, luv. They'd take you away, put you in cell somewhere and study you like an animal. They'd parade a never-ending line of Guardians through your life and study what happened. That alone could kill you. Your life would be over. You'd never be free. You'd never see your kids again; they'd be lucky to escape a death sentence, too."

It was all too much. I needed to back up. "Wait, how do we know I bonded to both of you?"

Everyone thought for a minute.

"Let's test it," Cal said. "A Muse can feel her Guardian's presence. How about Shelby closes her eyes, covers her ears; we spin her around a few times and switch positions within the room. If she can reach out to one or both of us, we'll know who is bonded to her."

"Agreed," Malcolm said. "It would be prudent to know for sure before we start killing witnesses. Not that we would kill you lightly, Kali, but we have to protect Shelby at any cost. You understand."

Kali stood up to face Malcolm. "I've been protecting Shelby for the last six years. I may understand better than you do, but I'll not let you kill me to relieve your paranoia."

"Perfectly understandable. First a test."

Kali looked nervous again but nodded.

They weren't sure how I'd know where my Guardian was, but I would know. So helpful.

I covered my ears, closed my eyes and Kali spun me a few times. Her hands stopped and held me steady before letting go. All I had to do was point with one or both hands to where the boys were standing. I took a deep breath and let my mind reach out. I don't know how I knew, but I felt something five feet to my left. I felt a little harder with my mind and could tell it was Cal. My energy brushed his and he bristled at the contact. Then, like a cat deciding it wanted to be petted after all, he relaxed and the connection became soothing and pleasant. Like stretching out on clean sheets. A rightness.

I reached out again and found Malcolm. His essence was different, more solid and darker. He didn't bristle when our energies touched. It was more like a pull, a magnetism that had always been there, something that made all the risks of being together seem trivial. I could see it now. A fundamental part of who we both were.

I had my answer. Standing there with my eyes closed and my ears covered I could reach out to both of them, feel them both as part of me at the same time. I'd bonded to both of them. I still wasn't sure what that entailed, but it felt right. Just like that, I made peace with it, accepted it. Sometimes you just know.

Now, what to do with the information. I could lie, say I only felt Cal or Malcolm, but Kali could read it out of my head. Hell, she could already be reading it out of my head. With that thought, I opened my eyes and uncovered my ears. All three of them were staring at me.

"Tell them what I found, Kali."

She blinked and swallowed. "She can feel you both. You're distinct and separate, but both there."

It was quiet for a long time. Cal and Malcolm looked at each other, something passed between them, and they both looked at Kali.

"I'm sorry, Kali. We can't take the chance." Malcolm moved towards her.

It was my turn to make a decision. Could I stand by and watch them kill my best friend, even at the cost of all the other people I love? I guess the more important question was whether Kali would really betray us.

I only had a moment to decide. Kali was trying to evade them, but she was outnumbered and probably outclassed. I didn't know the details of everyone's abilities, but even if she could read exactly what they were gonna do before they did it, I doubted she could react faster than Malcolm could move.

I stepped between Kali and Malcolm. "No."

Malcolm looked confused.

"She's not gonna tell."

"We can't know that, luv."

"I do, and it's my life. Kali would never betray us."

"It's not just your life," Cal said from behind me. "Are you willing to bet all our lives on that? Mine? Malcolm's? The kids'?"

This was hard. Not a week ago, I'd been ready to cut ties with Kali because she'd lied to me about being a Guardian. Since then I'd made peace with what she'd done. They're Guardians. They have no choice. I'm a Muse and that wasn't my choice either. I might not like it, but they did the best they could. I had to believe that. The longer we argued, the closer Julian was to danger. I couldn't do this on my own. I needed to trust someone.

I stepped closer to Kali and turned to face Cal. "Yes, I am willing to risk all our lives that Kali won't tell a single soul the three of us are bonded."

Cal wasn't happy.

"I'll forfeit my life on it," Kali said.

There was a gasp from Cal and Malcolm. Something in the air changed, got lighter.

"You'd really do that?" Malcolm asked.

"I will. I'll do it with Shelby. It'll tie me to her too and then we'll all be in this together." She turned to me, but I was backing up.

"Tie yourself to me?" I couldn't keep the fear out of my voice. Too many metaphysical things had happened to me in the last hour. Another one wasn't in my comfort zone right now.

"Not like you bonded with them, but it's a way of pledging my word to you. If I tell anyone you've bonded to both of them or someone finds out because of my actions, I'll die."

"You just fall over and that's it?"

"Sort of. I won't be able to pull life anymore; without it, I'll lose my abilities. Any Muse I'm guarding will die, too. In essence, everything I am will die and eventually it would take me too. I'm forfeiting my life. Everything I am or ever would be would come to an end."

I tried to wrap my mind around that. Her word was good enough for me. It was Cal and Malcolm who needed more.

"What do you guys think? Is this enough?"

" What about Andre?" Malcolm said still standing in front of the door, arms crossed over his chest.

"Yeah, where is he?"

"Picking up the food." I could hear a slight panic in her voice.

"Are you going to keep this from him, too? He's gonna be around us; he'll figure it out."

This was a whole other quandary. Could we drag him into this? Was it fair or right? Looking around the room at everyone, I didn't see another choice. Either he had to be informed and make some kind of promise or Kali would have to promise and then they'd have to stay away from us. I wanted to avoid the option that meant Cal and Malcolm killed both of them.

As if on cue, we heard the front door open downstairs and Andre's voice echo through the house. "Hello?"

34

Where art thou, Muse, that thou forget'st so long
To speak of that which gives thee all thy might?
—William Shakespeare

"You have ten seconds to decide, Kali. Either we bring him in and you both make promises. Or, you make a promise right now and you both leave and don't come back."

"There is that other option," Malcolm added.

I gave him a dirty look. "We're not killing anyone."

"What would Andre want?" Cal had that hard, flat look back on his face. It was unfamiliar, new. Not something he'd had before he left.

Kali swallowed, obviously thinking hard and fast. How do you decide this for someone you love? The decision only took a few seconds, but felt like an hour.

"We're bringing him in. No one hates the Authority more than he does. He'll promise, and I don't wanna lose Shel." She met my eyes when she said it and I wanted hug her, but this so wasn't the time.

Malcolm opened the door a crack, giving Kali a careful look. "Call him up here." If she did something dumb, it was all over.

Kali met his gaze with a calm one of her own. "I'm in this. You don't have to worry."

Malcolm gave her that guy nod.

She called out to Andre, and he said he'd be right up.

We waited while he bustled around in the kitchen, finally coming up the stairs. He came swaggering into the room like it was any old day.

Malcolm closed the door behind him and moved in front of it, giving Kali another nod.

She told Andre the whole story while we waited.

Excitement sparkled in Andre's eyes. "This could be the prophecy."

Cal and Malcolm moved uncomfortably, and Kali stared at the floor.

"What prophecy?" I asked.

"Before the last prophetic Muse died, she said there'd be a Muse with two Guardians who were brothers who'd bring an end to the Authority." Andre looked at Cal and back to Malcolm. "That could be you guys."

I looked at Cal and back to Malcolm, too. Something in my brain clicked, like a light going on, but I still couldn't see what I needed to see. My panic rose as the thought—the light—flickered and went out. It was like walking into a room looking for something and forgetting what it was when you get in there. You wait for your mind to give it up, but you don't remember until you go back to what you were doing before. Sometimes you never remember. Either way this thought was gone.

"Cal and Malcolm aren't brothers," Kali said, pulling me from my head.

"No, we're not," Cal said.

Malcolm nodded his agreement.

"Maybe it meant brothers in arms or something. It still could be you guys." Andre was still looking excitedly from person to person.

"It's possible," Malcolm said.

"Oh, I'm in. Totally in. I'll forfeit my life, my cock, whatever you want. I want in on this. The Authority needs some shaping up."

"You'll agree, just like that?" Malcolm asked, his voice deeper than usual. Was that disbelief I heard?

"Absolutely. I've been waiting for this." He took two steps forward, clasped my hands, and said, "Under pain or duress, in life and in death, I will keep your secrets, Shelby Hammond. Should I break this word, I forfeit my life and energy." He leaned into my face, his lips nearing mine. I thought he was gonna kiss me and tried to pull away. Only I couldn't and he didn't. He stopped just before my lips, my own lips parting of their own volition. He exhaled into my mouth. I somehow knew to inhale. A warm tingling energy filled me up, warmth spreading through me. The force of his oath made everyone shiver as it passed through the room, making everyone witnesses to it.

When the moment passed, Andre was smiling.

At least someone was happy about all this.

"Kali's turn," Cal said from near the window, still in nothing but boxers, still on guard. His posture was perfect, his hands ready at his side. Malcolm was the same. Both were watching Kali. This wasn't over until she gave her oath, too.

Andre stepped out of the way and, without hesitation, Kali stepped forward and took my hands. She repeated the same words, her mouth moving dangerously close to mine. I pulled in her breath. It was somehow warmer and sweeter than Andre's. Once again, the shiver moved through the room at the increase of energy, this time leaving peace and calm in its wake.

Kali didn't smile the way Andre did. She looked very serious and tears ran down her face as her words whispered through my mind. *You're the sister I never had. I'd never hurt you and yours. I love you all too much.*

I finally gave her that hug. "I know you wouldn't. I didn't need this. It was for Cal and Malcolm."

"I know."

Just like that, everything was normal again. Malcolm grabbed his shirt and opened the door; he and Andre walked out, talking about the rescue plan.

Cal pulled on pants and a shirt. He looked at me. "You, come here."

I put my hands on my hips and tried to look indignant. Some of the dignity was lost because I was still missing my own shirt. "Just because we're bonded now doesn't mean you get to boss me around."

" Fine. I'll come to you then." He took two steps forward, swept me into his arms and, before I could tell him to get his hands off me, he was kissing me.

I tried to resist, but that warm fuzzy energy that's Cal and home and all things wonderful and right swept through me, the kiss becoming soft and breathtaking.

I ran my fingers through his curly hair, reveling in the familiarity of it. I ran my hand down his cheek that had more stubble than I remembered, the lines of his face that were deeper, but it was him—my Cal.

He pulled back from the kiss. "I've wanted to do that for five years, six months and seventeen days. I missed you shelly-belly. I never wanted to leave and I'm never leaving again. I'm sorry, sorry for everything. I'll do whatever it takes to make it up to you. Name it and it's yours.

This was both my worst nightmare and my wildest dream come true. I really didn't know what to say, so I said the only logical thing my mind would allow.

"Help me save our son, Cal. There's nothing I want more."

His eyes narrowed, his grip on me loosening. "Julian?"

I'd forgotten he didn't know.

Kali spoke from the doorway. "Let's get Shel in the shower and I'll fill you in. We've got a plan, but we need to get moving."

Now that somebody mentioned a shower, I realized how icky I felt. My hair hadn't been washed in days. Sweat, blood and other things I didn't want to identify were still crusted to me, and I didn't exactly smell great. A shower sounded good. A shower would wash away Jerry and what happened. It would make me, me again. Me could save Julian; me could deal with all this. I started towards the door, but Cal grabbed me again.

"Let me unwrap your hand first."

I'd forgotten about my hand, still splinted and wrapped. It didn't hurt and, with all the crises in the last hour, it hadn't been important.

Cal sat me on the bed and started unwrapping it. "I don't know how much function you'll have. There was so much damage to your tendons and muscles, I'm not sure it will all repair." He met my eyes. "I did my best."

"Shel," Kali said. "It was trying so hard to fix your hand that nearly killed Cal."

I looked back at Cal and tried to comprehend what they were telling me, but my mind just refused to understand. Of course, my hand was going to be fine. Why were they so worried?

Open air hit my hand, and Cal's skin brushed mine. He was sad. Really sad.

Cal thought he'd failed. Failed to protect me and failed to fix me.

I put my free hand on top of his, stopped the unwrapping and looked into his eyes. "None of this is your fault. These were my choices. You did the best you could. It's enough."

"You may not be able to hold a brush again," Kali said.

Finally, it hit me, smashed into me, leaving me without air. I struggled to breathe. Not hold a brush? My mind reeled, my vision going in and out. Of all the scenarios running through my mind, not being able to paint again hadn't been one of them. My art was like breathing. I just do it. It's the most basic part of me. Not be able to create anymore ... I didn't know how I could or would cope with that.

"Shelby, Shelby, are you all right?" It was Cal, squeezing my good hand.

Kali rubbed my shoulders. "Shelby, take a breath. You're all right. We haven't even looked at your hand yet. It may be just fine. Take a breath."

I struggled and finally a stuttering breath came in.

"I'm getting Malcolm." Kali was gone.

I sucked another breath and looked at Cal. The hurt look on his face was enough to bring me back, to realize this wasn't just about me.

"It's not your fault," I said, but my voice was dead, just hollow.

The next thing I knew, Malcolm's warmth was sliding in behind me, his arms pulling me close. "It's going to be all right, luv. We're all here for you. Whatever happens, we'll get through it."

Distantly, I felt myself nod.

Cal finished unwrapping my hand and rested his own on my knees, not leaving me without his comforting touch.

I forced another breath and looked down at my hand. It was like seeing something alien on my body. A huge scar covered the back of my hand, still fresh and white, but underneath, things had gone terribly wrong. Most of the flesh was just gone. My hand not half of what it used to be. Without trying to move my fingers, I turned it over and looked at my palm. If I held it at the right angle, I couldn't see the damage on the other side. Like an umbrella stays dry on the underside, protected from the rain, my palm was untouched. I turned my hand back over and just stared at the damage. I put both hands next to each other and couldn't believe the difference. I don't know how long I just looked at them, but Cal's voice finally broke through.

"Try moving your fingers, Shel."

I did. I wiggled my fingers. They moved, and they didn't hurt. It made me smile. Sometimes the little things save your sanity.

Cal led me through a few more movements to test my dexterity. Those results weren't as encouraging. I couldn't make my thumb meet any of my other fingers, kind of a must for holding a pencil or brush. I squeezed Cal's hand as hard as I could, and it was pathetic. Two of his fingers filled my hand, but I could tell he barely felt my squeeze.

When he stopped guiding me through the tests, I felt my mind slip away again. He was saying something about how I should continue to heal, how the scar would eventually smooth over, but the missing flesh would take longer, if it ever fully returned at all. He kept saying my strength and mobility would get better, but I could barely nod when he asked me questions.

"Where'd you go, luv?" Malcolm said from somewhere far away.

Kali answered for me. "Think what she's been through in the last forty-eight hours. She was kidnapped, tasered, drugged, beaten, molested and mutilated. Then she was unwillingly bonded to both of you, learned she may be part of one of the most serious prophecies of all time and simultaneously oathed to both Andre and me. Now she's just learned that the one stable, constant thing her life—the thing that's always been there for her no matter what—may be gone forever. As if all that wasn't enough, her son's still in danger, and we're all sitting around wondering if Tiffany succeeded in breaking her for good. Let's give her a minute and let her mind catch up."

Somehow hearing all that and knowing that someone understood made me feel better. The fog lifted and I could see again. I could see Julian, his dark curls and big brown eyes trimmed in lashes any girl would envy. His dark skin, lanky arms and legs. And that one dimple on his left cheek that only showed when he really smiled, when he was really happy. I had to save him. Nothing else mattered.

I stood up. "I'm taking a shower. We're leaving as soon as possible. Kali, fill Cal in on Julian. Malcolm, Andre, go back to whatever you were doing. We need to get going." I moved towards the door.

"Shel, are you okay?" Cal asked.

"No. No, I'm not okay, but I can melt down later. Julian needs me now, and I'm not wasting another minute on things I can't change."

I walked out of the bedroom, down the hall and turned on the shower before any of them moved.

Nothing was keeping me from my baby. Not even a psychotic break.

35

A Guardian is only as strong as its Muse.

—Anonymous

Once I got in the shower, all I wanted was to curl up on the floor and let the hot water hit me until everything was all better. But nothing would be better until Julian was safe and for that to happen I had to get through the shower, not go to pieces on the floor of it.

I brushed my teeth, ran goop through my hair and pulled it back in a severe ponytail. My room was empty, clothes waiting on the bed. Black cargo pants, black T-shirt that said "I do it with canvas," black hooded sweatshirt, and black treaded boots. I had a feeling we weren't picking Julian up at the front door. My cell phone, keys and wallet were also waiting. I loaded up my oversized pockets and was ready.

All four Guardians were huddled around my dining room table eating pizza and looking at a roughly drawn sketch.

Cal hugged me. "We're gonna get him back safe. I promise,"

"Don't make promises, Cal."

"Sorry, I forgot." He handed me a slice of pizza.

I gave him a look. If he thought I could eat now, he had another thing coming.

"You haven't eaten in forty-eight hours. Eat or I'm putting you back to bed."

Later, when things weren't so convoluted, Cal and I were having a serious conversation about him ordering me around.

I took the pizza and started eating, begrudgingly. They waited until I'd eaten the whole thing before they jumped into their plan.

Andre pointed at the sketch. "We're gonna come in on this service road and park here at the end of it. Back in the day, it was little used; the same is probably true now. Malcolm's confident Tiffany doesn't know about the road, so any vehicles with her group should be stashed elsewhere. From there, Malcolm's gonna bring us in one by one using his speed." Andre indicated what looked like a section of roughly drawn trees and then a little circle on the map. "This is a good vantage point of both the school and the tunnel entrance. At that point, using my abilities, I'll be able to infiltrate the tunnel and the building undetected, scope out their resources and report back. Then we'll make a plan to overwhelm their forces. They're gonna want their people out before the big bang. Hopefully by the time we get there, they'll be down to minimal personnel."

"Why not just call the school and warn them?" I asked.

"We have no idea who's been compromised at the school," Malcolm said. "If we throw the alarm, they could increase security or set it off early. Tiffany said breakfast; that means 7 a.m. We're gonna need every one of those minutes to get there and stop the bomb."

"What about knocking on the door and, at least, getting Julian out?" I asked, desperate to see my son safe.

"We decided that wasn't a good idea either. Right now, Tiffany thinks you went with Jerry and no one knows about our plan. If Julian's pulled or you show up at the school, it could tip them off. Our best bet is a surprise attack."

"I'm not betting with my son's life," I said a little too calmly.

"I don't like it either," Cal said, "but this is the best plan to save everyone. Julian's not the only kid at that school. There're hundreds in there."

I blew out a breath and looked at the sketch. There was a square labeled school and a long path labeled tunnel.

"What's this tunnel?"

"It's an old drainage pipe that leads to a tunnel Cal and I built. It leads into the school's old bomb shelter," Malcolm said. "The shelter itself sits directly under the dining hall and kitchen. They were originally part of a bomb shelter design. After the cold war, they sealed off the shelter portion below. When Cal and I were at school, we found the entrance and used to hang out in there. Eventually we found the drainage pipe and realized we could connect the two. Gave us a way to sneak off campus and get into trouble. Tiffany knows about it because I dated her in school and we snuck out a few times. We're confident this is where they're planting the bomb. During breakfast is the perfect time, too. Everyone will be in the dining hall. Lunch and dinner are more scattered, people coming and going at different times. Everyone eats breakfast at the same time."

They gave me a minute to absorb, like they were waiting for my approval. "All right let's do it."

"Let's?" Cal asked. "You're not coming."

"Excuse me?"

"You have no training and you're in no fit state to help. You'd be a liability more than anything."

"Hey, I can hold my own and Julian is my son. If anyone's going, it's gonna be me, or so help me you won't like what you come back to ... should you come back without my son." There were no words for what would happen if something happened to Julian. "I'm coming or you can find yourself a new Muse and a new family."

Cal and I glared at each other across the table. Everyone else was smart enough to keep out of it. Finally, he shook his head. Cal-speak for giving up. I was going.

Andre clapped his hands together, startling me. He looked exhilarated, ready for an adventure. "Leaving in five. Let's move out, people."

Turns out each Guardian's trench coat is a color unique to their personality. Cal's was the same chocolaty brown one I'd been seeing him wear since he got back into town. Unsurprisingly, Malcolm's was black. Andre's was a very light grey, almost white, but not. Kali's coat was a surprise. If I had to guess I would've said she'd pick yellow, not canary or anything, but a nice light shade of yellow. It's her favorite color and, when she wears it, her eyes look Caribbean blue. Much to my surprise, her coat was a simple khaki color. That alone was weird enough.

I stood in my living room looking at four professional Guardians. It was too surreal. Less than two weeks ago, I swore I'd never have anything to do with a Guardian. Then I find out my ex-husband is one, my son probably is, too, and he's off at Guardian camp about to be blown to smithereens. Not only is my boyfriend one, but my best friend and her surprise husband are, too. Not to mention that I'm bonded to my ex and my boyfriend, not that I even know what that means, and the other two Guardians are oathed to me and can't betray me without shriveling up into little non-Guardians. To that little pile of information, let's add that I may never be able to paint or draw again.

I went for the door. Outside in the open air I could breathe again. I bent over, hands on knees, trying not to hyperventilate. I felt Cal's hand on my back. How did I know it was Cal's? I could just tell. Without seeing or hearing him, I could just feel it was him. I had to bend over a little further and will myself to count to two between inhaling an ex-haling. Cal's hand crept up the back of my shirt and I started to feel calmer. He was switching my chemicals around to soothe me.

I moved away from him. "Don't."

"Shelly-belly, it will help."

"Don't call me that, and I don't need your help. I'll need all my wits if this plan's gonna work."

"We're hours away from getting there; you can afford for me to help you stay calm. I can feel how wound you are. You're about to burst out of your skin."

"I'll drive. It'll give me something to focus on."

"That's not a good idea."

I looked up at him then. "I don't think you're in any place to be telling me what a good idea is. If it wasn't for you and all your lies, my son wouldn't be in this mess in the first place." I was angry. Angry was good. Anger I could harness and use. Feeling overwhelmed does nothing but make you feel overwhelmed. Yes, anger, I could use.

Cal didn't have a response and I didn't care. He and I could make up later. It was time to get my son back.

I surveyed the five vehicles in front of my house. Malcolm's supercar was there and a stick shift, but it was only a two-seater. Kali's Mazda was a stick too, but only sat four and we needed five, especially with a four-hour drive ahead. I looked in the window of Cal's fed-mobile, a big black SUV and the most practical choice, but it was an automatic. Blech! How I could've been in love with and married a man who thought an automatic was preferable to a stick shift was beyond me. Andre's car was a little white sports car I couldn't identify and didn't have time to worry about. It was a stick, but again, only two seats.

As everyone moved toward Cal's fed-mobile, I announced, "We're taking my car and I'm driving."

Kali turned toward my car without a word and Andre followed her.

Malcolm stayed where he was and seemed to struggle. "But you don't know the way."

I gave him a long hard look. "Don't you start that, too." I could feel the argument coming against me driving, but I wasn't budging.

Kali was the only one who knew me well enough to know I needed this. Andre was wise enough to follow her. Cal and Malcolm weren't going to be so easy. What is it with men needing to drive?

I got in the driver seat. Kali cleared the car seats out of the back seat and got in the passenger seat. Andre got in the back and scooted to the middle. Then we waited.

Cal and Malcolm just stood there next to each other looking at us. They were a stark contrast. Cal was all muscle and taller by about four inches, but Malcolm was wider through the shoulders, unnaturally broad. I knew his other ability was strength to match his speed, but he'd never told me how strong. I imagined the wide shoulders were a product of that. I could see thoughts whizzing though his head behind those sharp blue eyes. Cal was a dark tower, his sharp eyes and cheekbones made softer by the black curls growing past his ears.

"Shel, you really shouldn't drive," Cal said.

"I concur, luv. It's not a good idea," Malcolm said. At least they were finally agreeing on something.

"And why's that, boys?" I said out the car window.

"You've had a long few days. You should rest; let Cal help you keep calm. We'll be there soon enough, and you'll need all your strength."

Kali let out a heavy sigh and reached for her door handle.

I touched her arm. "I got this."

"Go easy on them, they're learning."

"No promises."

She smiled.

I got out of the car and faced them. "So you guys think because it's been a couple of rough days, I need to be carried around in a palanquin or something?"

They both shuffled uncomfortably.

"It's my ... er our job to take care of you," Cal said.

"So you think standing here and arguing with me is helping me? Helping Julian? He's the only one I care about right now, and I feel like I should be doing something to help him. I feel it so deep in my soul I could burst out of my skin and fly to wherever he is just so I can help him."

"We want to help him, too. We just think you should take it easy."

It almost wasn't possible for me not to scoff at that. These guys had no idea what it was like to be a mother. Pregnancy sucks the life out of you. Literally a molecule of nutrition at a time. Having the baby is even harder. All that effort, physical exertion, blood and pain, and then they send you home with this little dependant person. You don't get more than two hours of sleep at a time for months, a full-night's sleep for years, and it doesn't end there. I once picked Julian up from the principal's office when I had the stomach flu. My eyes were completely bloodshot, my face a sea of broken blood vessels. I threw up in Mrs. Brooks trash can and barely made it home again, I was so dehydrated. Where was someone to take care of me then?

The mental distress is worse. So many decisions, so many mistakes and never anyone to ask for help or to tell you it's going to be okay. I didn't even have a mother or friends with kids to call. There were nights I hugged my pillow and cried, sure the pillow was the only thing in the universe there for me when I needed it.

With the exception of a few months when Cal and I lived together, I'd raised my kids on my own. Never anyone to take over a midnight feeding, to let me get a full-night's sleep, or even take care of us because I was sick. I did it all, and I didn't need two men who knew nothing about what it means to be a mother, a parent, telling me what I could and couldn't handle.

I was shaking my head, trying not to lash out. A few choice things to say ran through my head, but I decided to go with the truth. "I like to drive. It's one of my favorite things. It's a stress reliever for me. Driving to wherever the hell we're going will relax me. I'll feel like I'm doing something. If the stress is being relieved and I feel like I'm doing something then maybe this feeling that the world is going to implode will stay at bay long enough to save Julian. Is it okay with you guys if I don't implode and we save Julian?"

Malcolm met my eyes first. "Sorry, luv, I forget you don't need a gentleman." He moved toward the car.

I touched his arm and he stopped. "Yes, I do. I just don't need him to carry me all the time." Then I thought of something. "Thank you, by the way. For carrying me when I did need it."

"I only wish I could've gotten there sooner."

"Next time we go in together."

"And this time, too."

I nodded and let go. He climbed into the back seat and left me staring down Cal, who had that menacing look back on his face. Who was this guy? He wasn't the Cal who left me any more than I was the Shelby he'd left behind.

"You're really not the girl I knew. I never imagined you'd change. I imagined a lot of things, but not that."

I made a gesture in his direction. "You changed, too. I don't know this angry person."

He looked away and I saw whatever changed him flash across his face. It was so many things: anguish, horror and just plain regret. The emotions were so strong I could feel them play across my skin like I was standing in front of a heater.

"What happened to you?" I almost took a step towards him, but stopped myself. For some reason I couldn't comfort him, not yet. I didn't have it in me.

Cal swallowed a painful lump and got in the back seat. I guess we were going without a fight after all.

36

Nothing shows a Muse's character more than what she laughs at.

—Johann Wolfgang Von Goethe

I drove, and I didn't do it gently. Every stoplight and sign was its own mini stress reliever. Only when you drive a stick shift do you really get the control to rev up the engine as high as you want, feel the power when you push the RPMs past what is "responsible" and the sweet release when you finally let off the clutch and are fired into space completely in control of where the ride will take you, but enjoying the feeling of being taken none the less.

That was the first thirty minutes of our ride as we made our way out of Corvallis, down Hwy 34 and finally onto the freeway heading north. Depending on how fast you drive and how many stops you make, it's a three-and-a-half to four-hour drive to Olympia. I'd been informed the school was just past Olympia on a privately owned piece of land with limited access. I planned to make it there in less than three hours. Even less if I could help it.

That first half hour everyone was quiet. Kali seemed satisfied with the way I'd handled the situation. She kept smiling and I couldn't help but wonder if she was hearing something in the guys' heads that made her smile. Then again, she and Andre could be having a silent conversation. Heck, for all I knew they could be having telepathic sex. I didn't think they were, but the notion kept my mind busy for a while and distracted me from the impending situation. Maybe my thoughts about Kali having telepathic sex were making her smile. You never know.

"Shel, take a deep breath," she said

"What?"

"I can hear what you're thinking. It's like you're hooked up a loud speaker. Try to relax."

"Not you, too," I muttered, but I tried focusing on my breathing. I'd learned a long time ago that the trick to handling any situation was in handling your breathing. If you can control your breathing, you can control anything your mind and body might want to do. Including panicking or murdering someone. Take murdering, if you let the feeling and the breathing take you away, you can use them to let your body do whatever needs doing. Thinking about killing made me remember the dark girl. I'd almost forgotten about her. I let my mind take a glimpse into the bottom of that hole she was hiding in. Much to my despair, she was still there. Smiling up at me.

"Shelby has a dark passenger," Kali said to no one in particular.

"She blew out a light bulb when she was upset," Malcolm said in a matter-of-fact tone.

"She has the pull," Andre said with that same awe in his voice from earlier.

Cal didn't say anything.

"What's that mean?" I was having trouble keeping my eyes on the road and catching everyone's reactions to what they were saying. "What's that mean?"

"It means, luv, that you have a very rare Muse talent. One that counters what we Guardians do. We pull life from the air. You pull energy."

I waited a whole ten seconds to see if he would say more before I asked what he meant.

Kali answered. "You pulled energy from Jerry. You made him weaker. That's how you were able to physically beat him. It wasn't his life force you took; it was more electric than that. Guardians move what animates us all. You move pure energy. It's overlapping, but not the same."

"Wait. I thought I pushed energy into people to influence their decisions, like I did with Isabella. You never said anything about pulling it."

"You push life, Shel; you pull energy. Think of the difference like what is inside us that makes us alive versus what's in a battery. They seem interchangeable, but they aren't," Malcolm said.

"Not to mention, no Guardian can pull life from a person," Andre put in.

I tried to let that sink in. "So why the dark girl? I thought she came from Jerry, part of his essence or something? He was ... dark, like her."

A few minutes passed and no one said anything. "Come on, guys; don't clam up on me now."

Again, Kali spoke. "The dark girl is part of you. You needed something to do with the excess energy. It activated part of your mind that was dormant or suppressed. She is you."

"No, I don't think so. I felt her come, felt the darkness that came off Jerry. I didn't know what it was then, but she definitely came from him."

"You may've felt the energy come from him, but *she* came from you. The situation you were in probably influenced what aspect surfaced, but she is part of you. You were in a violent dangerous situation; your mind reacted with something violent and dangerous to deal with the threat. Had you been in a situation where the kids needed you to care for them, the personality that surfaced could have been the ultimate nurturer or had the situation been sexual, something appropriate may have surfaced for that, too.

"So you're telling me she is my dark side and that if the need arises I may have other personalities that manifest?"

"If the situation's right, then yes, but we're gonna try really hard not to have that happen."

I could think of my own reasons why I wouldn't want that to happen, but I wanted to know Kali's. "Why do we want to keep that from happening, exactly?"

She didn't answer right away, so I looked over at her.

She was giving me a serious look of death.

"I don't want more personalities running around in my head either; I just want to know what your reasons are."

"You're already a vessel, constantly influenced by the energies around you," Malcolm said. "Having this ability can be overwhelming, you could ..."

"Go insane," Cal finished. It was the first thing he'd said since we got in the car.

"Well, that's lovely." I sat back in my seat and focused on the road. I could go insane. Who couldn't? Aren't we all? You'd get the kids if I did. A million other quick-witted remarks flew through my head, but I didn't share them. I'd caught the look on his face in the rearview mirror, could hear in his tone that this wasn't a joke.

"So how do I control it, keep it from happening?"

"You don't pull energy," Cal said.

I thought about that. "I'm not sure I can help it," I said quietly.

"Well you better learn, Shel, because I'll not lose the love of my life and the mother of my children," Cal said. "Not after what I went through," he added even more quietly.

I was tired of Cal making all this about him—how he suffered and what he wanted. "And what exactly did you go through, Cal? What was so terrible that you earned the right to be the world's biggest self-centered jerk?"

The look that meet me in the rearview mirror was akin to the light I saw in Jerry's face just before he'd hit me. A shiver went through me as my body reacted physically to my fear.

"Enough, Cal. Now's not the time."

"Time for what?" I had to know what would make Cal look like that, not just for curiosity's sake, but also as a matter of safety.

I watched horror flash across Kali's face and knew whatever she was seeing or hearing was from Cal and whatever it was had been horrible.

I looked at Cal in the rearview mirror again. "Tell me, Cal. Don't I deserve to know? You left me for whatever it was."

"Believe me, if I could've stayed with you, I would've. What I went through was ... not anything I want to share." His voice was hollow, his arms crossed over his chest.

I looked at Kali. Nothing.

There was silence in the car.

"You should tell her, Cal," Malcolm said. "You want her to understand, to give you a break. Maybe this is the way."

"I don't need you telling me how to live my life. Not in the past, not now and not ever. It's not your life. Although you are doing a pretty good job of taking it over."

"It's my life now, too," Malcolm said very calmly. "Whether we like or not we're connected through Shelby and each other. I imagine the life and death of it is the same as a regular bonding. You go, I go."

I didn't like the way that sounded. "You go where?" I asked.

No one said anything.

"This is getting old, guys. Just tell me."

"When a Muse dies, so does her Guardian and vice versa," Kali said. "Malcolm means if Cal dies, so will he ... and you, of course."

That took a minute to sink in.

"We're a unit, aren't we?" I asked them. "Can you feel each other the way I feel you? Sense each other and all that?"

Silence.

Then, "Yes," they both said quietly at the same time.

There was a half hour of silence after that. I drove at break-neck speed, pushing well past the posted speed limits and the capability of the car. It's an SUV designed for power, not for speed. I had to slow down as we went through Portland, navigate the heavier traffic and wind through the many forks and turns. Finally, on the other side of the Columbia River, we were in Washington State and the speed limit went up another ten miles an hour. I pushed the beast as fast as she would go and still keep us on the road.

As the sun set over the river, I thought of Julian sitting happily at a breakfast table with his new Guardian friends, laughing and eating. My mind started going to that awful place where you start imagining your loved one being blown into so much pink mist, and I nearly careened off the road. There was a screeching of tires and honking of horns as I righted us and slowed my speed a bit.

In that moment, with the image of him laughing and smiling, I couldn't get there fast enough. But not getting there at all would be so much worse. The sun had gone down. If we didn't stop the bomb before the sun came back up, we'd be too late.

My mind careened back to a world without Julian, not seeing him grow up to be a man, have children, have a life outside my arms. I felt myself going to place where no parent should ever have to. Ironically, it was Cal's voice that pulled me back.

"Have you ever heard about the Delta force training the Army uses to weed out the best of the best?"

"Is that the one where they get black bagged?"

"Yeah, they put the soldiers through every imaginable survival and combat scenario, testing the limits of their physical and mental capabilities." He took a long deep breath, "They made me go through something similar to guard you. At first, I thought they wanted me to be the best I could be. Artistic Muses are not an easy assignment. About halfway through my training, I realized it was punishment." Cal wasn't speaking very loud, but everyone was dead silent. Not even shifting in their seats. They wanted to hear as much as I did.

"Punishment for what?" I asked quietly.

"It could be a lot of things or maybe just one. They knew I wanted to guard you because I loved you and because we'd accidentally had kids together. I think they wanted me to earn it, and they wanted to punish me for fraternizing with someone who wasn't my Muse to guard in the first place. It's not allowed under the rules. Maybe they wanted to punish me because I didn't ever follow the rules, including going to a civilian high school in the first place. I'll probably never know, but I survived, and I don't think they were expecting that. I'm not sure what would've happened if, after all that they told me, I couldn't be assigned to you. It wasn't until a week before your birthday they finally told me I could. I was sure they were going to deny me, assign you to someone else. I don't think I could've lived with that."

"But they did let you come." I met his eyes in the rearview mirror. There was hope in them. God help us, there was hope in them.

"What'd they make you do?" Malcolm asked, an edge of wariness in his voice.

"At first it was just the usual advanced guard training. Profiling, facial recognition, the physical stuff. It was hard, but I could handle it. Then for some reason they decided I'd benefit from hold training."

Kali let out a gasp, Andre a groan. Malcolm didn't say anything, but I saw his face in the rearview mirror. It wasn't pretty.

The car went silent again. Being out of this Guardian loop was getting old. They all knew what he meant, but no one felt the need to let me in on it. I tried not to sigh.

"What's hold training?" I asked, since no one was going to tell me.

It took a minute, but finally Malcolm spoke, voice flat. "They give you a piece of information and try to torture it out of you. See if you can hold onto it." He went quiet again. "I'm sorry, Cal. If I'd known ..."

"There was no way you could've, and she needed you. I'm still gonna kick your ass later, but I don't blame you."

Malcolm laughed, a deep happy sound that raised goose bumps on my arm. "I look forward to it. Then when I kick your ass yet again, you can buy me a drink."

"Yeah, we won't have to sneak out for it this time," Cal said, laughing, too. "I can't believe you still wear that same cologne. I could smell it all over Shel every time you went near her."

"Hey, that's a French classic, and I seem to remember you asking me for a bottle once."

"I'd forgotten about that," Cal said, and they laughed again.

Their laughter filled the car for a long minute, contagious enough that the rest of us couldn't help but smile. I was glad they could get along, joke about our predicament. It meant there was hope for this completely convoluted mess. Maybe if we all worked together we could save Julian and make it home again. I had no idea what would happen next. I couldn't imagine a life with both of them as permanent fixtures. It was too much to take in. I put that thought aside into a box labeled "things to worry about when not in a crisis."

As the laughter subsided, I remembered the reason behind the joke in the first place. Cal and gone through training where they tortured him for information. Whatever he'd gone through had been bad enough the other Guardians didn't wanna hear about it. Right then, I wasn't sure I could handle it either. The laughter had been so welcome and warm I couldn't bring myself to break the mood and ask what they'd done to him, what he'd gone through so he could be with me, with his kids. I suddenly felt terrible for giving him such a hard time, for being so cold towards him. I couldn't say I'd treat him better from now on or that I'd break up with Malcolm to give him the chance he earned, but I'd try to keep in mind what he went through just to be here.

"Remember when we stole Cookie's spatula?" Malcolm asked, still laughing.

Cal laughed harder. "She made nothing but plain oatmeal for breakfast for a month afterwards."

"That was you guys?" Andre asked.

They both laughed harder.

"You know she only stopped doing it because Dodson threatened to fire her if she didn't," Andre said. "A friend of mine who helped out in the kitchen said, even years later, she still bitches about her spatula being taken."

They continued to laugh. "Do you still have it?" Cal asked Malcolm.

"Yeah, it's in a box at my house, along with our other trophies."

They laughed some more and the rest of us smiled along with them. They started going through the items in Malcolm's "box," reliving their childhood debauchery as school hellions.

Malcolm's twenty-eight, Cal two years younger. Andre, who fits into the year between Cal and Malcolm, remembered almost all of their antics and was fortunate enough never to be on the receiving end of any trouble. Kali, a year younger than I am, remembered a few things, but not much. It mostly took place before her time. She did, however, know both Cal and Malcolm by reputation before she met them in person.

Just wonderful.

37

Muses have to be clever, cunning, imaginative,
dogged and wily, whereas society merely has to lean
its weight a little.

—Anonymous

When Cal arrived at Vladimir Academy as a little ten-
year-old, Malcolm was assigned to mentor him. They hit
it off and became inseparable at the Guardian School.
Not to mention they'd run amok together for over five
years. I thought of Julian and cringed; hopefully, the "run
amok" gene passed him over.

When Malcolm finished school at eighteen, he chose
not to become a Guardian. Cal, then sixteen, didn't know
how to handle that so when Malcolm went his own way,
Cal left Vladimir's and reentered the civilian world....

I learned that Cal's "parents," whom I'd always
understood were his foster parents, were actually two
Guardians who'd chosen to be together rather than to
guard anyone. Kali and Andre were in a similar situation,
although Kali still had another year before she turned
twenty-five and had to decide if she'd take on a full-time
Muse.

I'd never look at Cal's foster parents the same again, but suddenly things made sense. Anita and Stanley Hammond, never had children, something Guardians can't do amongst themselves; they need a Muse. Two Muse parents can make a Guardian or a Muse. A Muse and a Guardian can make a Guardian, a normal kid or, very rarely, another Muse. A Muse and a normal person could make a Guardian, but usually they have just a normal kid. Two Guardians however can't have kids at all, and Guardians can't have kids with normal people either. That's why Cal thought he couldn't get me pregnant back in high school. When I *did* get pregnant, he knew, I'd be a Muse.

It's also interesting that two normal people, like my parents, can have a Muse child, but not a Guardian. I also realized that one if not both of Cal's parents were Muses. Why they would give him up is beyond me, but pondering that made a good distraction for a while.

When Cal left Vladimir's, the Hammonds took him in and he entered high school, my high school, to finish his education. That was how we met, and the rest was history. When Cal and Malcolm met on the sidewalk outside Isabella's, that was the first time they'd seen each other since Guardian school. That explains why Malcolm hadn't known about me or even that Cal had left Vladimir's. Everybody knows Guardians are supposed to stay at Guardian schools and normals at normal schools.

I listened while Cal and Malcolm relived their school years together, Andre throwing in a comment when he could and, to a lesser extent, Kali helped, too.

The solace from all the tension and danger was a nice break. Everyone knew it, too, so no one brought up what we were about to do or any of the things we'd have to deal with when the ride was over. We just listened and laughed, enjoying this little piece of calm.

As Olympia came into view between the trees, we were ready. Whatever happened next, we understood we were doing this, not only to save Julian, but also so the next generations of Guardians could have the experiences we'd all spent the last couple hours laughing about. So Julian could have them and so the system wouldn't be corrupted.

We drove past Olympia and took an exit into the woods. The guys directed me off the main road and down the rarely used dirt road. We followed it for miles until it finally ended. I stopped, turned off the engine and lights. The clock on my dash glowed 12:12 p.m.

The car was silent.

"Everyone ready?"

Three doors opened and everyone got out. I hastened to follow.

Kali set out the plan. "Malcolm's going to carry us in one at a time. Otherwise, it would be about a five-mile hike. He can get us all there within a half hour. From there we should have a vantage point of the school. Andre can go in to do some recon."

It turns out Andre can go invisible. Not like you just can't see him, but like no heat signature, no air movement, nothing. The Authority attempted to exploit his abilities when he finished school and that was when he'd dropped off their radar. He wanted to keep it that way. So, as much as he wanted to help us and what he thought was our cause, he couldn't show himself or do anything that would alert them someone invisible was there. Evidently, there aren't many people with his ability, and they'd be able to figure out who it was pretty quick. It worked out, though, because he could run recon and keep an eye on things, then communicate the information telepathically to Kali, who could get it to the rest of us. Talk about a perfect pair.

Cal and Andre were going into the new location first, so I was well protected when I arrived. Kali was coming in last with Malcolm, of course. Each Guardian had a backpack. I peeked into Malcolm's as he was checking its contents and saw weapons: guns, grenades, rope and other things I couldn't identify.

Being a single mom living alone with two helpless babies taught me a lot about paranoia. It got me into self-defense classes and shooting lessons at the gun range. I toyed with the idea of owning one, but I just wasn't comfortable with the things. Keeping one in the house with little kids wasn't a good idea. They say you're supposed to keep the ammo and gun separate so it's safer, but what if one night I got paranoid hearing sounds outside, loaded the thing and took it to bed with me? What if I fell asleep and the next morning Chloe crawled into bed with me and found it? I shudder to think what could happen.

I settled for the self-defense classes and then some Ninjutsu. I'd heard it was the most direct of the martial arts. I'd only made about one level above cannon fodder, but I slept better regardless.

"Are you really going to use those?" I asked Malcolm, as he pulled on a shoulder holster and tucked a gun into each side. The holster must have been a custom job to fit across his wide chest and shoulders.

"Probably not. As a rule, Guardians don't use guns, but we're going after guys that work for the Captain so we're not putting it past them to play dirty."

"The Captain?"

"The organization Tiffany works for is headed by a man who calls himself the Captain."

"So his flunkies are what, pirates?"

Everyone laughed at that.

"Actually they're his crew or just the crew. They'd be amused to hear you call them pirates though."

The laughing died down and everyone went back to getting ready. Cal, Andre and Kali each put on a similar rig with a gun. Then they covered the holsters and guns with their trench coats, tied at the waist.

Cal jumped on Malcolm's back and said., "Gitty up, horsey!"

Malcolm shook his head and muttered, "Just like old times." He couldn't hide the smile though. He was happy to have his friend back. He winked at me and they were off, leaving Kali, Andre and me standing in the dark near the beast.

"Shel, I need to warn you about something," Kali said.

I looked away from where I'd last seen Cal and Malcolm.. They'd disappeared faster than my brain could comprehend.

Kali looked scared. "I saw some of what Cal went through in hold training. They used you as tool to try to break him. If you get into danger, I don't know what he'll do."

"What do you mean they used me?"

"I think it was just your likeness, but he thought they were torturing you, trying to get him to give up the information so they'd stop. He never gave it up, but he really thought it was you."

Shit.

Kali nodded. I kept forgetting she could hear what was in my head.

"What do I do?"

"Don't risk yourself unnecessarily and, from what I saw ... avoid screaming."

"Screaming?"

She nodded with the gravest expression I'd ever seen.

There was a noise through the trees, and Malcolm was standing next to us. "Ready, Andre?"

"As I'll ever be." And suddenly he wasn't there with the three of us.

I blinked and looked around for him.

I heard him laughing. "You should see the look on your face, little muse." The sound seemed to come from everywhere and nowhere at once. Even the direction of his voice couldn't give him away.

"That's seriously cool, Andre."

"Why thank you."

Malcolm staggered a bit, obviously startled by Andre's sudden weight.

"You're next, luv." Malcolm said and then took off through the trees again.

That left Kali and me.

"I don't envy you, Shel,"

"What do you mean?"

"Cal and Malcolm. I don't envy the choice you're going to make."

"Can I even choose just one? I'm bonded to them both. What happens to the other?"

"I don't know, and I don't envy you finding out."

We stared at each other through the darkness for a while. Then I felt Malcolm's arms slip around my waist, his fingers finding the skin under my shirt. His touch was like slipping into a tub of warm water. I let it fill me up and soothe my frazzled nerves.

"Ready, luv?" he whispered in my ear.

"Yes."

He scooped me up and took off running, only it was unlike any running I'd ever experienced. He was so fast I could barely make out the landscape, but I could tell he was going slower than when he'd taken me from the warehouse. Perhaps it was the terrain, perhaps it was because I wasn't dying in his arms this time, but the pace was certainly slower. It only took a few minutes to reach the vantage point. When we stopped, I was still processing, waiting for my brain to catch up. Malcolm must have noticed because he didn't put me down right away.

Cal walked toward us, arms out. "I'll take her," he said.

Okay, I'm so not being passed around like a baby. "I'm all right." I swung my feet toward the ground, over swung and ended up nearly doing a face plant. Malcolm and Cal both caught me, the world spun and I leaned into them. So much for my dignity.

"I gottcha," Cal said. "That ride can be disorienting at first. It'll pass in a minute."

"Be right back." Malcolm was gone.

I let Cal hold me. Wrapped in his familiar smell, the disorientation cleared faster than I would've thought.

I looked around for Andre.

"He's gone to scout already. Wanna see?"

I nodded, and Cal lifted me up so I could see over a ledge. The view that met my eyes was breathtaking. The backside of Vladimir Academy was stretched out before me, maybe a quarter mile away. It wasn't a castle per se, but a huge brick manor house, bigger than any house I'd ever seen. It looked old and brand-new at the same time with grand turrets and even a tower making up the majority of its outline. Exterior lights illuminated much of its rustic-colored exterior. I filed the scene away to paint later. The sheer majesty of it would haunt my dreams until I took the time to recreate it.

There was just enough lighting to see a wide river and manicured gardens , but this side of the school was dark, a tall fence between the actual building and us.

Cal lowered me back down and I found I could stand unassisted as Kali and Malcolm arrived.

Cal's dark head peeked over the ledge to keep watch Kali and Malcolm took separate positions, kind of keeping me in the middle. I felt like a burden, but no one gave me a gun or asked me to watch a perimeter. Tensions were running high enough without me making a fuss. We'd taken too long getting this far. It was already two in the morning, and we had only five hours to infiltrate the school and stop the bomb. Time was literally ticking away, and we were all sitting around waiting for Andre.

Cal said it would be at least an hour before he got back, that he was going through the underground passage that would take him halfway across the school. Assuming he didn't meet any trouble, it was a half-hour trip. Then he had to get a good lay of the land before heading back and that's, again, assuming he didn't meet any trouble on the way back. Once we knew what we were up against, we'd make a final plan and move out. Now we just had to wait.

The two hours Andre was gone ticked by without so much as a rustle in the bushes. Everyone stayed standing, so I did, too. We were quiet, listening for people moving around in our surroundings. It was the longest two hours of my life.

"He's coming," Kali said quietly so not to startle anyone. Cal and Malcolm didn't, but I did.

Jumpy, who me?

"He's not happy," she added.

Cal and Malcolm shuffled uncomfortably and then Andre was standing a few feet from me. Finger to his lips, he pointed in the direction of the school and we all poked our heads over the ledge.

There was a troop of men and women leaving through a five-foot drainage pipe, not a hundred feet from our position.

All together, about twenty people were leaving. They were quiet, relaxed, not expecting trouble. We waited until they were out of earshot and then everyone but Cal popped back down.

"If I'd known that door would be used for such evil purposes. I'd have sealed it up before I left," Cal said.

"If I'd known, I wouldn't have shown Tiffany," Malcolm added.

Cal gave him a look.

"Hey, there's a great make-out spot about a quarter mile that way."

Cal shook his head.

"Back to business, little boys," Andre said. "That was the bulk of their forces moving out before the bomb goes off. I hurried double time to get out before they did so I could warn you they were coming."

"Had we been talking, they would've heard us," Cal said. "Good work, Andre. What else you got for us?"

"I counted seven more on the inside, including one at the tunnel entrance."

"Who?" Malcolm asked.

Andre smiled. "Victor."

Everyone turned to me.

"What?"

"Victor's a sucker for a pretty face," Cal said. "We could give her a gun and make him think she's here to double-check things He'd buy it. Tiffany won't carry. The Captain hates that," Malcolm added.

Cal gave a slow nod.

"I don't think they're expecting trouble. The guard is minimal and Tiffany is in there,"

Kali cut in. "She's mine."

Cal and Malcolm looked like they were about to argue, but Andre cut back in. "Maliki is in there, too, along with Chad."

Malcolm and Cal both slowly turned back to Andre.

"Maliki's helping Wendy with the bomb and Chad looks to be overseeing the operation with Tiffany. She didn't look happy about it, either."

"She took too long wrapping things up with Shelby; the Captain's keeping an eye on her," Malcolm said as he sat down on a boulder. All of the sudden he looked tired.

"What's the big deal with Maliki and Chad?" I asked.

" Maliki is the only other level four, like Malcolm, who's active. He and Malcolm have a history." Kali said.

"Level four?"

"Guardian's abilities are ranked from one to five. Malcolm is a four point three. Maliki is a four point two."

Cal looked down at Malcolm. "You're stronger than him."

"He beat me last time. It wasn't pretty," Malcolm said from his rock.

"You'll beat him this time," Cal said.

Was this a guy version of a pep talk? A "Don't worry everything will be all right" speech?

Malcolm nodded his head, blew out a breath and got up. "I'll beat him this time."

Evidently, the pep talk worked.

"What about Chad?" Kali asked.

"He can't heal others like I can, but he's pretty indestructible. Weak on the muscle side, but last I saw he could take a bullet at point-blank range without a scratch even when the momentum knocks him over. He makes a great shield, but he isn't a weapon. I can handle him. Malcolm can help if we get Maliki under control."

Malcolm nodded, still looking a little unsteady.

Andre continued with his report. "That just leaves Wendy, Scott and Tim. Scott and Tim are mostly patrol. I saw them all over the place, but they didn't leave when the others did. They're small potatoes, but they're also the only ones armed, other than Victor."

"We'll pick them off," Cal said.

"What about Wendy?"

"She's just there for the bomb. When the going gets rough, she'll bail. If not, between Cal and me, we can take her. Hell, Shel can help if she wants."

"Good to know I'll have something to do," I muttered and then thought of something. "What about the bomb? There's a plan for that, right?"

"Malcolm knows bombs," Cal said. "If we can clear the way, he'll take care of it."

Kali took off her pack and pulled out another holster with a gun in it. All guns pretty much look the same to me, so I couldn't tell you what kind it was. "Shel can help. I've seen her handle a gun, and she's taken me to the mat more than once at Ninjutsu."

"But Kali, you can read minds," Cal said, as if he couldn't believe I could best her.

Kali shrugged. "Her mind runs quick, changes fast. They don't lie when they say artist Muses are tough to keep a handle on."

Cal and Malcolm exchanged a glance I didn't like, but I ignored it. Kali had me take off my jacket, and we hooked up the shoulder rig. Five minutes later, we were finally ready to enter the tunnel. We had a little over two hours before the bomb went off. God help us.

38

The virtues, like the Muses, are always seen in groups. A good principle was never found solitary in any breast.

—Buddha

I took off through the woods all on my own. The plan was for everyone to be fifty feet behind me using their sneak ability. They wouldn't be seen unless someone was looking for them. It wasn't foolproof since the crew would be looking for intruders, but we were hoping Victor would be distracted enough by me that he'd stop looking long enough for Malcolm to knock him out.

According to Cal, I should enter the tunnel with a flashlight, thank you very much, and after about a hundred yards come to a door cut out of the cement. I should walk through that door like I owned the place, flash my gun at Victor and tell him the Captain sent me to check on the crew. Cal said, quite painfully, that I should flirt a lot, that Victor would eat it up and allow everyone else to sneak in and do their thing. No problem, right?

The woods were dark, but I kept my flashlight off just in case anyone in the school was looking out a window.

The last thing we needed was for some unsuspecting school employee to come check it out and be caught in the crossfire. I made my way to the tunnel entrance, only falling down twice. I thought I heard a chuckle behind me after the second fall, but ignored it. It was probably just Andre anyway.

The tunnel entrance was dark and ominous; the steady trickle of water coming out didn't help either. I swallowed my fear and took those first few steps into the darkness before flipping on my flashlight. With the tunnel ahead of me illuminated, I felt a little better. There was an inch of water moving in a little stream underfoot, but my boots kept my feet relatively dry. I walked down the tunnel bent at an awkward angle because it was so low at the top. I imagined Cal was bent double trying to make his way through.

After what seem like an hour, I finally came to the door they'd described to me. Back when they were at school, Malcolm had used a chisel and his amazing strength to cut a door in the side of the tunnel. They'd even added hinges and then glued sealant around the door to keep out the majority of water. Evidently, they'd had a plenty of spare time while at school.

The door was still there, intact and just the way they described it. Andre said Victor was stationed just inside. He was armed, but that shouldn't be a problem. Apparently Victor wasn't the brightest crayon in the box, but still not someone to mess with.

I put out my flashlight, unzipped my jacket so I could flash the gun more smoothly and tried to compose myself into the confident flirt Cal had coached me to be. Thank goodness for all my years as a Thespian. I blew out one last breath, smoothed my ponytail for good measure, opened the door and stepped through it, leaving it open in my wake.

What lay beyond was indeed a dirt tunnel dug about seven-feet high and five-feet wide. They'd really had a lot of free time.

Victor was right where Andre said he'd be. He was about the same height as Malcolm, six foot or so, with black hair and a thick mustache. To say he was armed was an understatement. His gun was huge, like something Rambo would carry. He was dressed in all-black military fatigues. Minus the clever message on my T-shirt, we matched.

He startled as I came through the door, but his look quickly turned to curiosity.

Showtime. I swept one hand back to rest on my hip, taking my jacket with it and exposing my gun in its holster.

Victor's eyes narrowed, and he started to point his gun at me.

Time for my lines.

"Victor, right?" I asked in my smoothest voice. "The Captain said to watch for you. Said you'd have my back if I need you." I tried to look interested and swung my hips as I walked toward him. This would've been so much easier in heels but, honestly, I didn't even own a pair.

"And you are?" he said in a very ordinary-sounding voice.

"Cecilia, Captain sent me to make sure things run smooth and to check up on Tiffany, said the bitch can't be trusted."

Victor laughed at that. "The bitch has already got Chad all up her ass. What're you gonna do exactly?" He pointed the gun at me.

This was the moment of truth. If I backed down or acted afraid, he'd know something was off and I could end up dead. I pulled up all my courage and took a step forward putting the barrel of Victor's gun to my chest. "I can be all kinds of useful," I said in my most seductive voice.

Victor's eyebrows went up and he lowered the gun. There was a thud, and Victor fell to the ground. As if my brain suddenly willed it, the others appeared around me.

Malcolm checked Victor. "He's out cold. Should come to in a few hours. He'll need a doctor, but he'll be all right."

I gave myself a shake and paced away from the crowd. "Now what?" I was antsy, ready to be done with all this. Now that we were here, it was worse. I wanted to move, wanted Julian safe.

"We move forward and deal with whatever comes our way," Cal said, taking the lead, which made sense since he was the bulletproof one.

Kali followed next, then me, with Malcolm bringing up the rear. I assumed Andre was somewhere, but I couldn't see him no matter how much I willed it.

The tunnel was dark, but Cal didn't turn on a light. Malcolm did,, a dim one with just enough light to make sure none of us tripped.

It was a long walk to the opening of the bomb shelter. We were ten feet from the entrance when Kali stopped, pulling us against the wall and relayed information from Andre. "Tiffany is with Chad, two rooms over. They're packing to leave. Just beyond them in the main chamber is Wendy with Maliki. Haven't seen Scott or Tim."

"Let's move around and come into the main chamber," Malcolm said. "Try to take out Maliki before we have to deal with Chad. Maybe the ruckus will make Wendy book it."

Cal nodded and Kali concentrated for a moment, relaying the message to Andre, and then she nodded too. We moved out of the tunnel and, to my great surprise, none of them pulled a gun. We moved through one empty dusty room and then through another before coming to a door where Cal stopped.

"This is it. The main chamber is on the other side." This time Kali pulled a gun. We exchanged a few more nods. With my heart in my throat, I pulled the door open and everyone ran out ahead of me.

When I made it through the door, Cal and Malcolm were already on who I could only assume was Maliki. Malcolm was trying to land a blow while Cal distracted Maliki. It was like a dance, Maliki always one move ahead of Cal and two ahead of Malcolm.

I couldn't stand there and watch, though; Kali was calling me over.

She was holding a gun on someone who must have been Wendy. I had no idea what to do until she told me to keep my gun on Wendy while she tried to help the boys.

I got my gun out and just as I pointed it at Wendy, the side door opened and Tiffany and someone who must have been Chad ran in. When Tiffany spotted me, she had an odd look on her face; it wasn't a smile, but she looked happy to see me all the same. Weird.

"She's mine," Kali called and ran toward her.

Tiffany raced across the wide chamber. The two women disappeared around a corner, and I was left holding a gun on Wendy while Cal and Malcolm grappled with Maliki and now Chad, since he'd entered the fray.

The way we were positioned, I couldn't watch what was going on and keep an eye on Wendy so I looked for a better vantage point. A group of tables was set up where Wendy was curled into a corner. There was quite a bit of gear, wires, plans and various other items I couldn't identify on the fly. I looked around for the bomb and was surprised to find it attached to the wall five feet above Wendy.

I shot a glance at the blueprints on the table and saw the bomb was attached to the main support beam for the dining hall above. When the bomb blew, it would take out the whole floor some thirty feet above us. Anyone who wasn't killed in the blast would be pulled to their death by the fall. Ingenious and sick.

I threw everything off one of the tables and tipped it on its side just in case I needed some cover. I shoved Wendy in front of the table so I could watch her and the fight at the same time.

What met my eyes was mind-boggling. Malcolm and Maliki were locked in a high-speed grapple, neither of them able to land a real punch. From what I understood, they were both super strong, but neither was indestructible. If one of them managed to land a full blow, he could easily kill the other. I watched, hypnotized for a moment, as they wrestled at high speed, becoming blurs and then stopping, only to take off again.

Cal was at a similar stalemate. Chad was impossible to hurt, but so was Cal. Cal was smart enough not to try landing blows; he had caught one of Chad's hands with a choke wire. They were in their own weird dance as Chad tried to avoid Cal and get his other hand free.

I must have shown how enthralled I was in the fight because Wendy chose that moment to throw a kick and knock the gun from my hand. It skittered across the floor, and she tackled me. I landed an elbow to her neck trying to hit the nerve bundle there like I'd been taught in Ninjutsu, but she evaded and rolled away, coming to her feet again.

She swung a kick at me and I ducked. She did some kind of fancy kick-spin-punch move and I avoided it, landing a hit to her gut. She dropped to her knees, winded, hunched in pain, disbelief etched across her face.

"Who are you?"

Who was I? I was a Muse, but that didn't mean much to me, at least not yet. I was a student, a woman, and a friend, but why was I here? Once again, I decided to go with the truth.

"A mother," I said and sent her spinning with a kick to the face. She slumped to the floor and didn't move again.

I was tying her up with some wire when shots fired across the chamber. I pulled her behind the table I'd knocked over, finished the job and shoved her under another table out of the line of fire. By then, I'd found my gun and peeked up over the edge of my cover.

The shots were coming from one of the far doorways. I could see two men with guns just around the doorway as they fired and reloaded. They seemed to be aiming for Cal, the bigger target, but he was all but bulletproof and so was the guy he was fighting. I took aim and tried to hit one of the guys peeking around the door firing. The first two shots missed, but I noticed one of them would pop his head out at exactly the same spot each time and then aim and fire. For whatever reason they hadn't noticed me yet or fired in my direction, so I took a moment to set up my shot, sighting down the barrel the way they'd taught me at the shooting range. When guy number two poked his head out again and started to sight up his own shot I fired.

It was a direct head shot. He went down in the doorway, a pool of bright red visible even from thirty feet away.

Guy number one finally realized there was a threat in the room other than the huge Guardian trying to take down his boss and the lightening fast blur that was Malcolm and Maliki. He started firing in my direction, blowing a bullet through the table not inches from where I was sitting.

I started to move when the sounds around me changed. There was a series of quick shots ... then nothing ... and a frustrated roar that sounded like Malcolm. I poked my head above the table again and saw Maliki, a very broken pile on the floor. Malcolm was dragging himself across the floor toward me. Shooter number one was very obviously dead on top of shooter number two, and Malcolm's chest had been hit with multiple bullets. I knew Malcolm healed faster than a normal person, but he was losing so much blood I didn't think he'd make it long enough to heal.

Cal and Chad were still locked in their dance. Everyone but Tiffany had been taken out, and Kali hadn't returned so I had to hope she was taking care of her. I ran to Malcolm, pulling off my sweatshirt as I went, skidded to a stop next to him and pressed the jacket against his chest.

"You're gonna be all right. We just have to slow down this bleeding," I said, trying to see the wounds well enough to cover them all. There were so many that panic rose in my throat.

"Luv, you have to stop the bomb." Malcolm said through a couple choking breaths. The sound of his voice through all the pain was enough to make me cry.

"I can't. That's your job," I said, stricken as I watched blood soak through my sweatshirt.. Blood was soaking into the knees of my pants as I knelt in a puddle of red, my arms bloody up to my elbows.

"Five minutes, luv. ... Look at the timer." He was gasping now.

I glanced up and there it was in glowing digital red letters: a little over five minutes.

"I don't know how."

"Use your pull. Pull the energy from the battery. If the battery has no charge, it can't go off."

"I don't know if I can do that ... and you told me not to use the pull. You said it was too dangerous."

"You can do it, luv. There's no other way." He was fading now, his skin white. I hated to leave his side, but the timer was down to four minutes. If I didn't go, we'd all die regardless of whether I was holding his hand when it happened.

I tried to get up, slipped in all the blood and landed hard on my knees. I let out a shriek, a frustrated cry and tried again. I moved across the room, my heart breaking. Malcolm was dying. I pushed a table under the bomb and climbed on top, leaving a bloody trail in my wake. By the time I reached the bomb, we were down to three minutes left. Cal was still grappling with Chad, and it didn't look good. Cal struggled for breath. Chad had the choke wire around his neck and was pulling from behind.

I pulled my attention back to the bomb, took a deep breath, cleared my mind and laid both my hands on it. I don't know how I knew what to do, but I could feel all the currents of energy moving through the various parts of the little box.

Cal was making horrible choking noises behind me, but I couldn't help him. I willed myself to block out the sounds and focus on the energy in front of me so I could feel where it was going, how it was circling and where the bulk of it was staying. When I found the battery, I opened my mind to it, willed the energy to come out of it and into me.

Nothing happened.

Cal continued to struggle behind me. I threw a glance at Malcolm. He wasn't moving, but he couldn't be dead. Cal and I were still alive.

I focused on the bomb again. There was little over a minute left. My bloody hands shook as I tried again to will the energy to leave the device and come into me. Still nothing.

I thought back to when I'd done this before, when I'd done it by accident. What was happening? What was I thinking? When it happened in the bedroom, I'd been angry. I hadn't directed myself at anything; the light bulb had just popped. When I did it with Jerry, I'd just thought "pull" and the energy had come.

That was it.

I simply thought "pull" and imagined a string of energy coming into me. Finally, it started to come. Twenty seconds to go. I opened myself up and tried to pull it faster, but the battery didn't want to let it go. The current was fixed by the mechanisms and wires. I pulled and pulled, but it wasn't enough. The timer flicked 3 ... 2 ... 1 ...

I was reading "zero" when a rush of energy hit me like a tidal wave. Only it wasn't a physical wave that tore apart my flesh, but an influx ... an explosion of energy. The battery had released its energy and the explosion had taken place. There was a bright flash of light, and I was on my back, vibrating with energy and screaming. I felt like I was on fire, writhing with the pure contained energy inside me. It needed out. I had to put it somewhere. I felt something around my neck. ... I was choking. My eyes flew open. Chad was above me holding the wire around my neck. All this effort to stop the bomb and I was going to die like this?

Then it hit me. I knew exactly what to do with the energy.

I put my hands around Chad's neck, the more nerve endings touching and all that, and let the energy flow into him. I didn't push it. I didn't fire it at him. I just let it go, and it went. I was a full vessel and Chad was quite empty. A mass of energy moved into Chad and he let me go. He tried to pull away, but I held on. I could feel the moment his body couldn't take any more energy, but still I held on. He collapsed, and I let go.

I didn't stop to take his pulse; I crawled towards Cal. I could still feel his essence. He was alive, but I couldn't see him breathing. I could still feel Malcolm, just barely. If I could revive Cal, he could save Malcolm. We'd be all right.

I started mouth-to-mouth resuscitation on Cal. After two good breaths, he was breathing again on his own. He opened his eyes, and for the second time in twenty-four hours, I was so glad to see him awake and alive. I smiled at him and he smiled back. The moment passed, and I crawled awkwardly toward Malcolm. A lot of the excess energy was still in me, making my muscles do weird things as it ebbed and circled within me, but I could shuffle across the floor on my hands and knees.

"Shelby, what's wrong with you?" Cal asked, getting to his feet.

"I'm fine. You have to heal Malcolm. He's been shot and he's barely alive." I reached Malcolm, and still Cal stood there watching me, something intense on his face that I couldn't identify.

"Cal, he's dying. You have to heal him!" I pulled Malcolm into my lap. He was almost gone. I could feel the little spark that was his essence within me start to flicker.

"Cal, if you don't save him we'll all die. He goes, we all go. Remember?"

Cal just looked at me. "I'm only supposed to save you, Shel."

"Cal!" I screamed with everything I had, screamed like my soul was being ripped from my body, because that's what it felt like. A piece of my soul was dying. ."If you don't help him, there won't be anything left of me to save!"

And just like Kali predicted, the screaming did something to Cal. He started moving. I cried into Malcolm's shoulder as Cal knelt beside us. Cal looked like he was in shock, but laid his hands on Malcolm, closed his eyes and simply breathed.

I felt Malcolm's heart start beating harder and faster. He took a real breath and then another. Something rolled across my lap. Bullets. Malcolm was healing. I pulled away my jacket and watched as the holes closed themselves. I counted five bullets and, as they rolled away, I picked them up and tucked them into the pocket of my pants.

Malcolm moaned and shifted in my arms. He was waking up and it hurt.

Cal fell away from Malcolm, and I went to him.

"So much damage. I need to bond," Cal said with raspy breaths.

All I could think was "Here? Now?"

He chuckled—a faint, strained noise.

I put my hands on him, the blood red of my hands stark against the skin of his face and neck.

I focused on the scene of him fighting Chad, fighting to save our son who was now safe, thanks to all our efforts. Julian was safe. I let that feeling of wonderful fill me up and then I pushed it into Cal. It had some extra oomph because of the extra energy flowing through me, and Cal felt it, his eyes going wide. I felt it fill him up, but before he was full, I stopped. I didn't want to hurt him.

I pulled my hands away and Cal sat back up and put his hands on Malcolm. Within seconds, Malcolm's eyes were open, his color back. He started to sit up.

"Him, too," Cal said.

Without a word, I laid my hands on Malcolm and let that energy flow smoothly into him until he, too, was nearly full. Once I got the bonding energy flowing, it seemed to work on both guys. I didn't need a new thought to keep it going for Malcolm. When I pulled back from Malcolm, the three of us sat there staring at one another. Malcolm opened his mouth to say something, but at that moment, the bond hit us.

A shiver ran through my body and Malcolm was suddenly holding me. Not kissing me or searching under my clothes, just holding me, hugging me, so tight it would've hurt if it didn't feel so amazingly good. Cal was there, too, and we all held each other. The bond rode us, itched across our skin, begged us to make something of it, but we just held on, rode the waves and weathered the storm in one another's embrace.

39

And strictly meditate the thankless Muse.

—John Milton

When the storm passed, we were all huddled in a pool of Malcolm's blood, soaked in it. Had we all not been so near death in the last ten minutes, the bonding would've taken us, regardless of the place or situation. I'd be sure to remember that in the future.

Multiple bodies lay around us, and we still didn't know what had become of Kali and Andre.

"What happened with the bomb?" Cal asked, as if we all hadn't nearly lost our lives and then used every fiber of our beings to avoid having a threesome in a puddle of blood.

"I tried to pull the energy from the battery, but I couldn't make it come. The bomb went off while I was pulling and all the energy went into me." I felt hollow inside and suddenly very tired.

They just looked at me.

"You're telling me you absorbed all the energy off a C4 explosion?" Malcolm asked.

I just nodded.

"Are you okay?" Cal asked, incredulous.

"I wasn't. I had to find somewhere for it to go. Chad offered himself up."

We looked over where Chad lay not twenty feet away. Definitely dead. I'd killed another person. Including shooter number two, that made three people all together. Three lives I'd taken in the name of saving my family. I tried to tell myself it was necessary, that they'd have done worse to me, but I just felt more tired.

Cal blinked and shook his head a bit. "And the rest?"

"I put it into you guys. It worked better than I thought."

Malcolm got to his feet. "Yeah, I feel great. Bet I could break my speed record right now."

I looked around at the carnage. "Do you think you could beat it while cleaning up this mess? I doubt we should leave it like this ... and where's Kali?"

They both just shrugged. We'd find her, but now we needed to clean up the mess and get out of here. They could be miles away by now.

Malcolm said he'd take care of the bodies. "Cal, you know what to do with the blood." Just like that he was gone, not even a flash, just disappeared.

Cal and I got to our feet, kind of. I was so tired I couldn't even stand on my own. I leaned against Cal, and he put a hand on me.

"You're exhausted. That energy took a lot out of you, huh?"

He took me over to the wall and I slid down it, coming to a rest with my butt on the floor.

Cal took off his jacket and laid it over me. "Rest, I'll take care of this."

I felt myself nod—the last thing I remembered.

"Wake up, luv. It's time to go." Malcolm's voice reached me in a sleep so deep it hurt to come out of it.

I got up and looked around. The blood and bodies were gone, the bomb and the tables too. It looked like the empty room it was supposed to be, albeit cleaner ... an empty, gore-free chamber once again.

"Come on, Shel, let's get you cleaned up. Then we can pick up Julian. You're a little too macabre to go walking into the school."

"Did Kali come back?" I managed to ask as they led me towards the door.

"She did. Tiffany got away. It's a long story, but let's tell it later. She went to get us a hotel room as she's the only one not covered in gore."

I nodded and shuffled my feet. I wasn't moving very fast and I knew it. It hurt to be awake, like I hadn't slept in a week and was struggling through the fog of it.

"I think I could use that palanquin now, guys. I'm not gonna make it."

They both chuckled.

"As a lady wishes." Malcolm scooped me into his arms. He moved a few steps and my brain fell back into sleep.

The next time I woke, I was in a bed, Malcolm and Cal on either side of me. My bloody clothes had been stripped off, including my underwear. I was naked. I wondered how they got me undressed without me waking up, but then I remembered Cal could keep me asleep if he wanted. I couldn't complain. I'd needed the sleep and all that gore had probably gone into a bag to be destroyed.

I crawled out of bed and into the shower. I scrubbed blood off most of my body and spent a long time with a washrag, trying to get it out from under my fingernails. At least I knew all of it was Malcolm's. When I finally shut the water off, I could hear the boys talking. Good, they were up. I was ready to get my son and head home.

I wrapped a towel around myself and opened the bathroom door.

They both just looked at me.

"Are there clothes for me somewhere?"

Malcolm pointed towards the little closet. "In the suitcase."

I'd forgotten Kali packed me a bag before we left.

"How long was I out?"

"Only about six hours. We're ready to leave when you are. We know you want to get to Julian as soon as possible."

I found what I needed: jeans, a bra, underwear, socks, a red thermal and a sweatshirt. I took it all back to the bathroom. I left the door open a crack so we could still talk.

"So what happened with Tiffany?" I said through the crack.

"Funny story actually," Malcolm said. "She wants to cut us a deal."

"What deal?"

"She likes you, wants to turn spy for us."

I stepped out in bra and panties, towel still in hair. "What'd you say?"

Malcolm smiled, and Cal tried not to.

"Really, she wants to cut a deal. Says she's changed her ways, wants to be a good guy. Thinks you're the one to follow."

My mouth fell open.

"After what she did to me? You've got to be kidding. ..."

"Why don't you give it some thought. We don't have to make a decision today." Cal said.

I tried to shake it off and walk back into the bathroom, but my shoulder hit the door jamb. I righted myself and walked into the bathroom where I dressed in a haze.

I came back out, dug through the suitcase and found some shoes.

"I can't deal with this right now. I need to see my son."

"Our son," Cal corrected.

That stopped me. I met his eyes. "Our son." He'd earned it.

"Do I want to know what happened with the scene? The survivors?" I asked, tying up a fresh pair of Cons.

"We left Wendy and Victor tied up in one of their vehicles," Malcolm said. "I'm sure Tiffany has found them by now and they've been returned home to lick their wounds. The bodies have been similarly taken care of, the scene cleaned. No one will ever know we were there. Just like the warehouse where Jerry kept you. It's been taken care of."

I hadn't thought about the scene with Jerry. "You took care of that, too?"

Malcolm nodded. "Andre helped. We had a bit too much fun actually. He has a thing for fire."

"You burned it down?" Why hadn't I thought of this before?

Malcolm nodded.

Not real inventive, but effective nonetheless.

We packed up the room and filed out to the beast. I said goodbye to Kali and, with my mind, told her to say goodbye to Andre. He was staying incognito. She'd rented a car and they were driving back without us, as there wouldn't be enough room in the rig once we picked up Julian.

I let Malcolm drive us to the school and I personally led the way up the steps to the front doors, opened them and looked around for someone to tell me where my son was.

Malcolm and Cal came through after me, both of them in new trench coats. They looked slick and professional coming back to their old alma mater. They were both grinning

A woman appeared, walking at a brisk pace in heels across the marble-tiled foyer.

"Excuse me? I'm looking for my son."

Her eyebrows went up, but she seemed to regain herself. "Down the hall, first door on the left. They should be able to help you."

I thanked her and proceeded down the hall, Cal and Malcolm following.

I stepped into what looked like a very nice waiting room where a woman was sitting behind a desk.

I walked right up to her. "I'm sorry to bother you, but I'm looking for my son, Julian Hammond."

"Oh wow, you're here already. I'll tell the dean."

She picked up her phone and pressed a button. "Ms. Hammond is here to see you." Silence for a few beats. "No, sir. I only left her the message a few minutes ago."
        More silence.

"Yes, sir. I'll send her in." She hung up. "He can see you right now. Julian's still in there."

I almost asked what for, but figured it would be faster just to see for myself.

"That door there." She pointed down a hallway.

There was a plaque outside the door that said, "Dean Dodgson," and I got a bad feeling.

I opened the door without knocking and found Julian sitting in a large wingback chair facing the desk, a wiry-looking woman with a red spatula in her hand was pacing back and forth behind him. A man, whom I assumed was the dean, sat behind the desk with a concerned look on his face.

I didn't wait for an introduction, I just rushed forward, wrapped Julian in my arms and squeezed. He squeezed back, not even telling me I was hurting him.

"You! I knew it!" I heard the wiry woman shriek. "It all makes sense now. He's one of your spawn, isn't he? Isn't he?" She waved her spatula in Malcolm's and Cal's faces. "Malcolm Dixon and Calvin Smith, two of the most unruly ragamuffins to ever cross this threshold, and now you've reproduced. God help us all!"

"Ms. Sheppard, kindly control yourself," the dean said from behind his desk. "In fact, I think that's quite enough. You may leave us now."

"He's yours isn't he?" she said, pointing at Cal. "He's got those calculating eyes."

"Ms. Sheppard." The dean had warning in his voice.

She made an indignant noise and swept from the room, leaving the scent of tomato sauce and pepper in her wake.

"Ms. Hammond, I presume? Please come in and have a seat. Mr. Dixon, Mr. Smith, what can I do for you?"

"It's Hammond now, and I'm Julian's father," Cal said, coming to stand behind my chair.

"Very well. And you, Mr. Dixon. It's been more years than I can count since the two of you were in my office together. To what do I owe the pleasure?" He didn't sound like it was a pleasure, but there was a bit of amusement in his voice.

"I'm with them," Malcolm said and moved next to Cal.

"I see." The dean then launched into a story about a frog and a pot of spaghetti and how Ms. Sheppard—

"Cookie" to Cal and Malcolm—had opened the pot and been sprayed in the face with sauce when the frog jumped out.

So much for Julian not getting the "run amok" gene.
...

I could feel Malcolm and Cal behind me, trying not to laugh. They did an acceptable job of holding it in.

The dean talked on, but it was Cal and Malcolm I was thinking about. The three of us here together. A unit. How even Malcolm, who by all rights should've felt like an outsider, had not only made a place for himself but was confident he belonged in it. I wasn't sure how I felt about that, but for now, it was all right. He'd nearly lost his life helping us. He'd earned his place.

The dean talked some more and it was decided Julian would come home with us. He would be invited back and, when he came, he'd have service to do to make good with Cookie. But today he was going home.

His stuff was brought down to us and before I knew it, Julian was tucked into the back seat between Cal and me, with Malcolm driving us home. We stopped on the way and picked up Chloe. I saw her smiling face peering through the blinds when we pulled up and realized she'd been right. It had all turned out okay. I rode home between the kids, Cal up front with Malcolm.

We even stopped for ice cream, just like Chloe predicted. The only thing she'd said that didn't come true was that Cal and Malcolm would get Tiffany. Then again, getting her could mean many things. Maybe it hadn't happened yet or maybe Chloe really didn't know what was going to happen. Only time would tell.

When we got to the front door of my house, two presents were sitting on the porch: Julian's favorite stuffed animal and Chloe's favorite doll, the ones Tiffany had taken to threaten me with. A peace offering. I still wasn't sure what to do about her, but right now I had other things to worry about. I got the kids settled in and unpacked, fed them some dinner and got them to bed early. We were all tired and glad to be home.

Andre had been by to install surveillance cameras all over my house. He and Kali had known I wouldn't be okay with Cal or Malcolm staying over. I just wasn't there yet and I felt safe enough. Malcolm was only seconds away with his super speed if something happened. Not to mention that we'd pretty much killed all the bad guys. If Tiffany came looking for me, I'd have no problem taking care of her myself.

Cal showed me how to work a GPS wired panic button, and he and Malcolm left together after giving me long hugs goodbye. Whatever understanding the two of them had come to about me seemed to be working. Thank goodness for little miracles.

I'm not sure what I'm gonna do about Cal. He nearly did what all Guardians are supposed to do and what I just can't forgive. He'd almost let Malcolm die because he thought he was just supposed to save me. In the end, I think he saved Malcolm because he was sure if Malcolm died, we'd all go with him. Did that mean he wouldn't have, if we hadn't all been attached? If that was true, it was unacceptable, and I needed to do something about it. I just didn't know what.

I think I'm still dating Malcolm, but that's all kinds of confused now and I haven't had the energy to examine it. He said he had something important to show me, that it couldn't wait any more. I told him I needed a break from new information for at least a few days and then he could tell me anything he wanted.

An hour after the guys left, Diane beat down my front door and started yelling about not hearing from me for days and days and a hundred voicemails I never answered. I assured her I was fine but exhausted and we'd talk soon. Then I pushed her back out the door.

Ten minutes later, my head hit the pillow.

I don't know what's going to become of my hand or the art show or if the kids will even go back to school. And what about basketball practices? It all seems like another life now. One I'm not sure I can go back to. I don't know what tomorrow will bring. I don't know if I can do this—be a Muse, have two men in my life, and balance it all with the kids and school and the life I want to have for myself—but it looks like I'm going to try. Cal will be there to help, and Malcolm. Kali will do what she can, and Andre will be amused by the whole thing. Diane and Johnas will be my rock of normal in this sea of insanity and somehow it will all work out. Right?

Susie M. Hanley is a native Oregonian where she has always slept best curled up with a good book and the sound of the rain pounding against her window. Her love of worlds beyond her own led her to complete a degree in communication and cultures and to begin creating worlds of her own for others to enjoy.

When not working on Shelby's next impassioned quest, she can be found chasing her kids, cuddling her hubby, and randomly organizing everything into submission. Visit her official website at www.susiemhanley.com.

www.ingramcontent.com/pod-product-compliance
Lightning Source LLC
Chambersburg PA
CBHW070208260626
47160CB00002B/491